Mine Work

JIM DAVIDSON

Mine Work

a novel

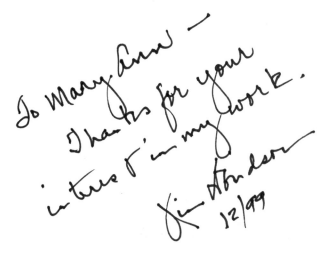

To Mary Ann —
Thanks for your
interest in my work.
Jim Davidson
12/99

UTAH STATE UNIVERSITY PRESS
Logan, Utah
1999

Utah State University Press
Logan, Utah 84322

Manufactured in the United States of America.
Typography by Lito Tejada-Flores
Cover design by Michelle Sellers

03   02   01   00   99   5   4   3   2   1

Library of Congress Cataloging-in-Publication Data

Davidson, Jim, 1943-
  Mine work : a novel / Jim Davidson.
  p. cm.
  ISBN 0-87421-275-8
  I. Title.
  PS3554.A92556 M56 1999
  813'.54—dc21
                                    99-6251
                                    CIP

CONTENTS

To my father, a miner from age fifteen until the year he died, and a carver of fine, mystifying wooden chains. I'm amazed, still, at the things he could create with his hands.

PROLOGUE

Just north of the border between Colorado and New Mexico, the desert slashes in from the west, blunting the southern nose of the Rockies, cutting the mountains off and pushing the Continental Divide to the east. Change here is sharp and abrupt: in some places, little more than 30 miles separate glacier-fed headwaters from bone-dry arroyos, separate elk herds from scorpions. A red-tailed hawk can sail off a rocky and icy ridge above timberline, then glide south on the crown of thermals that surge up out of the steep canyons, and finally make the hot desert floor almost without a single movement of wing.

Wild rivers spill out south and west, gouging canyons and cutting walls, laying open the plys and veins that tell the story of all the tides and volcanos that made the land. It's much harder to see now, but this confusion of layers carries silver and copper and zinc and lead. Even traces of gold nest in those rocks, although the gold runs mostly in flakes, buried in the river gravels.

Those words—gold and silver—spoken a few times loudly, have always drawn anxious crowds. Particularly in the late 1800s. With outstretched hands and poorly-focused eyes, swarms of the hopeful clawed their way into those rugged canyons. And near the sources of most of those furious rivers—the San Juan, the LaPlata, the Dolores, the San Miguel, the Uncompahgre—mining camps were cut into the meadows and hillsides, wherever the land would sit still for it. Ragged and wild, optimistic well beyond good sense, these towns and their people prospered during the early years, taking the easy stuff—deposits on the surface and veins that were simple to follow and scrape clean.

But as the holes in the mountains grew deeper, and as the holes in the graveyards began to crowd the wrought-iron cemetery fences, bad luck dimmed the shining eyes. Markets collapsed and the mines played out. One by one, the mine buildings were boarded-up and the tunnels blasted closed. Always without fanfare, sometimes in the night, those people of the calloused hands and the patched coats slipped quietly away. Houses stood empty, falling apart.

Some towns would survive, prosper even, when later generations of the rich came back to play. Others would simply vanish, leaving behind scraps of tin and boards, and ironic place names on old maps. Like Nirvana. Joyful. New Eden.

Still others, like Madero on the Helado River, would just wait, feeding off the scant highway traffic, ignored. Always in decay. Always about to be gone.

PART ONE

Neal

1

I'M GLAD I HAVE WATER.

The desert dust is boiling up behind me, spilling off into the sage and rabbit brush as I drive along. It hangs in the air for a long time, floating and drifting with the wind, before it settles down into a dull coat on the prickly pear and the red rock, before it softens the edges of my own tracks.

I meet and pass nobody, nor do I see another car. It's a silent world, and empty, and I wonder, vaguely, how much distance and time separates me from another living soul. They're out there, and I know it. They're just hidden, distant, out of my sight.

Each time I turn off of one road onto another, the trail gets smaller and rougher and less traveled. Toward the end, sagebrush growing up between the tracks scrapes and digs at the bottom of my truck, and forces ragged images of pieces being pulled apart.

I know where I'm going. But I've already taken a wrong turn or two and ended up back on some road I've driven earlier in the day, confounded to come upon my own tracks. It's nothing new. I've been through this before.

It's vast, endless, this old ocean floor. The redrock cliffs out in front of me don't seem to get any closer, no matter how long I drive, and sometimes I think I'm being toyed with and fooled. But that's just the way it seems. All deserts know that trick.

These lesser roads were not built, but rather just worn into place by feet and wheels, with a little help from the wind. They go through nothing and around everything, so they twist and dive and climb and veer like a tangled rope thrown, in disgust and dismay, off into the brush and rock.

Suddenly down. Into a dry, ragged arroyo, across the smooth bedrock, and up and back out again, up and over a sand bank where spinning wheels have cut the road into a trench.

I've stopped looking at the buttes. Too many have passed me by, these massive, million-pound sandstone fists and fingers, gesturing toward the sky, towering over me. They're too high, too sheer and they throw up too many faces. From over there, one looked like a bishop's cap, but from here, it's a leaping fish. So what's its name? Each one is a puzzle, thus, and for me, now, puzzles are in long supply.

He's not expecting me, not at any particular time. Or ever. But I drive on.

It's not hot. This is February, early in the afternoon. But I've been here in August before, when breathing burns, and heat dancing up out of the earth makes the whole world waver and slide in and out of focus.

No, it's not hot now, but it is dry. Dry like ground bone. Any rain, any falling snow sinks presto into the ground, and whatever springs might be running now won't run for long. Friction causes easy fire, but dead wood turns to rock out here, before it has time to soften and rot.

A half dozen cows stare at me, big-eyed and dull. Ganged together alongside the trunks of a grove of bare cottonwood trees, down in a sandy creek bottom, they want something from me. I can see it. Water probably.

I have some. But not enough to help us all.

Finally, I'm up against the tip of one of the high mesas. Boulders, huge slabs of rock that have sloughed off the mesa walls flank me on one side, like blown-up grains of sand. Walls close in on me, but slowly, patiently. They mean no harm.

And as I push back into the short, rough canyon, the road itself, my trail, begins to climb. Up, up, along the rough sidehill, toward the flattened top of piñon, juniper, and cedar trees. Through the cake-layers of old ocean floor—some red, some orange, some yellow and brown. Crumbling, always changing shape.

The sun is bright, straight, yellow. Not so hot, but resting, waiting for the equinox. I know that. I've come to this place before.

2

THE OLD MAN'S NEST IS STILL HERE. THE BEAT-UP LITTLE TRAILER STILL sits on the edge of the cedars, backed up against the twisted trunks like an old tin can nailed to a stump. Its windows are held together with tape, and its skin is bleached the color of a cow's skull. I'm not surprised. No. But each time I come here and see it, I think: it's too naked, too flimsy, and someday a good desert wind will blow it over the edge of the canyon. It will disappear, and become little more than curious trash down below in the rocks.

The wood skirting is all but gone, gnawed away in some spots, dry-rotted in others, and the tire that is left uncovered has turned flat, cracked and grey. Tufts of dry grass reach out through the holes and cracks. Something under there makes a scurrying, scratching sound.

Most everything else is junk. An old compressor with half its innards gone, buckets of salvaged pipe fittings, pieces of heavy chain, a stack of rails, the wheels and buckets pulled from old mine cars. Shovel blades and hammer heads and rotten hose. A copper miner's junk, pitted and bleached and rusted, some of it half-buried in wind-blown sand. A graveyard.

The steps leading up to the trailer door are solid—two short chunks of tar-blackened pine, cut from mine timbers and wedged in between rocks—and they give me a footing, a reliable base that I need, as I stand there and knock.

There's no answer.

I knock again.

Still nothing.

Then I see him, topping a set of old stairs built down into a crack in the rock, little more than a ladder, bringing him up from a mine portal below the canyon rim. He sees me, and in that instant he tries to straighten up, to look taller and stronger. But he's a little stooped and a little slow, anyway, and he uses a round-pointed shovel like a cane.

I walk toward him, and he stops and takes off his sweat-crusted straw hat and wipes his forehead with his sleeve, even though there's no real heat in the air. His mustache has grown longer, bushier, and is mostly grey and white. His skin is red and wrinkled from the sun.

We stand there, four, maybe five, feet apart.

"Thought I heard an ore truck up here," he finally says, his voice harsh and a little too loud, the way loners talk.

"No truck," I say. "Just me."

He nods.

"What do you want?"

Not it's good to see you, or it's been a long time, or even how the hell are you. Just what do you want.

"I don't know," I say. And that's partly true. Or it's mostly true. "Maybe I just wanted to see if you were still here. If the buzzards had carried off the last of your bones."

My father doesn't smile, nor do I.

———

"It's gettin' late," he says a short while later, after we've tried to talk, but haven't been able to say much of anything at all. "Damned near supper time. You stayin'?"

He's surprised when I say I am. Nothing really shows in his quick grey eyes, but the slow way he turns around tells me. We both know: I've never been here after dark, never spent the night before.

———

He sits outside at a table made from an old cable spool, smoking and staring out into the space over the canyon, while I carry the dinner dishes back into the trailer and wash them off. I look around as I scrape and scrub. Like the outside, the inside is patched and bleached, and not much attention has been paid to the dirt and sand that must drift in and out with the seasons. But everything has a place—every plate, book, boot and spoon goes just so, allowing him room to reach the bed, sit at the table, stand at the stove. No space can be wasted. None is.

It's not in perfect order. An old book lies on his unmade bed, its leather cover stained and worn around the edges. It's an 1880 government report, I see. *Report on the Geology of the High Plateaus of Utah,* by someone named Dutton. Several bookmarks peek out, as though he's chosen to subdivide and emphasize in his own particular way: how he would have done it had he written the book. That's the way he is.

His old lever-action .30-30 lies there, too, with the chamber open, the hammer let down. Once before when I came, he'd said he had trouble with coyotes.

"Crazy bastards," he'd said. "Got to keep 'em back. Otherwise, they learn ya. Then you can't drive 'em off anymore."

By now, I think, they should have made peace. How could he not have become part coyote? He could hear the same hard silences, the snapping of a twig, the rolling of a rock, the shifting of the wind. He knew when the moon was precisely full, and when it would be gone for a night or two.

And the coyotes, how could they not have learned a sort of etiquette that allowed them to slide by him without friction? Stay out of his sight, and his firelight, and his garbage. Don't wake him up, or drink his water. That's all.

He said little during dinner, except that if we don't get done before dark, we'll have to use the lanterns. His generator is low on gas, he says, and he doesn't want to use it up before he can get back to town. He didn't fill the cans last time in, he says, because he bought a bottle of whiskey, and then he forgot.

He lights another Camel, and I see a tremor in the hand that holds the match. Then he coughs, and it's with his whole body, and I wonder how much dust has gotten down in there by now, and what it's done.

There's a weathered old bench, high, right on the edge, and I sit with a cup of coffee, come to watch the evening drift and slide. I don't want to be comforted. I want to keep my edge, to stay tight with my skin stretched thin across the margins. I'm here to trade pain.

But perched on this bench, looking down on the floor of this dried-up sea, looking down on the buttes like round-shouldered soldiers marching off into the haze, looking down on the mythical edge of the world, I can't quite keep my bile up. We're small, the two of us, like pissants in this hard, awesome place. And soft. The coyotes will get us in the end.

I sit, sipping my coffee, hearing birds I can't see. Birds that sound like jays and crows. Raspy, talking tough. Their taunts bounce around in the rocks like hard rubber balls.

I listen for other sounds. But there are none. And when the birds are gone, there is nothing. Silence, pressing down hard, holding the world dead solid still.

I want a rock to fall. Or a leaf to rattle. Or the two-note song of a chickadee to slip out of the fading light.

But the desert calls for a moment of silence. So I try not to breathe, try to stay mute and still and invisible. And for a quarter of an hour I can do that. Sit and watch and listen to nothing.

When he walks my way, I know it. He can't move without grating the sand, without rubbing against the air.

I don't turn to look, barely look his way when he sits on the other end of the bench, holding his own cup.

He squints for a minute, head bent toward the canyon. Then he points, but I can't tell at what.

"Coyote," he says. "Can't see him now."

"Your eyes must still be good," I say, but he doesn't answer, so we sit and watch. How long, I wonder, how many evenings, until you no longer see the desert at all, but instead just see the end of another in a string of numberless days? How long before you can barely fight back the urge to jump?

"What's on your mind?" he asks, after several minutes have passed heavily. Blue-black shadows have started to lie down behind the boulders in the canyon, and long, thin shadows stretch out on the easternmost sides of the buttes.

"You know that Neal is dead."

His answers never come quickly.

"I got your letter," he says finally.

"I didn't know for sure. You never answered."

"Meant to."

"It doesn't matter," I say, and that's true. I never expected to hear from him.

"I would have come for services, had you let me know in time."

"Didn't make any difference," I say. "He didn't know whether you were there or not." My mother's sister, the one that had seen Neal and me through the second ten years of our lives, would not have wanted him there. No one from that side of the family would have wanted to see him standing there, beside the grave, hat in hand. Thirty years was a long time, and for much of it, he'd been holed up out here in one old mining claim or another. Who knows what he might have done? Or what they might have done to him?

"Besides, that old truck of yours would never have made Tucson."

He doesn't say anything for a while.

"Am I supposed to do somethin'?"

I'm making him uncomfortable, but that's all right. He knows that more than a month has passed since Neal died, and he wonders what we're really talking about, what is hanging unformed in the air. This is his life, his land, and he doesn't allow complications here.

"No." I mean yes, but I can't start in with him that way. Can't ask him for much. "I just wanted to talk to you about something."

He looks a little annoyed, as though I'm about to cause him trouble. Maybe I am.

"What do you want?"

"Time is running out for us," I say. "For the Cottins."

He stares at me. Maybe I'm making no sense.

"You and me. We're all that's left."

Wrinkles roll up across his brow, and he spits on the ground. When it comes to talk like this, he wants to make it as hard for me as he can.

"But I want to know something. Before we're both . . ." I stumble here. This is a heavy rock to get rolling. "I want to know whether this name is worth saving before we just let it die out."

He chews on that for a minute before he answers.

"Just a name. What the hell's a name?"

"Is it? That's all it is to me. A name. No faces. No tombstones. No stories."

He just stares out across the canyon, like maybe he's gone deaf. Like maybe he's never going to answer again.

"You want me to save it, you do something for me. You tell me who the hell you are. Who you were. Where you came from."

"Why's that?"

"So I can decide. If there's anything in this blood . . ." It's hard to go on. " . . . that's decent. Or whether it's meant to end with me."

He turns his head slowly, and looks at me.

"That's a bunch of bullshit," he says. "Blood's blood."

I don't really expect him to help me with this thick, heavy rock. I know I'll have to keep pushing by myself.

"Okay," I say. And I unfold a single piece of paper out of my shirt pocket and hand it to him. "Just give me a little help, here. Tell me about little things like this."

It's a bad photocopy of two small newspaper clippings. They tell how he's gone to jail for dynamiting the workings of a company called Cable Minerals. Twice.

He reads, and I watch his face for a sign, and I see one. A little drop in the corner of his mouth. A deepening of his squint. He stares hard off across the canyon again, and I can see the muscles moving in the tops of his jaws as he clenches and releases his teeth. His fingers clamp tighter on each other.

"Let me tell you somethin', mister," he says after a long while, his voice rough and flat. "This means nothin' to you. Nothin'. It was a long time ago."

I wait on him for a change.

"If this is the kind of crap you want to pry into, well, you can just pack your shit and head 'er right on down the road. When I figger you need to know somethin' like this, I'll tell you about it."

"Neal and I, we waited a long time," I say. "Waited for anything from you. But it never came. So now I'm here. And I want to know what kind of a man does this. Runs. Hides out under rocks. Won't talk." I pause to catch my breath. "You've never told me shit."

"Not gonna argue with you, boy. It's my business, and if I wanna bury the son of a bitch, that's just the way she goes."

He stands up and dumps his cold coffee onto the rocks, and starts to walk away in the growing shadows. Then turns around and looks at me. For a few heartbeats, he says nothing.

"Go home," he says finally, louder than before. "Go home and ask all those sunsabitches on the old lady's side of the family what kinda blood you got. They have all the answers, them suck-asses. They always did."

He walks away into the junipers, breaking his way through the shadows, not waiting for an answer.

———•·——

I sit for a while, feeling a cool breeze come up and sigh its way along the rim. The rustle of the needles. Silence broken. It would have to start this way, I think. Even if he wanted to talk to me, to tell me everything that had happened, it would have to start this way. That's just the way we are, the way we always are.

Finally, I get to my feet and throw my own cold coffee over the edge. And as I do, the coyote down in the canyon starts up a sharp bark, a comment that I can't read.

I walk down the rim fifty yards, then cut back through the dim junipers and piñons to my pickup. There, I dig around in the back, throwing boxes and tools around until I find my little pack and my sleeping bag, and I toss them out onto the sandy ground. I find a tarp and a pad and toss them out. As I lift my head, a glimmer catches in the corner of my eye. A match. A lighted lantern, and then it disappears as the trailer door closes with a thud.

Just before the darkness closes in, the coyote signs off with one short, fading howl. A reminder, I think, about who owns what.

3

MY BROTHER SHOT HIMSELF IN A MOTEL ROOM IN LAS VEGAS. ALL ALONE, facing another round of drug charges he knew he couldn't run from and couldn't beat. Nobody heard the shot. The night was wet and miserable, and nobody heard much of anything over the hiss of the rain and the roll of the thunder.

It could have been a hammer, or a slamming door. It could have been most anything.

Two days passed before they found him, and they took another two days to figure it all out. Still, the call came in the night. Calls like that always do. Maybe the job always goes to somebody on the night shift, somebody low down on the sheriff's totem pole.

I couldn't be surprised. In our few conversations over the past three years, he'd always seemed to be posing the question: what's the use? What's the fucking use? It was in his choice of words, in his tone of voice, in his long, heavy silences. And when he wrote, rarely, he always seemed to say, "One town's like another. The nights are all the same. Then I stop watching, and things turn bad. I don't know how it happens or when it's coming. I only know that it does. And when I wake up, things are worse than they were before." So what's the use?

He'd been in jail twice before. Once for beating a woman he'd picked up in a bar. Another time for holding up a liquor store with a stolen gun. With coke in his pocket.

No, I couldn't be surprised, but I could be hurt. Hurt in a way I could never explain. After our mother died, when he was ten and I was twelve, years after our father had faded and faded until he disappeared into the rocks, Neal and I stood together back to back, leaning hard against the tides and the winds and the blackish clouds. We propped each other up, and made promises to each other in bed at night. We talked about the day when we would have our go at the world. But even then, I could tell that he barely believed. He seemed to know that the storm dogs would always come back again. And eventually they would bring down the sky.

And now, he was gone. It was a hard, confusing pain.

A week later, they left his belongings at my door. Five boxes. That was all. Maybe truck drivers for cowboy bands never do have much, I thought. Only what fits in the empty spaces, around the speakers and the mixing boards and the costumes. Life reduced. Defined by spaces in the back of a truck.

Clothes mostly, and towels from everywhere. Chicago. Dallas. Calgary. And there was a box of books. Some serious reading, like Kerouac and Conrad. And some not, like L'Amour and MacDonald. Beyond that, not much.

But there was a note. It simply said good-bye and sorry for the mess. He was tired, worn out, and things looked dark and bleak and every day it seemed to rain. He wished he could do something about the goddamned rain. But he couldn't, and he was getting out before the storms got worse. That's what he had to look forward to. Darker skies. Harder rain. More time in jail.

And there was this: "You were always the hawk, Markus, and I was always the crow. I was born to be the crow. It's something you will probably never understand. Maybe about both of us."

And this: "I found this stuff in mother's boxes a long time ago. I always wanted to show it to you and ask you what it meant. I've looked at it a thousand times. And I'm tired of it. My gift to you."

His note was clipped to an old brown envelope, and on it, in her distinctive, floral style, our mother had written, "Save for the Boys."

Inside, two short clippings from unidentified newspapers. One with the date Aug. 9, 1971 inked on the top, saying that Andrew Cottin had been found guilty of dynamiting a Cable Minerals mill in New Mexico and had been sentenced to six months in jail. Little more.

The other, about the same length, was dated June 8, 1972, and said that Andrew Cottin had been found guilty of dynamiting a Cable Minerals mill in Colorado, and sentenced to two years in jail as a repeat offender.

And there was a yellowed, brittle photograph that had been clipped out of a different newspaper. Old. Much older. In it, a thin, gaunt-faced man in handcuffs was being led up a set of stairs by a bigger man. Old halftone grains took away the eyes, but not the look of the lost. No date. No caption. No hope.

It wasn't our father. But it was somebody we were supposed to know. Or, at least, know about.

4

THE NEXT DAY, I GAVE HIS CLOTHES TO THE SALVATION ARMY AND LEFT for the desert. Toward Dos Cabezas and the Chiricahuas, out there where I could slow it all down and sort through it and let it lie there in the dirt.

A sleeping bag, a brand new bottle of tequila, and Neal's note. Some matches and a cup. I put it into a little bag and drove east, not seeing the traffic on the road, not hearing the white lines saying hello/good-bye, hello/good-bye, hello/good-bye. Not smelling the rain that was trying to form in the sky. Just driving. Going east.

———————

Maybe the little town I stopped in wasn't a town. It didn't have a name. At least I don't remember seeing one. But I stopped there anyway, at a run-down little store, because I was out of gas, and so it didn't matter where I was. After I'd pumped the gas, I bought a couple of cans of black-eyed peas and a loaf of bread, a package of wieners and a jar of orange juice. A jug of water. There wasn't much else on the dusty shelves, except for packages of hard dry rolls and boxes of candy bars, and I didn't want any of that.

The old man behind the counter took my money and said thank you in a careful, practiced way that told me those might have been the only English words he knew.

I was loading the stuff in the back end of my truck when I felt something touching my leg. A light touch, just barely there. When I looked down, I saw that it was a hand, a very small, very dirty hand, on the end of a very dirty arm that belonged to a big-eyed little girl. I guessed that she was four, maybe, or five.

"Chewin' gum?" she asked, looking up at me with big round brown eyes and holding out a box that contained perhaps six little pieces of wrapped gum.

"No thanks. Don't use it."

She set the box carefully on the ground and dug into an old, wrinkled paper bag.

"Buy my Bible?" she asked, holding out a book. "Please, señor."

It was a Bible, all right. One of the hotel/motel type, with a red paperboard cover that was scuffed and partly torn. Something she'd found in a ditch along the highway, I guessed.

"No thanks," I said. "Can't read."

"Please, señor. Ees bery nice."

I looked at her eyes. Looked at the dirty little dress she had on. Looked at hair that hadn't seen a comb in days.

"How much?"

"One dollars?" It was a question, not a price.

As I drove away with my Bible, I could see her in the rear view mirror, dragging her sack and running on happy legs as fast as she could back toward the store.

———•———

The back roads grew smaller and rougher, in stages, just as I wanted. Finally, I'd gone far enough, and I stopped in the bottom of an arroyo crossing and backed my truck up next to a half-dozen cottonwood trees. Then it began to rain. Not a heavy rain, just a squall blowing through, but steady for a while. I jumped out, grabbed the tequila and the orange juice, and climbed back in.

The drops pattered down in a rattle that killed all other sound, in a rhythm like life ticking away on a clock, only faster. I drank about that. Water running down the windshield played tricks with the shape of things. I drank about that.

Storm dogs brought down the sky. I drank about that, too.

———•———

The clouds broke just as the sun was going down. For two minutes, maybe four, everything glistened and gleamed. The rocks. The slabs and barrels of cactus. The yucca leaves. And the air was sweet, and it could be felt and tasted.

Then the sun dropped behind a hill, and the colors muddied and went flat. The red rocks turned brown, and all the greens faded off into a dull grey. The rain nectar left with the light.

I stumbled and almost fell when I climbed out of the cab. My thoughts were clear enough, just fuzzed at the edges, but my gyro was off and my legs had lost their bones. I walked around, picking out the flat spots, sleeping places, fire sites, and as I did, the tracks I left stumbled off to the left, then the right, and back again. Random. Chaotic. Circular.

By the time I'd gathered a pile of cottonwood branches and limbs off the ground, little remained of the day. Shadows had gone deep black, and even the high rocks had gone a dark reddish grey. Off somewhere, an owl warned the mice to move quickly and to stay close to home. Hoo-hoo. Hoo. Hoo-hoo. Hoo.

I hooted back, and waved, but he didn't answer.

I made a pile of twigs, but even in my semi-numb hands, they felt wet to the touch, and I knew they wouldn't light. I needed paper. First, I took the cellophane off my wieners and bread, wrapped the food in a spare tee shirt, and crammed that paper under the wood. One match, a whoosh, a couple of crackles, and it was gone. Too quickly burned to help the wood at all.

Then I tried a couple of old envelopes that I found under the seat of my truck. This time, the paper burned longer, and I could blow on it and move the wood around. A little plume of smoke, an instant of flame, a fading spire of vapor, then nothing. Burned out. Gone.

I took another pull out of the liquor bottle, straight, and thought about just crawling into my sleeping bag for the night. I was starting to feel chilled, lost, confused about the time and the place and why I was there. A half moon was up, but that looked cold, too. And the owl had gone away.

Then I remembered my one-dollar Bible. I took the book, and couple of wieners, a few slices of bread, the tequila and the orange juice and sat down next to the small circle of rocks that I'd made.

Then I dug out my pocket knife and began to slice my way into Genesis, and pile the paper on. Somewhere in Exodus, the fire took hold.

The warmth, the food and the juice, and time cleared my head a little. I sat there, cross-legged, layering on wet wood and scripture, staring at the flame. Thinking about the day. About the year. About Neal and my father and all that I knew and didn't know.

Leviticus. Numbers. Deuteronomy. Joshua. Judges.

When ancient philosophy burns, where does it go? Does it just hang there in the air, waiting to be collected and organized again? Or does it blow away on the wind, a word here, a thought there, and take root somewhere else? Or is it just gone, gone, gone? Destroyed by a man with cold hands.

Ruth. The Samuels. The Kings.

We, three kings.

The Kingston Trio.

Threes. A handy, triangular way of looking at things. A pattern, like on an Indian rug. Everything tied to everything else. More wisdom for the fire.

The Big Three: the Father and the Son and the Holy Ghost. Capitalized. That stuck with me for awhile. What about the father with the small *f*? The son with the small *s*? The holy ghost that had once been a brother, my brother, but who was now just ether, new heat on the inside of the earth?

It was getting late. My mind was getting bigger than my head. But this was the stuff I'd come there for, my way of spreading life out on the ground, opening it up for a closer look.

We did have the father. A horse's ass, no matter what direction you sliced the bacon. Out of step on purpose, just to screw up the parade. Mad. A man who liked to stick his chin right in people's chests and spit and yell. Better left alone.

"It wasn't unusual during those first years we were married for him to come home in the middle of the day with a black eye, or bleeding from the nose. After a while I just stopped asking. I knew."

That was my mother's take, her little history. One of the few memories of him she ever provided to us. Fired again, or quit. The mining engineer who would be regularly undone, over and over and over again. By his stubbornness. By his anger. By his hatred of authority.

"He could never tell me why. He wouldn't even try."

Within five years after they were married, she'd told me one night as I dried dishes for her, he'd fought and argued his way out of every decent job opportunity he would ever have. Blackballed. Embargoed. *Persona non grata.*

But he didn't starve. He could still work and make a day's pay. But as a miner, not a boss. As a laborer, not an engineer. They could handle his anger and his distrust so long as he hauled out the ore, so long as he was pounding away down there in the dark, out of sight and far enough away from their ears. They just didn't want to have to sit around a table with him.

And every job seemed to take him further and further away from home. And then he was gone, too far removed to ever be coming back. And in that leaving, that slipping away from us, he left us to learn to change tires and carve turkeys and catch ground balls on our own.

We didn't speak of him often. We had nothing kind to say.

By then, the wood would have probably burned well enough by itself. But I was caught up by that little ritual of burning up philosophies that I knew nothing about, playing with names. Getta Job. Jeremiah Johnson. Amos 'n Malachi. I continued to cut out the pages and toss them in. Evening mass, sung by St. José of Cuervo.

And we did have the son. One now, where once there were two. And what of him? He wrote books on art and paid his bills. He had nightmares, but not always. He was average. He had lost his wife.

"Frankly," that wife had said one night when we'd taken turns cursing the darkness we found in each other, "I hate poetry. I don't even like books."

And I don't like you, I thought, staring into the fire. I wish there was a chapter named Allison in the New Testament. I'd rip it out carefully, ritually, and burn it page by page.

"I didn't write poetry," I said to the owl, as though I had to explain, somehow.

———·•·———

I layered on more wood, and laid back down with my head on my sleeping bag, watching every star in the northern hemisphere wink on and off. I wanted to finish the conversation between myself and the owl before I ran out of Bible. About Neal. The third point on my triangle, the leg that once seemed to hold everything together. A holy ghost, now, in every sense that I cared about . . .

But I passed out. Somewhere between Peter and John. When I woke up, sometime in the early hours of the morning, the fire had burned out and I was stiff with the cold. The half moon was gone. I unrolled my bag in the darkness, pulled off my boots, and crawled in, helpless in my shivers, with a throbbing in my head. Then I began to warm up slowly, and just before I fell asleep again, I heard the owl one more time. He said that he'd once been a crow, too. But now he was in charge of the nighttime sky. Hoo. Hoo-hoo. Hoo.

———·•·———

I took a walk the next morning, up the dry wash, then higher, through the prickly pear and broken rocks, climbing the ridge. My head hurt some, and my arms and legs ached, and I was hoping to find a crumbled mission, maybe, or at least an old shack. Something old to sit on, some rotting board that proved that every plan gets changed, every glory finally fades away. Ashes to rise out of. Perspective. But I found nothing, so instead I walked until my legs gave out, and I sat down next to a big warm rock.

The day was new, and my mind was raw from the scrubbing it had gotten. I felt a vague guilt, somehow, over my drunkard's Bible school, but I felt cleaner for it, too.

So I sat there, letting the mysteries evaporate. Letting light shine in, brightly, until it hurt. Letting the meat of the matter dry a little, and shrink closer to the bone.

———

I pulled Neal's note out, and I read it again. Then again. I looked at the clippings and the old photograph. I held them out in front of me, and let them all sit in my hands. Waiting for something to leak out of the paper and through my skin. Waiting for a whisper that I knew was there. Waiting to hear.

A little lizard crawled onto a rock next to me, and sat, turning just the right color against the rock, stalled in the warm morning sun. For five, maybe ten minutes, we watched each other watch each other. Barely blinking. Locked in and at rest.

"It's something you'll probably never understand," Neal had said. But as I let myself go numb and still under the stare of the lizard, let myself fade out of my own focus, I thought I did. I thought I understood.

I'd gone to see my father three times in the past ten years. It took some asking, some hunting, but I'd found him. Alone. Civil, but always a little on edge. Each time, we'd talked for an hour or two about little things. Each time, I'd lost my nerve, and could barely bring up the past. I'd gone there pulled by some sense of duty that I couldn't describe, and then I'd failed badly at it. We'd shake hands and turn away, and I'd promise myself never to pick at old scabs again. Even old scabs bleed.

But Neal hadn't seen our father since the last time he walked out the family door. Never. And I'd wondered about that. Once, when I asked him about hunting our father up, his eyes clouded over, and he wouldn't answer. He just turned and walked away. There was anger in his steps.

And now I thought I saw into it all. The package of his good-bye, the collage built around his note, was his final message to me. A picture, drawn to replace words he could never allow himself to form or write or say. Look hard. You have to see it, though the light is dim and going fast.

After spending so many years chasing himself around in the dark, hiding and seeking both, Neal had finally escaped: he'd found someone, something else, to blame. It was our old man. And maybe all the Cottins who had ever lived before him. Guilt replaced by dirt in the blood. Poor crops sprung from bad seed. Destiny.

Was he saying a touch of madness came with the Cottin name? Or was it a touch of evil? That much was not clear.

Was he warning me, or just pleading his own case before some drugged-up dream of a final judge? That wasn't clear either.

But as I pictured him there in his last hours, trying passionately to force little fragments into some kind of a whole, I saw a man who got it all mostly wrong. Neal's problems were his own. Unique to him. Coming from him. And it was not our father, or his father before him, who pulled the trigger in Las Vegas that night.

But in a way, he got part of it, something of it, right, too. There was something in the darting, shifting greyness of the old man's eyes. A touch of madness? A touch of genius? Or was it just a touch of plain old dimestore fear?

———·•·———

Only two remained. And one lived where the rocks and the coyotes and the heat waited to take him down. Another week, another month, another year? How long would it be? Time was passing, and the light around the truth was fading fast.

In his own way, Neal had pleaded for answers. For his own sake, it seemed to me, he wanted to be proven right. And for my sake, I wanted him simply to be wrong.

Biased though I might be, I was the only one left who could gather the evidence. Make the case. Sit, finally, as judge.

PART TWO

Old Tom

1

I WAKE UP EXPECTING TO FIND MY FATHER OUT ON HIS BENCH ON THE RIM drinking coffee and soaking up the morning sun. Watching the ravens glide below him, and listening to their squawks bounce off the canyon walls. Watching the sun climb over the tops of the Abajo Mountains and wash its way across the desert floor. That's the way I would start my days.

But even before I open my eyes, I know there is no sun. The wind gusts and stops, gusts and stops. I hear grains of sand rasp as they blow across my sleeping bag, and I feel the wind and pine needles crossing through my hair. And when I do ease my eyes open, I see white boiling clouds, and flat light. The reds are almost purples, and the browns and greys have become the same color.

He's not around. I knock on the trailer door, and when he doesn't answer, I let myself in. Coffee perks on his little stove, and I pour myself a cup and wait for a minute or two. No sounds, except for the wind and the rattle of his windows, and the banging of a loose piece of tin on the trailer roof. I wonder how he tolerates that.

Then I go back outside and climb down the rickety stairs that drop through the crack in the canyon rim, down to his mine. He's there, sitting on another old bench near the portal, squinting, hard at work with his hands. When I get close, he looks up with those flashing grey eyes, and I can see that he's crimping blasting caps onto the ends of long cords of fuse with a pair of pliers.

"Morning," I say.

He just nods, and looks back at his work.

"What's up?" I ask.

"Gettin' out of that goddamned wind," he says. "Besides, I got work to do. Holes are all drilled. Got to get 'em loaded and get 'em shot. Maybe this afternoon."

He grabs the caps out of their red box and jams the fuse in the end with a clumsy indifference, and I suspect right away that his recklessness is just a little drama staged for me. He did that same trick to me once before. He knows it gets me.

"What happens if you squeeze the other end of those caps with your pliers?" It's not a dare. Just a way of saying I don't care, one way or the other.

He looks up at me, as though he's never thought about it.

"I guess you could give all your gloves away," he says. "Wouldn't be needin' 'em."

"That's all?"

He finishes one and drops it on the ground, in a pile with several more. I can't help myself. I flinch.

"Sometimes it kills ya. Blows your eyes out, maybe. Depends." He's laughing inside. I know it, and it rubs me a little raw.

I watch him for a while longer as I sip my coffee and act bored. Let my mind pretend he's just sticking fuse cord into the end of little lipstick tubes, or big .22 shells. Unclench my toes. Watch a cobweb sway and strain in the swirling wind.

"I'll be heading out, here pretty soon," I say after five minutes or so.

He grunts, I guess, just to make a noise.

"But I need to talk to you first."

He looks up, and stares at me blankly.

"Talk."

"You're busy," I say. And I don't want your mind and your hands to get too far apart.

"I'm done," he says, standing and walking into the little shack next to the portal. "Got a pot of coffee waitin' for me in here anyway."

He's waiting for me to start, and now I'm not ready. The wind has stirred up dust inside the shack, and I taste it when I breathe. The door is not fastened, and it squeaks back and forth on its hinges. I feel cobwebs in my hair.

I sit on an old powder box turned on end, watching him watching me, and I sort through my words, taking my time. I have to take my time.

"Asked you yesterday," he says, tired of waiting on me. "What do you want?"

What do I want? Other than to get the hell out of here? I want a lot of things. But first, I want to know what I'm up against. I want to know where I stand and how far away that might be from where he's hunkered in.

So I take a breath, let it go slowly, and tell it to him as it comes to me. The lack of a family truth works like a vaccuum, a black hole, and it invites nightmares. Without real stories, we make them up. And sometimes the ones we make up are darker and deeper and more misshapen than they need to be.

He looks at me, and he says nothing.

"A man who dynamites ore mills is part of a story. And when he does it to the same company twice, that's maybe a different story. But we don't know about it, so we make up our own . . ."

"Stop wastin' my time." His voice is hard and cold.

"What?"

"I said go home. This is none of your goddamned business. Now get your goddamned nose out of my life before I twist it off." The longer he talks, the louder he gets.

"That's about what I thought you'd say." Already I can feel the back of my neck getting hot, my mouth getting dry, but I try to hold on.

"I don't give a shit."

"I know that."

He hears all that those words are supposed to say, and it stops him for a moment.

"I got better things to do," he says, a little more quietly, and moves toward the door.

I jump up and block his way, holding on to both sides of the door frame. My legs are shaking, like they want to give out.

"Who gave you the right to own the past? Huh? Who gave you that right?"

"I don't ask for permission," he says, angry again now. "Not from you or any other bastard. Now get your ass outta my way."

"Remember me?" I ask, yelling at him now, and poking my finger into my own chest. "Remember me? I'm your own goddamned kid. Not some other bastard. A kid you let grow up alone. Where were you? Huh? What were you doing with those years that were supposed to belong to Neal and me?"

He starts to push me aside, and we both know he can do it.

"Goddamn it!" I yell finally. "Don't I have a right to know?"

He looks me in the eyes and his face and voice grow colder still.

"Maybe you got a right to ask," he says evenly. "But I got rights, too." He spits the words out, one at a time. "I got the right to tell you to stick to your own goddamned business."

He shoves his way past me and climbs the steps back up to the rim, back into the wind.

I start to follow him, but I can't. I don't have the strength, and my legs are shaking, and my lungs are pumping hard, needing more air.

———————

I'm loading my stuff into the back of my pickup when I hear him walk up behind me. I don't turn around. For a minute, I hear nothing else but the wind.

"I'm going to go to those towns where you were put in jail," I

say, still facing the bed of my truck. I don't have to work to put flat
determination into my voice.

He doesn't answer.

"And after that, I'll go hunt up your goddamned birth certificate,
if that's what it takes."

Still no answer.

"You went to school," I say. "I'll find out about that, too."

I hear him shuffle his feet, but I hold my place.

"You think there's some big story hidin' out there, don't you,
boy?"

Now I don't say anything. I just let that big silence and the wind
answer him back.

"Well there ain't. There ain't nothin' but a bunch of fools. A chain
of fools. Each one worse than the one that come before."

I turn toward him, and he's just standing there, with his hands at
his sides.

"Maybe people figgered me for the biggest fool of the bunch,"
he says. "And maybe I am. But them people . . ." He pauses. "They
ain't met you."

I start to tell him that the biggest fool is the one that dies alone,
in the night. But Neal died alone and in the night, and I cannot label him that way.

"You know where Madero is, do ya?"

It sounds as though he's changed the subject, but I know he hasn't.
This is still about fools. I nod. It's about three hours away. In Colorado. High up. Where my old man lived as a kid. My mother pointed
it out once on a map.

"Well, you need to just go on over there. Haul your ass up that
particular road."

I stand there with my arms folded.

"You just stay there for a while. Dig around in that old shit. And
you just keep diggin' until you turn over Tom Cottin. He's there,

somewhere, livin' in his shack. And you go see him. Talk to him. Ask him to tell you how we've all spent our lousy goddamned lives. Tell him you want to see tombstones left behind by all those fools."

Even if I want to answer him now, I can't. His words have stunned me, left me dead at the nerve ends just as surely as if he'd hit me in the back with a hard, heavy board.

His last words to me before he turns and walks away: "And when you're done doin' that, when you've heard it all and thought about it, you just ask yourself if you wasn't a smarter man when you didn't know nothin' at all."

2

OUR GRANDFATHER. ALL THROUGH OUR LIVES, OUR MOTHER HAD LET US believe he was dead. Maybe she'd never said he had died. Maybe she'd just said he was gone. But she knew what we believed. And we believed a lie: that we had no living ancestors on our father's side, beyond the old bastard himself. It was not so uncommon in this age, to have no wrinkled hands to hold, to know life as being only one or two generations deep. Small, shallow-rooted family trees.

But at the same time, we'd wondered why there were no photographs, no stories, no real family lore. Like all kids, we'd plundered the dusty boxes in the attic and thumbed through the fragile, yellowed pages of old books. And we'd found my mother's parents and uncles and aunts hiding among the cobwebs there: clippings of birth and death, favorite poems, soldiers and sailors staring fearlessly toward unseen cameras, souvenirs from the World's Fair. But from my father's side, nothing.

And I'd wondered about this: why did we act so deliberately as though they'd never lived? Why were their names not scratched into some kind of wall somewhere? Was that what death was supposed to mean to the few who were left?

But the old man was alive. Not dead. Not the victim of some mining camp black death. Not rotting away in some unmarked grave.

Alive. Of this time. Within reach. Not dead. Echoes off the canyon walls and back again. Not dead.

———•+•———

As I drove down off the mesa, following the dirt tracks that led out of the rimrocks, my mind ran out ahead of me, slinking through the sagebrush like an angry and hurt and confused she-dog, waiting for me, the explainer in me, to catch up. But it couldn't catch up. There was no way for me to know, to understand, why we'd been led astray for so long. What that had been meant to do.

There was no way to know whether that truth was supposed to have been shoved into the envelope, too. The one marked "Save for the Boys."

3

"WINTER'S THE SHITS."

A tall, lanky, empty-eyed kid was pumping gas out of the station's single pump, talking toward me through a blue-grey cloud of exhaust. He coughed, and his words were broken up by the rattling hum of the old pump and the rumbling idle of the car's engine, but I couldn't help him. The day was too cold and the snow banked too high around us to make me willing to shut my truck and its heater all the way down.

He'd been dozing on a bench next to an old kerosene heater when I'd driven up, and I had to wait and watch while he fought far enough through his stupor to slip a greasy coat over his coveralls, tug a cap down over his ears, and work his hands into a pair of heavy mittens that had shriveled and crusted from being left too close to the heat.

So he knew better than to tell me I owed it to him to shut my engine down.

"No place to stay here after dark," he said as he counted out my change with one bare hand. "Not this time of the year, anyways."

How did he know? Or was it just the kind of warning he routinely passed out to strangers who might, later, try to take away his heat or his bench?

———•+•———

Snow had been piling up since November, and it filled the narrow Helado Valley like white sand poured into a deep trough. A pale ribbon wound down the center of it, the only sign of a small, quick river gone under the ice. Along the watercourse and a third of the way up the steep hillsides, the colorless, lifeless aspens spread in a thick flank of black and white lines, before giving way higher up to the feature-less wash of dark green spruce and fir. Higher still, jagged peaks and cliffs of granite took over, leaving only cracks and pockets for the snow to claim.

Because there was little sky between peak and peak, the days were only half long. The feeble sun arced low to the south, barely getting up from behind the east ridge before it crossed the canyon and ducked behind the peaks to the west. Long blue-black shadows laid down along the north sides of the trees and across the north-facing slopes.

The main road through town, connecting the gas station on one end with the town's only cafe on the other, a full six blocks, was well plowed, but with a high ridge of snow down the center of it. A hole had been cut through with shovels, letting those who needed to cross between Ike's, the tavern on one side, and the general store on the other. The post office/liquor store sat at an intersection on the west side, and the highway maintenance barn was across to the east. Everything else on that street was boarded-up, locked, forgotten. Dry goods store, pool hall, garage, offices, bank: all gone. Others had no names or labels. No proof of what they were, or had once tried to be, and their faces were buried deeply behind drifts of grimy, sooty snow.

If the highway, the main street, was the spine of the withered, little town, the side streets were its ribs. And those ribs, on the west side, plunged down toward the river sharply, keeping the angle of the mountain face, and crossing only one other flat street. The other ribs, on the east side, climbed just as sharply higher, crossing two flat streets and ending in a confusion of drifts and mine dumps and a retaking of the land by aspen trees and clumps of snowbound brush.

The grid was clear and marked in places, where the snowplow cut clean lines and left behind dikes of crusted snow. Other streets had been plowed once, or twice, but had since gone to deep ruts and scattered, formless mounds of hibernating cars. Other streets had closed down to mere foot trails, and still others were unbroken, clean dunes that would wait, silently, until winter had tired of the valley, and had moved further north.

King, Silver, Eureka, Commerce. Names on a few old bent and rusted signs, barely poking through the sweeping mounds of snow.

Old mine buildings sat mostly on those back streets and ragged edges of the town. Stone walls with no doors or windows or roofs, filled in now with the wind-blown leavings of the season. Tin sheds, rusted and rattling, but still good enough to hold a horse in summer, or old car parts, but now becoming just drift fences, trapping waves of snow. Concrete pilings and pieces of wooden walls that could have been parts of anything, but which were nothing now. Nothing more than markers, reminders, land-buoys sticking up through the sea of snow.

Where once three hundred houses might have stood, only about sixty remained. Side-by-tight in some places, spaced out across abandoned lots in others, crowded mostly in ragged rows up against the shoulders of the streets. But most were boarded up, waiting for summer use. Only here and there were roofs cleared, wood piles tarped and trails cut by shovel through the waist-deep snow.

Icicles like walrus tusks, and drifts that swept up and over everything. Those things were the punctuation at the end of a long, somber sentence that said winter.

The first day was a test, but not a surprise. The old cabin that I'd rented over the phone from the postmaster's brother was just as he had warned: worth about forty bucks a month. Rough. Small. Weathered. And it was blown under, not ready for a winter tenant, forcing me to shovel all one day just to free the doors, find the windows, and cut a trail to the wood and coal sheds.

It was good enough. The old wood-burning heater warmed the two rooms with ease, and the chipped and stained coal-burning cookstove would fry my eggs and heat my bath water. Six quilts and blankets on the hard, flat bed would see me through the coldest nights.

The next day, after staring out the window for an hour, wondering where and how I could find anything underneath this heavy cover, this great silent overpainting of winter, I made the only move that came to mind. I walked the four blocks down to the town's only store, and while I paid for soup and coffee and a large sack of beans, I asked about him. Where he lived. When he came in. What he looked like. Richert, the storekeeper, looked at me as though my dialect was way wrong, somehow, and his eyes and brow knotted up in a painful curiosity, but he answered my questions anyway. Without asking any of his own.

So I stood the next afternoon in a light snow, and watched him from a distance, watched him shuffle slowly up the road from his shack, watched him pass me by, unaware. Moving as if suspended on strings. And I felt as though I was alone in a vast white movie theater, watching an old, old film of history being made.

———•———

The next day was Sunday, a cold snowy Sunday, that would, in normal times, have kept me inside. Would have allowed me to read and oil my boots and think. But I was not there for those kinds of days. I was there to brush the snow aside and to uncover what time had left frozen underneath.

I took a stool at the street end of the bar in Ike's Place, and nursed a beer I really didn't want. The coldness of it felt wrong in my hands. A television screen crawling with little basketball players threw off a smokey glare that turned the other four customers in the run-down joint into raggedy-edged silhouettes. I looked up when they clapped or moaned, in time to see the replay. But mostly, I just thought about the ticking by of the hours, and about the connections I still hadn't made, and about the snow swirling and piling up outside.

I didn't care about the game. The teams, from New York or Chicago or maybe Houston, wouldn't change the shape of much of anything. But it was a way of doing something, moving, reaching, being there. Inside my head, though, a troubled vacancy, and the day and the game were going on without me.

So I watched it snow, intrigued by the fury, by the speed with which it layered over itself. The snowplow had gone by an hour ago, but the street looked as though a week had passed. The plow was barely gone, before its tracks were wiped whitely and completely away.

That's when I saw Tom Cottin, and I saw him fall.

He had just materialized, taking shape as a slowly darkening fusion of the flakes, limping along, a hunched over grey question mark, carrying two canvas shopping bags that barely cleared the snowy ground. But as he came enough into focus so that I could tell who he was, part of the hard truth I'd come for, his legs seemed to fail him. He pitched sideways, into a drift.

When, after five or ten or fifteen seconds, the old man failed to move, I pulled on my coat and walked out, with the sound of ". . . from downtown, but it's . . ." cut abruptly by the slamming door and howling wind.

Old Tom lay there, breathing in big, raspy gusts, his hands still locked onto the handles of his canvas bags. A few pieces of lump coal had spilled from each, making deep black holes in the snow.

"Let me give you a hand up, old man," I said gently, just loudly enough to be heard over the wind, holding out my hand.

The old man just laid there. His chest rose and fell. His feet kicked uselessly at nothing. Snow had already began to stick and clump on his greasy old ragged coat and gather on the side of his head.

"Here, give me your hand."

Another few seconds of silence before the old man spoke. "Don't need no goddamned help." The words came out in a loud, creaky rasp.

"Well, you'd better get up soon, then. Otherwise, you'll be covered over until spring."

A faded and dirty stocking cap, pulled as far down on his face as it would go, butted up against bushy grey eyebrows that scowled and had begun to gather clumps of snow. Underneath, old eyes shifted back and forth, and were hard to see.

Then a grin broke through and pushed some of the folded skin around and back, showing a flash of bits and pieces of teeth. Dark gaps and stained enamel. Rectangles and triangles and unnamed shapes.

"Heh, heh, that's right," he cackled. "Rise and shine you lazy suminabitch. Ain't gettin' nothin' done layin' on your ass in the snow."

He stretched a mittened hand up, and I pulled him to his feet. A hint of rancid air hung on the snowflakes between us.

"Yessir, yessir, got some jobs to do. Got to check the jail. Check on them Navajos," the old man said, slapping at his coat and pants to knock the snow loose. He set his bags upright and carefully placed the lumps of coal back inside.

"Nice talkin' to ya. Can't keep old President Harry a-waitin'. Prob'ly wonderin' where I went with this here goddamned coal. Prob'ly freezin' his old ass."

Navajos in jail. President Harry. *A chain of fools.* My father's words were ringing back there in my mind, like somber bells, making a song that was dark like the day, cold like the wind. I wiped them away, and went on.

"How about letting me carry those bags for you?" I asked, as the old man straightened up with his load. "I could use the work."

The old man looked back over his shoulder, studying me. Or pushing me back with his eyes.

"Told you. Don't need no goddamned help."

And he limped on down the deserted street, past the tavern, past the post office, past a couple of boarded-up buildings. His shape faded and fell apart and he disappeared into the storm.

———·——

I walked another way, up a steep side street that hadn't been plowed since the day before, kicking my way through dry, light snow that reached nearly to my knees. The afternoon was fading fast, from a dull white to a duller thicker grey.

Lights flared as yellow blurs from the innards of some of the houses. Somewhere in there: people with little or no money—a few oldtimers, artists and fugitives of one passion or another. Among the few that lived in Madero year-round. Other houses, mostly summer places owned by people from the hotter latitudes, fishermen who came and went—just brown, darkened backdrops to the dancing cloud of snow.

Two blocks up, two blocks over. The path I'd shoveled before I'd walked to Ike's was already filled with another six inches of winter. I swept off the porch and steps of the cabin, hauled a load of firewood, and closed myself in for the night.

The fire I'd left banked in the heater took off with a soft pop when I opened the vents, the flames dancing up and around the chunks of aspen, while I filled a teakettle and set it on the stove. No sense building a fire in the cookstove, I thought to myself. I have an ache where my hunger ought to be. Soup will do.

While the water heated, I turned on the radio, but the signals were few and weak. Agents of the Lord, promising redemption. Whining western music, promising to never drink and drive trucks again. I snapped it off and put on a tape, instead, something from Bach, with cellos and violins. Long, slow, deep notes. A fugue for the day.

Then I remembered the brandy, the cheap brandy, that I had hidden away. Outside, the sheets of white were disappearing behind the thicker sheets of falling darkness, and I could hear more of the wind.

My hands were shaking, like my hopes, as I poured an inch of liquor into the bottom of the cup.

4

THE STORM BLEW OUT DURING THE NIGHT, AND THE NEXT DAY CAME ON clear and crisp, capable maybe of taking the edge off of the pathetic. Shortly after noon, the snowplow rumbled its way past, throwing clouds of snow into the cold, hard air.

I bound myself up in my heaviest clothes and set off to see Old Tom. I walked down the deserted street, past rows of buildings lost behind the mounds of snow, to the state highway. Then a quarter mile north, where an unplowed, winding road cut west to the river, down past the old man's shack.

When I got within thirty yards of the half-buried cube of weathered old boards, I could see grey smoke curling out of his rusted stovepipe, and I could see the dirt-smudged windows that were cracked and patched with tape, and I could see the narrow path he'd worn through the snow.

But I couldn't go to the door. Couldn't walk up there and knock and wait to be invited in. Couldn't try to tell him who I was and who he was. Couldn't ask him any questions at all.

I turned, wishing I was stronger, more able to take these unknowns by the neck and beat them until they cried out some of the truth. I walked back up the hill, back to the walls that had so little to say.

That night, in air that was cold and clear and still, I got up, put on my robe, crammed more wood into the stove, and knelt on the couch, looking out at the deserted white street, at the empty houses scattered down the white hill. And I asked, of whom I did not know: what in the hell is going on?

A couple of days later, as I walked from the post office, I saw Old Tom sitting on a bench in front of Ike's Place. The sun was out, stronger than usual, and the day was far less cold. But Tom had the same old stocking cap pulled down around his face, and the greasy pea-type overcoat looked the same.

Without thinking, without trying to prepare for what I might do, I walked over to him. He watched me approach, staring at me out from under his bushy eyebrows, showing no emotion at all.

"Remember me?" I asked, sitting down on the bench beside him. "Remember when I helped you up out of the snow a couple of days ago?"

He just stared at me, as though he hadn't heard a word.

"Are you doing okay?"

He started to say something, then paused, then started again.

"Ain't got no goddamned coal." I'd forgotten how creaking and raspy his voice had been.

"You had some the other day." I wondered if there was something that I ought to do, if he was trying to ask me for help.

"Ain't got no goddamned coal," he said again. "Come to get some from the store. That's where I get it. My goddamned coal."

I remembered the bags full that he'd been carrying through the storm. And I wondered why he didn't have a shed full, like other people in town. But then, he didn't have a shed.

"Can I help you get some?"

He just sat there, not answering, staring across the street at the store, as though he was waiting for a signal, or someone to bring his coal. I wondered whether I should ask him again.

"Piss poor, too," he said before I could speak.

"What's that?"

No answer. He stuck his hands down deep in his coat pockets, and went back to staring across the street.

Still, I wanted to get the old man to talk, so maybe I could get closer to something I needed, something I could grasp. I had no way of knowing whether my questions were getting through, but I tried again, nevertheless.

"You think it will start getting warmer one of these days?"

He thought about it for a minute or two.

"What if it does? What if it don't? All of us be gone one of these days, anyway. Nothin' left in Madero but dog shit and Navajos."

I didn't know how to answer.

"Snow melts. Ever' year. Dog shit ever'where. Dog shit and Navajos."

"I guess I haven't been here long enough," I said. "I haven't seen any Navajos."

"They's a hidin'," he said, and winked at me. Enough of a grin so that broken teeth showed through. "That's when they getcha, when you think they's gone."

Then he laughed: that same screeching, cackling laugh I'd heard earlier. I couldn't stand to look at his face, so I took my turn at staring across the street.

When the laughter had stopped and I did glance over, a serious look had slipped down through his eyes.

"You ain't a Navvy, are ya?"

"No," I said, seeing an opening. "I'm just like you. I have the same name as you. Cottin. We're . . ."

I stopped short. A scowling, angry sort of a look had taken over the old man's face. He seemed to stiffen up.

"Names don't mean nothin'," he said. "'Sides, my name's Tom. Tom Navajo. Cottin ain't nobody. Never was."

With that, he stood up and ambled across the street, stumbled over the pile of snow plowed up in the middle, and went into the store. I watched each of his steps, his stooped back, his limping legs, until the door closed and he was gone.

Twice more I tried. Twice more that same week I found Old Tom sitting on that same bench, perched like an iced-up bird waiting for spring, and twice more I struck up conversations with him. They all went about the same way. I'd try to follow along, and then to lead him toward a name or a time or an event that he could recognize and talk about. But he'd give me only bits and pieces, phrases and words, odd names like Tom Mix and Jack Dempsey, nothing that matched. I'd ask questions, and he'd never answer any of them.

Then, without really thinking, I asked him if he knew anything about Cable Minerals, the company that figured so strongly in my father's foggy past.

"Sunsabitches," he said, and his scowl deepened, and he seemed to be chomping his back teeth together, quickly, like a controlled chatter.

"Why do you say that?"

"Sam Benally." A Navajo name.

"Who was Sam Benally?"

Nothing. I tried again, and still he wouldn't answer. He seemed to be glaring back at the past, lost in some kind of private anger.

I left him alone, then, for several minutes, until he seemed to be thinking about other things. Looking around again, his eyes wider, his face more relaxed. I didn't want to push him, to upset him again, but I had to get on with it. So I asked him if he'd had a son named Andrew.

"Yep," he said quickly, almost eagerly. "Died when I was in jail, back in '50."

But when I tried to take it further, to ask him what happened to his son, to ask him why he was in jail, he just stared back at me.

"Navajos," he said finally, as though that was the answer to everything.

When I tried to get him back on course, he just drifted away.

"Goin' to Mexico," he said. "Gonna catch my horse and go to Mexico."

Then he laughed again: that same unnerving shriek.

"Shit, I ain't got no horse. Dumb suminabitch. Ain't that right?"

"Well, I don't . . ."

"Remember when the army came?" he asked.

And I could tell from the look in his eyes that my answer wouldn't matter at all. He'd slipped away to a place where I did not exist, and some other kinds of dialogue were going on. So we sat there in an uneasy silence, far away from each other.

"You make my ass tired," he finally said. Then he got up and walked down the cold, deserted street. A small, dark, slow-moving stick caught in a big white river of time.

That night, I thought about the newspaper photograph that Neal had sent to me. Showing a gaunt, frightened man in handcuffs. I couldn't know for certain, but I believed, then, that the man was Tom Cottin.

Some time in the night, well past midnight, I heard the sound of steps on my front porch. Slow steps that thudded against the frozen wood and squeaked in the icy snow. Back and forth a couple of times. Then, before I could get myself out from under the blankets and get to a light, the footfalls moved away and left a hard silence in their wake.

Just before dawn, snow fell again. Whatever tracks might have been there were covered over and gone.

My questions, maybe, had made it hard for him to sleep.

5

During those days of big questions and small answers, February slipped away. The ides and the urgencies of March were taking over winter, and the days warmed and lengthened steadily, and the wind stopped howling in favor of a softer, more subtle humm. That inevitable change.

There was no point in going on. I could see that clearly enough. And I began to suspect that my father had been right: that we might be little more than a family of fools.

No matter how many conversations I might have with Old Tom, I wasn't going to gather anything new. Whether I'd seen what my father had intended, or whether I had not, it made no difference.

There would be nothing more.

—————

Early one evening as I sat reading, I felt the entire subset of Madero existence turn over, just as water in a mountain lake turns over to bring nutrients to the top. Although the sun had gone down, and darkness was coming on for the evening shift, I could still hear water dripping. The snow-melt was continuing, even without the sun, and heat was lingering into the night. It was a sign, a clear and vital sign: the icy grip was giving way.

That meant an ever-earlier morning light. Longer days. Snow fields would become snow patches, and the patches would shrink until, one day, they might never have been. Drifts would remain on the north sides, in the shadows, but the soggy ground would begin to take on a faint greenish tint.

And it meant it was time for me to go.

———

The day was Monday, and I decided to leave on the third or fourth day following, when most of my cabin rent would be used up. I'd already stayed longer than my patience and mood could stand, not because I felt as though I had to squeeze out every penny's worth, but because I wanted to get around to one last flailing stroke. I wanted a photograph of the old man.

I couldn't say how the picture would be used, if it would ever be used at all. Who would I show it to? Neal? My old man?

But I had the gear. And the know-how. And to overlook it, to be driven out by impatience and gloom, would be to gamble recklessly, to risk a later, desperate need for something I could have so easily had.

Though nothing that he said might ever come clear to me, he still stood for something that, somehow, we'd all together done wrong. So I still wanted to be haunted by that look in his eyes. I didn't want him to let me forget.

———

I approached his shack from below, from along the river. Much of the snow had melted along the river bank, and I could get around easily enough, except when drifts or big rocks forced me back into the willows and blue spruce. The snow was deeper there, and crusted, and hard to wade through.

I rounded a short, sharp bend in the river and crossed a deeply worn trail, worn through the snow down to the bare dirt. On one side, it led down the bank to where a short wall of loose river rock had been piled out into the water, creating a quiet and deep eddy, a tiny man-made lagoon, free of ice. On the bank next to the water, a stool made from a short section of sawed log sat next to it's backrest— the gnarled and twisted root end of an old stump that had washed ashore. A rusted coffee can was tied with a thin rope to a nail driven in the cut log.

Going the other direction, the trail disappeared into the thick willows, off in the direction of his shack.

It was the place where Old Tom got his water.

I stood there silently for a minute or two, forced by the scene to feel and consider the pain and sweat of the old man's life. I thought of him fighting just to keep a roof and a bite and a drink. And I thought of him in the dead of howling winter, keeping the ice chopped back so that his water hole wouldn't freeze solid, and dragging heavy buckets back through the snow. Without knowing why, I felt uneasy and guilty, like all along I had been ignoring some vague duty of humankind, or even of kinship.

I stood there a couple of minutes more, wondering which of us had the greater will to live. Then I started east through the willows, on the trail to the old man's house.

He was sitting on a wooden chair, leaning back on the west side of his shack in the warm sun, when I saw him through the camouflage of the thick brush. He wore a ragged old brown shirt, and the familiar dirty pants and old boots. For the first time, he was without hat and coat.

His hands were busy and sure, and wood shavings were piled up in the mud and snow around the legs of the chair. Whatever he was carving had his full attention, and I could hear him singing softly to himself as he notched and sliced and shaved.

He was as perfectly placed as if I'd drawn the picture, then asked him to live it, to become it.

Surprised to come upon him so abruptly, I thought at first about slipping back into the willows, pulling out my camera and getting shots of him quietly, stealthily, without him knowing. But I dismissed the thought as soon as it came. I wanted to take only what he wanted to give, in whatever shape and manner he wanted to give it, not to steal an image he wouldn't even know that he'd lost. So, instead, I coughed and stepped out of the willows, so he could see me.

He looked up quickly, partly confused and partly shocked, and almost fell in his effort to right himself and his chair. For a moment, his eyes darted wildly to the left and right, as though looking for a place to run. Then, he just stared at me, with another glance at the corner of his shack, as though he still might make a break for the door.

"Tom," I said, loud enough so he could hear but as gently as I could frame the word. "Don't go. I just came by to see if you were all right."

"Who says I'm not?" he responded loudly, as though I might have some problem hearing him, or as though he had to defend himself. "Who in the hell says I'm not?"

"Nobody," I said. "I was just coming down the river and thought I'd look in." I moved forward a few more steps.

From there, I could see that the piece of wood the old man was holding in his left hand was taking the shape of a wooden chain. Three or four of the links had been freed from each other, and they turned and rattled as he moved his hands. Other links emerging from the short, weathered piece of two-by-two were merely roughed out in alternating planes at right angles to one another.

"What are you making?" I asked, feigning a gentle ignorance.

"A mess," the old man said with another of those squeaky, self-amused chuckles. "Makin' one hell of a mess, ain't I? No difference, though. Dyin' one of these days. Makin' a chain to lower me down, mess and all, where old farts go to rest."

"How do you do that?" I asked, wanting to get him lost in himself, make him forget about me.

"By makin' the nights longer."

He was starting to confuse me again.

"Can I see your chain?"

"Hell no. You ain't gettin' my chain. Ain't gettin' the others, neither. You people keep to yourselves."

I had the feeling he'd used that sentence before.

"How about letting me take your picture, then?"

"Whafor? I ain't done nothin'. Old Tom ain't done nothin' wrong." His eyes were widening, and I could see a lingering fear starting to bunch up.

"That's not what I meant, Tom. I always wanted a picture of a man who knew how to carve chains, that's all. It doesn't have anything to do with anything else." I pulled my camera from the bag, and loaded a roll of black and white film as I talked, up front, so he could clearly see.

He looked squarely at my camera, as though it were some strange and threatening weapon, saying nothing.

"It's how the world gets to see your work."

At first it seemed to have an effect, and his jaw softened for a moment. But then the old suspicious look flashed back into his eyes.

"Share? Old Tom doin' just fine. You're just out to get me, find out what I got, sneakin' around here. Go on, get outta here. This here's my place."

I didn't want to leave without this shot, growing on me as even more powerful and important than I'd originally thought. But I wanted his serenity back, so I tried again.

"Tom," I went back to my gentler voice. "President Truman asked me to get a picture of you. He said he wanted a picture of you and your chains for his desk." The lie was a big gamble, I knew, and I felt a little ashamed of the cheapness and easiness of it. But I was about to lose him, anyway.

"Did not," Old Tom said, but then he smiled, suddenly pleased. "Harry woulda let me know. Did he?"

"Yep," I said. "It's important."

Abruptly, then, he sat up square in his chair, tilting his head and looking off to the side of me, as though he'd forgotten about my presence, and was thinking of his old friend Harry.

Then a tear rolled out of the corner of his eye, streaking the dirt on his cheek.

"I'll be damned," he said, unconsciously wiping the tear away with the sleeve of his shirt. "I'll be goddamned."

He looked at me, looked down at his hands, and sat quietly for a moment. Then he began to whittle again, humming softly to himself.

I shot one frame, then a second and a third. He never looked up at me again. I shot two more, and quietly slipped back into the willows, going back the way I came.

That night, I got out my cans and reels, my packets of powder and my empty jugs, and developed the film. In the dark, in the kitchen sink, holding my breath against the possibility that I might have lost my touch. But when the negatives were fixed and washed and I held them up to the light, I saw that some mysterious luck had been with me: they were perhaps the finest shots I'd ever made.

Because they'd been shot in the late afternoon sun, the wrinkles on his face, the drama of his hands, the grains on the carved wood, the textures in the boards on the side of his shack—all were in hard focus, all in deep relief. And the silent images, freed from the chatter and tics and jerks of our poor attempts to talk to one another, spoke their own language: a gentle weariness, a sorrowful confusion, an uncertain pride. The live, screeching, smelly Tom Cottin seemed, somehow, less than a human being. The captured, silent, visual old man seemed, somehow, more than one. The images grabbed and held, with a strength not left in those gnarled old hands.

Two days later, the old man was dead.

I heard about it when I went to the post office to turn in my key. Old age, they said, like it happens when an old body is just all worn out. I took the key back. I couldn't leave him now.

6

THE GRAVE WAS EASY ENOUGH TO FIND. THE COUNTY'S RUSTED BACKHOE was still there, parked behind the mound of fresh dirt that stood out starkly in the patches of snow. A little tin sign with plastic letters marked the last stop for Thomas A. Cottin, and a single paper flower was laid across the freshly-turned earth. How had they known his full name? Who had left the flower?

How wasted and unfair, I thought as I stood there, that a man would go into the ground alone. No words or mourners. No rain or snow. Nothing appropriately somber or grey or remarkable about the day. Only the birds sang, and they were the same old songs.

The county had buried him that morning, hours before I'd even found out about his death. A sad consistency. He'd lived most of his life away before I'd found out about that, too. I was late and help-less and ignorant, and knowing that only layered a greater, shapeless despair over the day.

Looking down at the crumbled brown earth, I felt an unexplain-able loss. And that confused me. For what had I had? Nothing, apart from what might have been: the piecing together of a past, an un-derstanding of how we fit together back in time.

So I stood there, talking to him, asking him for answers to ques-tions that I didn't even know how to ask. And I told him I was sorry that something, somehow, had gone so very wrong.

Two kids had found the old man, the sheriff's deputy told me, sitting on his stump down by the river, a half-filled water bucket at his feet. Cold and stiff. A heart attack, probably, or perhaps a stroke.

No need for an autopsy in a case like that.

Just as I was getting into my pickup to leave the cemetery, I saw a dented and bleached old truck, paint all but gone, stock racks swaying back and forth, windshield cracked like a spider web, pull up outside the iron fence.

An old man got out, dressed in bib overalls and a baseball cap, and looked around slowly. Then he made his way, limping badly, almost shuffling, along the trail up to the fresh mound of earth. He removed his cap, stood silently for a couple of minutes, then picked up a small clod of fresh dirt and tossed it on the grave. When he hobbled back toward his truck, I was waiting there.

He was wind-worn and wrinkled, much like Old Tom, unshaven with white thin hair that poked in sprigs out from under his cap.

"I'm Markus Cottin," I said, holding out my hand. "Tom Cottin's grandson."

His handshake hurt my fingers and jarred my shoulder.

"Arvo Belke," he said. "Used to be a miner from around here."

He said it with pride, as though it explained everything and was the only credential he'd ever need. It had become, obviously, the best way he could define himself. He started to say something else, perhaps about me or about an old man who'd been discarded like a worn boot, but he stopped himself short.

"You were a friend of his?" I asked, feeling the weakness in those words, but not knowing where else to start.

"Long time," the other man said. "Me and Tom came here together, back in '41 or thereabouts. From Nevada. Long time ago."

It started as a quick little tightening of my innards, then became heat on the back of my neck, then a small tremor in my hands: here was hope, a sort of found book alongside an overgrown trail. Arvo Belke could probably tell me more in five minutes than I'd learned in all my time in Madero.

"Do you live here?" I'd neglected to look at the license plate on the front of his truck, and I couldn't see it now.

"Not here, no," he said. "Haven't lived up here for more'n thirty years. Got hurt and had to move down outta this damned cold. Live down the canyon now, just outside of Three Rivers."

I asked him whether he stayed in touch with Old Tom.

"Did for awhile. But . . ." He hesitated. "Tom, he got pretty messed up, you know."

"How did you find out he died?" If I didn't know, how could a man who lived forty or so miles away?

"Read it in the police report in the paper," he said. "Comes a time in a man's life when he starts watching them things, obituaries, hospital news, shit like that."

Arvo Belke was reaching for his truck door.

"You, uh, work for Cable Minerals?" I asked, wanting to keep him there, keep him within reach.

"Yeah" he said, "I worked for the bastards." A touch of venom edged his voice. "We all worked for the dirty bastards, one way or another."

"Look," I said as he eased his bad leg up onto the running board, "I need your help. No one has been able to tell me about the company, or Old Tom, or anything else. I know you could. I know you could clear up a lot of questions for me."

And I asked if I could visit him at his place in the lower country.

"Hell yes, shore, any time," the old man said. "Don't get many visitors anymore."

He gave me directions, and I wrote them carefully on the back side of a poem I'd copied down, but couldn't bring myself to read over the old man's grave. It was about crossing over, a Buddhist thing.

———

Yes, the county coroner said, I could certainly handle the disposition of the old man's property. In fact, he was damned glad somebody had come along. The shack was worthless and built on mining company land, and would have to be torn down. As for what was inside: "Best get it taken care of before the kids and dogs get in."

The doorknob was the old white porcelain type, and it hung partly loose in the beat-up old door. Nonetheless, when I turned it, metal parts clicked, and the door pushed easily open. It was dark and cold inside. Though the shack had a couple of windows, they were so covered with smears and stains that only hints of light got through. Suspecting that it would be that way, I had a flashlight in hand. But there was electricity, and as soon as I located a grey string hanging down from the ceiling and gave it a tug, a small bulb threw shafts and shadows around the single room.

I stood there, looking to the left and right, too overwhelmed by the chaos to say anything for a minute or two, feeling like I'd just opened the door to a bad dream. The shack, just one fairly large room, was a packrat's museum. The hoard, some of it interesting, some of it disgusting, was hung and piled and stacked and strewn everywhere. Only a narrow corridor, running from the door, past a table with a single wobbly chair to his rusted old coal-burning cook stove, could be easily traveled. A shorter route branched off to his bed, hidden under a mound of filthy cloth. Every other cubic foot seemed to be under a stack or a pile. I thought of people who live under bridges.

"Look at all this . . . shit," I said aloud, compelled to say something, to get a voice echoing around the room, to get sounds at work against the cobwebs and silences that hid in the dark corners.

I wasn't sure where to start, what to dislodge first, so I just let my eyes work through the dim places.

That's when I saw the chains. Hung on nails along the wall behind his bed were loops and lengths of hand-carved wooden chains, the same type as I'd seen him carving that afternoon outside the shack. The chains were all tangled together, but the links and hooks and solid pieces seemed to be of several different designs and sizes and materials. They could have been gold, and I could have been Howard

Carter in Egypt, for the sensation they sent running up my spine. From where I stood, as close as I wanted to get for the moment, they looked to be flawless, unlike anything I'd ever seen before.

"Amazing," I said, "amazing, amazing." I still felt like I had to carry on a dialogue with the shadows, to convince whatever might be hiding there that I was not to be fooled with.

Then I noticed that, apart from the dirt, most of what I was walking on was wood shavings, several inches ground into the floor, pulverized by his countless trips from bed to table to stove.

Why chains, I wondered. Why not animals or kachinas or ships in bottles? Why the same thing, more or less, over and over again? I thought about it for a minute. What would be going through his mind? He couldn't remember how to do many things, but he could remember what people had once appreciated, probably. So he played it safe. He knew that if he was going to make it, he had to keep life narrowed down, predictable, simple. He couldn't risk getting lost.

Although the place was filthy, with an inch or two of dust covering much of what was piled around, at least nothing was rotting. From the looks of things, he carefully washed his one plate, his knife and fork, and his blue enameled cup after each use, laying them with some order beside the little wash pan he apparently used for dishes. Several dozen cans of beans, soup, corn, stew and the like were stacked on a shelf next to the stove. Food scraps, when there were any, must have been thrown out to the marauding dogs.

I didn't want to go near the bed, which was piled a foot deep with the same kind of greasy, dirty clothes that I'd always seen him wear. Presumably, under there somewhere, were blankets, but it was difficult to tell.

I reached for the nearest and easiest to move, and carried a stack of old magazines and newspapers out into the cold daylight. As I picked them up, dust exploded into the air, leaving me hacking and coughing harshly.

Denver Posts and outdoor magazines—*Field and Stream* and *Outdoor Life*—dated randomly from the late 1950s. Strange, I thought to myself, I could never imagine Tom Cottin as a sporting man. I guessed that the magazines had come from someone else's trash.

Then I rifled through the newspapers, quickly, just to make sure I wasn't throwing away old scrolls, valuable documents, anything critical to the piecing back together of Crazy Tom. There was nothing. Just old news.

The next load was a small but heavy box of books.

Although certainly the old man had been able to read throughout most of his life, I wondered if, toward the end, he really could follow the trail that sentences left. The books didn't tell me much. Each one was a well-worn Zane Grey western novel, all with hard covers that had, at one time or another, been damaged by water. All were 1940s editions. Keepsakes, I thought, treasures left over from a time when life allowed a fanciful cowboy read.

Much of what I hauled out that morning was similar: boxes of old clothes, old *Life* magazines, two boxes of old beer bottles, Christmas decorations, a box of chipped and broken plates, numerous pairs of disintegrating rubber boots, parts for a sewing machine. Some of it was puzzling, some merely garbage that he might have meant to throw out before he misplaced it, some probably just junk he'd drug home from the alleys for a closer look.

I kept thinking about possibilities, hoping that every box or bag would be the one that broke the code, that made the connections. Each, though interesting, was little more than detritus, flotsam on the old man's beach.

Finally, there was nothing left but the bed. Carefully, tentatively, I drug pieces of disgusting clothing out to the refuse piles. Then the bedding, which was slick and nasty to the touch. Finally, the mattress, which stunk badly of odors I didn't even want to think about. I dragged it all out into the yard.

After waiting a few minutes for the dust to settle and the stench to blow away, I went back in to see what remained. There, under the bed frame, coated, almost buried, in layers of dust and cobwebs was a small cardboard box, bound up with string.

The beginning or the end? I wondered silently. There was nothing left beyond wood shavings and dirt. If the box held buttons or pretty rocks, the trail back through these hard times would remain very, very dim.

I put the box on the front seat of my pickup. After all these months, there was no hurry now. Besides, a sharp wind was whistling in from the west, and I couldn't risk having the contents, whatever they were, lifted off and blown down into the river.

Then, remembering the wooden chains, I dumped some old shoes from one of the boxes into the foul heap, and carefully brought the chains down, packing them into the box. There were eight in all, none shorter than eight or ten feet. As I handled each one, I could easily see that the detail work was better than good. The links, precise in their shape and size. The hooks, as perfect and real as if they'd been molded in iron. The thousands of knife strokes, all but hidden by hours and hours of patient sanding. This box I placed carefully on the seat of my truck. At the first opportunity, I wanted to ponder the chains, one at a time, and give each piece its proper pomp and circumstance.

Finally, holding back only a few old bottles for souvenirs, I made a large pile out of the rest of the old man's belongings, ready for a trip by dump truck to the landfill. That final, depressing, melancholy job I couldn't do. Hired help, paid by the county, would come the next day.

As for me, I was finished, and I headed for home with the few prizes I'd found among the bits and pieces that were the last awful years in the life of Old Tom.

That evening, I cut the string and opened up the box. Inside I found two envelopes. Each large, yellowed, and dog-eared, the clasps broken off long ago.

In the first, photographs. Family pictures, once framed probably, but now just crammed together carelessly in the old, yellowed envelope. Numerous turn-of-the-century couples glared out at me, posed stiffly in their finest togs, flat-mouthed or frowning, swooping mustaches and full bosoms. People I didn't recognize, had never known. The vague resemblances that I thought I detected meant little. Everyone, after all, had ancestors like these, people with fused spines, people who couldn't smile.

In the other manila envelope, more photographs, but recognizable in a way that caused my hands to tremble a bit, and my pulse to pickup speed. The first: a medium-built man of serious intent, in a store clerk's apron, with his arm around an attractive thin woman with short hair tightly curled around her head and a mischievous look in her eye. Perched on the store counter, a little boy in bib overalls and high-laced leather boots. Tom, Anne Marie and Andrew, said the pencil writing on the back.

And another: the same three, but dressed in their best, standing on a depot platform with an out-of-focus train coming on from the rear. She in a dark dress and wide-brimmed hat, waving and laughing at the camera. He in a light suit with big lapels and a tie that blew in the wind, holding sternly onto a small suitcase. The boy in white shirt and slacks, twisting his head around to see the train. Our trip to Durango, the back said.

Other pictures: Tom among other men I didn't know in wide-brimmed hats and baggy pants leaning nonchalantly against vintage automobiles, smoking, posing, looking gallant. Anne Marie among other women, in dresses and wide-bottomed riding pants, but with a wink or a grin that always stood out. Andrew catching a fish, sitting on the hood of an old truck, in his first pair of glasses. Always, mine dumps and tram towers and head frames in a soft, blurry background.

And there was one more, a later photograph: Tom and Andrew standing with a giant elk head between them. The boy, who looked to be about fourteen, holding a rifle in his right hand, and an antler in his left, looking more somber than the occasion should have called for. Tom with dark and sunken eyes, as though he were shackled by a grief that hadn't let him sleep for weeks. Behind them, an ore truck, half in and half out of the picture, with the words "Cable Minerals" clearly painted on its side. It was, I guessed, the last picture taken of them together.

But Tom had appeared in one more: in the newspaper, looking scared and alone, with handcuffs on. I was certain of that.

———•———

The photographs affected me in a strange and powerful way, one that I didn't wholly understand. Perhaps because they put those people into contexts—placed them next to each other and fixed them in time—the photographs seemed more alive than life itself. Hadn't those people just walked in through the backs of the photographs to strike their poses? It seemed so.

Who was more real, the little boy who sat upon the store counter, or the man who dug rocks in the hot desert sun? Who was more enduring, the young father on the train platform or the old man who saw Indians in the dark?

There was something else: a sense that there should have been more photographs, ones with a skip forward in time, allowing me to be the boy looking for the train and my father to be the man with the blowing tie. But where would Neal be?

For a second, I wished for a cut-out picture of myself, one that I could just paste in among the family images. How appropriate: inserting myself into the family picture. Wasn't that, in a way, exactly why I was there, and what I was trying to do?

PART THREE

Arvo Belke

1

WE SIT, MY FATHER AND I, AROUND THE OLD CABLE-SPOOL TABLE. We each have a cup of coffee in front of us, but neither is drinking, and the coffee has long grown cold. It's early evening, not quite dark, and a half moon has come up already, and looks down on us like a half-closed eye.

I've just told him that his father is dead.

At first he just stares, like he doesn't hear me, or doesn't believe me.

"Goddamn it," he says finally, and shakes his head back and forth, four or five times. Then he stands, jams his hands into his pants pockets, and walks out onto the rim. For a second, just a second, I wonder if the darkening maw of the canyon might be calling to him. But then I know better. He and the rocks have had a great deal of time to talk these things out, and they know that survival, not sentiment, is all that counts.

I give him fifteen minutes or so, and then I walk out and sit with him on the bench. He keeps his eyes fixed on the growing darkness in the bottom of the canyon.

"You didn't miss the services," I say. "There weren't any."

He doesn't answer.

"The county buried him. Even before I knew about it."

He never looks at me. Always away, and down. A long time passes before either of us speaks again.

"He didn't leave much behind," I say, finally. I tell him about the chains, and about the photographs.

"Do you want to see them?"

"Nah," he says after a while. "Tomorrow's good enough. Better light."

It's dark now, and I've pumped up a lantern and lit it. Moths and millers swarm around, bounce against the lantern glass with a tiny ring, and drop soundlessly onto the table.

He comes back from the rim and goes into the trailer. I hear him rummaging around for a minute, before he comes out with a half-empty fifth of Jim Beam. He dumps his cold coffee on the ground and pours himself a shot. He doesn't offer the bottle to me, but I pour myself some anyway.

"Hope you've seen enough," he says after he's sat for five minutes or so, sipping at his whiskey.

"Didn't see much."

He pulls his smokes out of his hip pocket, takes a bent cigarette out, and lights it with a kitchen match that he strikes on a bolt head on the table.

"Didn't hear much, either," I add. "He talked, but he didn't make any sense."

He seems to be studying the smoke that comes streaming out of his nose and floats off into the night air.

"Tell you about his Navajos, did he?"

"Mentioned them. But he mumbled and just talked. It never amounted to much of anything."

In the lantern light, the eye he gives me looks a lot like disgust. He pours another big shot of Beam into his cup.

"Then you didn't learn shit."

"That's about right."

No answer.

"What the hell was I supposed to do?"

He still doesn't answer. Instead, he fishes his pocketknife out of his pants and starts digging at the dirt under his fingernails. He's talking to me with his hands, and he's saying that his life is still none of my business.

"He said he went to jail."

He looks up at me, finally.

"Well," he says. "You learned a thing or two."

"Is it true?"

He seems to be nodding his head, but barely, and I can't tell whether he's talking to me, or keeping some rhythm or agreeing with his own conclusions.

"For what?"

He snaps his knife closed and lays it on the table. Then he takes a long drink out of his cup.

"He killed somebody." His voice is flat, low, a little thick. He could be asking me to pass the bread, and a few more of those beans, and oh by the way, he killed somebody.

I'm stunned. I didn't know what he might say, but I didn't expect that. My mind loops back, trying to connect the fact to the face and voice and hands that I knew. But I can't see it. I can't see the pathetic old man who sat on the town bench, huddled up in his pea coat and stocking hat, with that kind of an urge. I can't see it in the young store clerk, or the man on the train platform, or in all the other pictures. Except maybe for the last one. The one with the boy and the elk and the man with sunken eyes.

"Who?"

"Don't remember," he says, too quickly, and I know it's a lie.

"Try." I let him know by the tone in my voice that I'm not buying it, and he's starting to wear on me again.

He doesn't answer me.

"Why'd he do it?"

"Maybe you shoulda asked him."

"Now, goddamn you . . ." I'm ready to jump him now. I've had enough. But he cuts me off.

"It don't make a shit, anyway," he says, standing up and grabbing his bottle by the neck. I can see that he intends to go in for the night, to leave me hanging, to tell me nothing more. And that causes my mind to flash, and my blood to boil out of its pan.

"It matters, goddamn it," I say, louder, getting to my own feet. "You can't just say that and walk away."

He turns and shoves his face toward mine. I can smell the whiskey.

"I told you once. I'll tell you again. You don't goddammit wanna know."

"The hell I don't."

He looks at me hard.

"The old man shot somebody. Then he went crazy. With Cable Minerals shit on his hands. On his skin. A stink ain't never gonna clear the air."

It's my turn to say nothing.

"Get your foolish ass on back to Tucson, son. Get it on back down the road."

We stare at each other. A melting contest.

"You're not scaring me off." I hold my voice down, level. Trying to take control.

He turns away.

"I'm not through yet."

"Just keep out of my way, you hear? I got better things to do than argue with you."

He climbs into the trailer and slams the door closed behind him. I hear him hacking and spitting inside, and I wish he'd choke.

———•———

This trip, I don't spend the night. I don't unpack my gear. I drive down off the mesa in the dark, slowly, trying one more time to figure out why things are the way they are. Trying to make sense out of the few things I know. Trying to decide what to do next.

About ten miles down the road, a coyote runs across the road in front of me, stops and barks once, and disappears into the sage. I take that as a good sign, and I pull over for the night.

I make a little fire and sit for a while. Thinking. Listening to the night sounds. Turning it all over again. And I can see that there was more he wanted me to find out in Madero, but it was just too late. He wanted me to sicken myself right off the job. To cover my eyes and turn away. And right now, here, I could almost do that. Quit. I'm tired and I'm hungry and I'm spent from fighting with him. And everything I've seen so far has been ugly. Just like he said.

But he's the one who feels the sickness. The one who can't stand to look. I'm beginning to see that, now. And to understand that he may never help me. Because he may never be able to stand hearing his own voice telling his own truth.

I wish I had the rest of that bottle of Jim Beam.

2

I SAT AT THE KITCHEN TABLE IN THE OLD FINLANDER'S RUN-DOWN farmhouse, watching while he carefully sprinkled Prince Albert on a brown cigarette paper, licked the edge, twisted the ends, and lit it with a kitchen match. We were drinking coffee he'd made on a hot plate—so strong that it might have been weeks old, just rewarmed and added-to day after day, time after time. I suspected that he'd given me his favorite cup, one of those heavy old tan truck stop mugs, stained and well used. The one he drank out of was too dainty, and chipped.

As the bitter smoke came streaming out of his nostrils, he coughed and choked a little, then began to talk again. I'd thought about questions I could ask him, obvious questions, but I'd let them fade away when I could see that he wanted to talk, and that I'd learn far more if I just let him go.

He'd cover it all, sometime, in his own way.

"Yessir, me and Tom was a workin' together out in Nevada, in a little gold outfit Cable Minerals had there. Damn neart kids, then, just takin' whatever we could get."

He took another sip of coffee, then leaned over deliberately and tipped his ashes into the rolled-up leg cuff of his faded pants.

"Then the vein petered out, and they told us we could come on over to the Madero workin's, or haul ass on down the road. Didn't matter to them, one way or t'other. Depression was on. 'Kin you load this pile of ore by noon?' they'd ask. 'If you kin't, there's thirty guys waitin' outside the fence that kin.' So we caught the train east. Any work was a good job. Even for them bastards."

He held the home-rolled smoke between the tips of his thumb and first finger, and stared absently toward his old coal-burning cookstove. No fire there, that day, but I could see how he spent the long winter days and nights. Hadn't I just came from that place, that season, where fire had a soul and a name, and it could be talked to, and it answered?

"Actually I came along first," he said. "Tom, he wasn't a goin' to come. He wasn't that much of a miner you see. He worked mostly in the warehouse, and he didn't want to come out here and run a muck stick. His wife didn't want him a workin' underground, and what she wanted was generally what she got. Maybe 'cause they had that young boy . . . what the hell was his name?"

"Andrew," I said.

"That's right," he said. "Andy. I'd call him that, and Tom's old lady would say Andrew. Anyways, she thought Tom ought to be doin' better'n that. Workin' outside. Me, I was single. I didn't give a shit."

I thought about the woman in the pictures. And it wasn't difficult at all to imagine strong will and ambition, to see a wit and a guile that had always found their own way.

Belke poured us more coffee, though I'd hardly gotten through half a cup in half an hour. Then he threw his little stub of a smoke into a bucket and stood up. As he did, an ugly scowl of pain flashed across his face.

"Goddamn this leg!" he said, and bent to hold it for a moment. Then he hobbled over to the old round-edged white porcelain sink to hack and spit and run his shirt sleeve across a face that hadn't seen a shave in more than a week.

"Lookin' at it now, you'd be hard pressed to believe it's the same damned town," he said, still on his feet. "Them streets that's plumb empty now was so crowded with people you couldn't hardly get around. Every mine that was worth a tinker's damn was a workin' and a man had a helluva time even findin' a place to live. Two mills was runnin', and two trains came in every damned day. The only things missin' from the real old days was the hangin's and the whore houses. That's what them old boys used to say."

"Because of the war?"

"Yep. The government was a buyin' ever damned ounce of lead and zinc and copper we could get out of the ground, and they was a payin' whatever it took. We was all doin' pretty good."

He picked up his cigarette papers and his Prince Albert again, and stopped to look down at his hands.

"Sometimes I wish we woulda just stayed at war."

———————

Arvo Belke had seen miners and mines, but he hadn't seen the pace or the passion of Madero. When the four o'clock whistle blew, they came streaming out of a dozen or more portals, a small army of men marching down the hillsides and back toward the heart of town. With faces and hands covered in mud, often dressed in black rubber coats and pants and dull-red hard hats, they were long strings of black ants headed back to the colony, the workers bringing the bread back to those who tended the eggs and played the other roles. They joked and laughed, these burrowers, and swung their lunch buckets, but their steps lagged and plodded and their eyes didn't dance.

At six o'clock, once the smoke from the day shift blasting had cleared, the night shift went in. Another more somber string of ants, facing the same darkness that turned all time into nighttime, they were different only because they slept poorly or not at all in the clamor of the day, and because they silently resented being out of step with the rest of the town.

And there was clamor. The normal rattle and grind of a hellbent, agitated industry was layered over with the song of the trains— whistles that echoed down the canyons as the narrow-gauge transports hauled away the ores that were the guts of Madero's mountains. Those same whistles wafting up-river meant that the beans and whiskey and baby shoes and radios that were the prizes for the work would be stacked on the depot planks, ready to be carried home. Coming in, the two or three passenger cars were always filled with the smell of the hopeful and a little din of old country languages. Going out, the smell was more of money and the language more of war.

On the streets, cars and trucks coughed and groaned until the gasoline ration stamps ran out. Then horses and mules filled in and around, hauling coal, pulling the fire wagon, moving the caskets.

At night, the taverns rang with stories and fist fights, and they were filled with pool sharks and single old men who'd made a long career out of migrating from camp to camp, border to border. Gold or lead, it all took the same kind of hole in the ground.

Underneath it all, a background noise crackled from the old Philcos and RCAs: the blow-by-blow call as Joe Louis hit Max Schmelling, the honey-sweet clarinets of Benny Goodman and Artie Shaw, the creaking door as Boston Blackie made his way down another shadowy street.

Madero was noisy, but for the time being, alive.

"Sure, I got work," the hiring foreman had told Belke, looking up from behind a table piled high with assay reports. "One helluva a lot of work. You ever run a jackleg?"

"Nope."

"You ever run a muckin' machine?"

"A little."

"That'll do," he said, handing over a clipboard with a simple form attached. "I'm short a mucker on the night shift in the Baltimore Tunnel. Pickup your diggers and your carbide light at the warehouse and catch the man trip at six bells."

Belke hesitated before he started writing.

"How much?"

"How much what?"

"Pay."

The man looked up at Belke, as though puzzled.

"Day's pay here is four bucks." He spit brown tobacco juice on the muddy wooden floor. "Helluva lot more than some of these jack-asses are worth."

He paused and stared at Belke.

"That suits you, don't it?"

Belke nodded, wrote down his name and a few numbers, and turned to walk away.

"Oh, and Belke."

"Yessir?"

"You got to provide your own rubber boots."

3

WHEN YOU'VE LIVED ALONE MOST OF YOUR LIFE, AND YOU COME TO COUNT and think and talk in terms of ones, you slip into the easy assumption that everyone lives that way. Alone. It happens without thinking: picture a person, and you picture him surrounded by space, or trees, or perhaps just a foggy nothing. It's a habit.

Consequently, I hadn't asked whether Arvo Belke lived alone. Or whether my visit might be disturbing someone else. But once I was there, sitting in his kitchen, the question would have seemed foolish, and probably awkward. The calendar on the wall was three years old. Dead flies littered the window sill. Small foul smells crept out of cracks somewhere. Doors to all the other rooms were closed. There was no one else, at least not anymore.

The old miner stopped talking while he made himself another cigarette, deliberately, then lit it with a kitchen match he struck on a metal button on the bib of his pants. He dropped the spent light carelessly on the red and white checkered oil cloth. Dozens of burn holes suggested that he'd always done the same.

He blew out another plume of hot blue smoke and watched it gather into a layered haze.

"But after I'd been here a few months, our warehouse man froze to death. Went off into the river in the supply truck in a blizzard and just froze up tryin' to walk back to town. So I sent a telegram back to Tom, but by the time he made up his mind and got to town, the job it was already filled."

He paused.

"So after a few months of muckin' out the shit ditch and freezin'

his goddamned feet off, he took the job of runnin' the company store.
I guess you could say he got smart. Tom he was good with numbers,
you see. Quick. Do everything in his head. Cable Minerals was good
at milkin' ya for what ya had."

He scratched the back of his neck and half smiled.

"Besides, it suited the missus a little better, you know."

I could see that. It even suited me better, this thought that Old
Tom, at least at one point in his life, had been not only a common
man, but something more. I could see him standing there behind
that counter, see him feeding and clothing the whole town, grant-
ing and denying credit, shuffling Madero's money.

"In fact, as the years went on and we started buryin' miners 'bout
as fast as we was diggin' out ore, that job in the company store looked
like one of the best places to be."

"What do you mean?" It was the first question I'd asked in a long
time, and my voice, with its clipped words, sounded strange to me.
It almost made me want to look around, to see who else might have
slipped into the room.

"Well you see, things turned to shit after the war ended." He
paused to look directly at my face. "We celebrated just like everybody else, you know. Hitler was dead and Tojo was in the cooler.
Then one day we woke up, and it was like wakin' up with a helluva
hangover. They didn't want our goddamned metals anymore." He
always left a pause between god and damned, even if he had to slow
the sentence down to do it.

"Companies were damned neart givin' lead and zinc away. Hardly
took six months, didn't seem like, before mines started closin' down
and people started pullin' out. Then the Stanley mill closed, and the
train cut back to three trips a week."

He paused.

"We weren't celebratin' anymore, mister. I can tell you that for
goddamned sure."

He pushed his coffee cup back and forth between his hands, and I thought about all the dried bones I'd seen in Madero, pieces of old mining skeletons pushing up through the snow.

"That's when we found out what Cable Minerals was made of. When we found out what good for nothin' sons a bitches was runnin' that town."

Absently he flicked his finger at a fly that settled down on the rim of his cup.

"They figgered they could still make 'er pay. All they had to do was stop spendin' money. When a pump went out, they just didn't pump no more. When somethin' else broke, they just threw a patch on 'er until she broke again. And again and again. Rotten timber? Ah, hell, ignore it. Gas in the drifts? Work around it, you dumb bastards."

He stood up and put his hands flat down on the table top.

"A man's life was in his hands ever' damned time he set foot in them holes. And that ain't maybes I'm givin' you, mister. Look at this goddamned leg. You wanna know why I walk with this goddamned limp? You know how many crutches and canes I've broke?"

There was anger in his voice, a heat that came rushing forward from a long time back.

"It ain't right, is it, when another man makes money offa your broken bones?"

———·+·———

"You're sure as hell lucky you got outta that tunnel and into that store. You're lookin' some smarter all the time."

The August sun was as warm as it got up that close to timberline, leaving a patina of sweat on the backs of Arvo Belke and Tom Cottin. Each was on one end of a long lumber saw, alternately pushing and pulling the jagged teeth across the trunk of a dead ponderosa pine laid up on sawbucks, next to the woodshed in Cottin's backyard.

"I guess," Cottin said with a grunt, straining to keep the blade moving and free from the sticky pitch resin that was the mixed bounty of that kind of wood: it burned with all the heat in hell, but gummed up axes and saws until neither would cut.

Belke wasn't the first to remind him that the storekeeper's apron was a robe of sorts in some eyes—a sign of office, a suggestion of difference in the way wages were made. And he appreciated the reminders. After years of standing behind the counter, there was a dull pattern to outfitting miners and their families, a routine about ordering in meat and rubber boots and double-bitted axes and coal, a mindlessness about selling school tablets and bullets and wash tubs and yarn. Still, at least his legs weren't broken, or his lungs full of dust, or his fingers blown off.

"It wasn't never safe," Belke said, "but you damn well know how it is now. I swear to Christ each month gets worse than the one before."

They stopped work and leaned against the big log, wiping their faces with their shirts. Both men were strong, but it was apparent which one worked with heavy mining equipment all day long.

"You thinkin' about Hockaday?"

"Yeah. Him and others. Only been about two weeks since I was workin' on that number five stope where he got caved in on. Coulda been me, sure as hell. Just not my time."

Not my time. Determinism. It was the theology they all lived by. A single-doctrine faith. When the time came . . .. Inside there, in the guts of the mountain, things would happen, events and processes that could never be planned for, even by the wisest and most careful of men. Falling rock. Poison gas. Rock dust. Live blasting caps drilled into. Bad luck. Who would be chosen? And when?

"How'd it happen?"

"Rotten timber. The whole mine's full of it, and it's gettin' older and wetter and weaker by the day. Some of that shit's fifty years old, and Cable Minerals has made it pretty fuckin' clear they ain't gonna spend a dime to fix it."

Cottin knew Belke was scared. The Finlander had told him that he didn't sleep at night anymore, that he kept feeling bridge timbers breaking under his feet, seeing himself falling helplessly down into the blackness of a shaft, seeing his own carbide light spinning around and around and around, getting smaller, smaller still, spinning his soul out into the universe, way beyond the reach of helping hands.

"Then I wake up, sweatin', and stare at the ceiling until it starts to get light. I pack my lunch and go, and all the way under ground on the man trip, I can feel my legs a-shakin'. And I know I'm not the only one."

No, Cottin knew, Arvo wasn't the only one. Hardly a man could go under ground, day shift or night, without thinking about Martinez and Boydd, who'd died on the spot when they drilled into a pocket of methane gas. Or Schneidermann, who'd been found with only his feet sticking out from under a ten-ton slab of rock. Or Garro, who'd been buried when the door broke loose on a loading chute.

They still laughed and told jokes, and talked about the future and saved what they could. They made serious plans, and laid out serious dreams. But their eyes ached from trying to see around the next bend.

———·•·———

"Why don't you quit? The Jackson bothers did, and Joe Riley, and whats-his-name Everitt."

They were sitting on Cottin's back porch, drinking beer and looking contentedly at the stack of pine rounds they'd managed to slice off with the heavy saw. It was late afternoon now, and shadows had begun to sneak out from along the east sides of fences and trees. The boy Andrew was rolling the pieces toward the woodpile. Most were too heavy for him to lift.

"Yeah, Arvo, why don't you just get out of Madero, go some place where the company's not so tight, where things are not so dangerous?"

The two men looked up with surprise. Neither had heard Anne Marie come out onto the porch, though neither had said anything that she hadn't heard before, or wouldn't hear again.

"I don't know," Belke said without much conviction. "Ain't much better other places, from what I hear. Least not in the mines. Jobs are dryin' up and wages are gettin' slimmer all the time. Besides, this here's pretty fine country. And I got no family anymore. Don't know where else I'd go."

He paused to sip his beer and look up-canyon, where the shadows had grown darker still.

"Besides, they keep sayin' they're going to make some changes when zinc prices go up a few pennies more."

"Do you believe that?" Anne Marie asked as she stepped over their legs and walked on out toward a shed in the back. From behind, her waist looked small, her lean hips lost somewhere in the bulk of her brown pants. She held her hands well away from her body as she walked, as though she was stretching her arms.

Tom watched Arvo's eyes, stepping with her as she moved. He was used to it.

"And if enough of these tough old bastards quit," Belke continued, turning back toward Cottin, "they'll have to do somethin'. They can't run this outfit with nothin' but bums and drunks, can they?"

"They might try."

"They might. But they'll pay for it in hell if they do."

4

THE OLD MINER STOOD LOOKING OUT THE WINDOW, OUT TOWARD THE odd collection of farm machinery junk and car parts that littered his yard, toward weathered buildings that sagged at the roof line and gaped on the sides, all shrouded in weeds.

"Sure, there was talk of a union," he said in answer to a question I'd just asked. I didn't know when miners won the union wars in the West Virginia and Kentucky coal fields, but I knew it had been back in the '30s and '40s, well before Madero's problems. And didn't the unions always win, and the companies always lose, because these were questions of justice, of saving lives? Why not in Madero? Or was it just that way in the movies?

"Hell, there'd been talk of a union off and on for two or three years. Lotta men who'd worked in silver in Idaho or iron somewheres else, they'd been union men, and they talked big in the bars."

He turned and stuffed his hands in his overall pockets.

"Kinda like the farmers around here," he added. "They talk loud in the feed store, but then it don't rain, and their damn beans don't turn out big enough to fill a good size piss pot."

He smiled, but out of sarcasm, out of a mild disgust. Then he seemed to realize that he'd gotten just off track, came too far forward too fast, and his old eyes turned serious again.

"But it was a little different in Madero. Lotta men, they lived in company houses, and had for years. Went to the company movie house. Used the company telephones. Damned near every one of us, maybe all of us for all I know, owed money at the store. And some with a buncha kids to feed owed one helluva lot."

He wiped his mouth.

"In them days, talk was cheap. Bullshit always is."

He paused.

"And Cable Minerals had us by the nuts."

———————

At noon on the Fourth of July, the fire whistle blew one long blast, and three Cub Scouts hoisted the stars and stripes smartly to the top of the post office pole. In the vacant lot next to the Mason's Building, most of the miners of the Madero district had already turned out, and they jostled around, shifting their feet, laughing, waiting. Wives were there, too, and children ran in and out of the crowd. Within the knots of men, pint bottles of Old Crow and Jim Beam and Seagram's Seven were slipped from hand to hand like secret notes, tipped up and savored, and moved along with appreciative nods and crooked little grins.

It was Independence Day, a day for sack races and egg throws and music in the park. Ice cream and cake. But for the miners, it was the day when they competed in the games only they knew how to play: the mining events. Most of the men were merely there to watch. But others, bolder maybe, or inspired by the Jim Beam, or with reputations to defend, were there for prizes—small amounts of cash, bragging rights, maybe a little place in the memories of all those who were there on that day.

On the surface, they were games, yes, but since they called upon the same muscles and tricks that kept the men alive and respected, they were more than games: more like muscle-flexing and parodies and mating dances, all rolled into a not so simple ball. This, they said with their sweat, is how it's done.

———————

Hand muckers, stripped to the waist and armed with their favorite shovels, heave loose rock from the back of one truck into the back of another, shoveling furiously and with abandon, on adrenalin and at a pace that can only last for minutes. One man shovels north to south, and the next man shovels it back the other way. Truck to truck, back and forth, as the crowd cheers and claps. Fastest man wins.

At the "go," a jackleg driller runs forward, clamps a drill steel in his rig, and drags it and its hoses to the face of a massive boulder. Then the fight begins. With its stinger stuck in the ground and surging longer as the air is turned on, with its drill-steel proboscis attacking the rock and spitting water, the drill looks more insect than machine, and it bucks and chatters, frantic to escape. The driller wrestles and shoves and leans, until the bit takes hold, until the steel begins to sink into the rock, until it's deep enough. The air is cut off, the weary miner drags his gear back and strips it down, and the judges consult their clocks. Fastest man wins.

Hard-hatted machine muckers gun their machines, little more than crude front-end loaders that throw their ore up, over and into a car behind, down a short section of track. Ram the bucket into a pile of broken rock. Throw it into the car. Ram the pile again. Swivel left and get the rock there. Swivel right. Then the whistle blows, and the judges step up to measure the load. Fullest ore car wins.

But it is the hand drillers, the traditionalists, that draw the biggest crowds and the loudest applause. Like John Henry, these are steel drivin' men.

——— · ———

Tom Cottin was standing with his son Andrew at the edge of the crowd, watching Gus and Alf Olsen, two giant Swedes, built like wrestlers but with greying hair and a solemn patience that sprung deep in their eyes. The strength, accuracy and trust that came together in the hands and backs of traditional drillers came together at their best in the Olsen brothers, and no one had beaten them in decades, or so the myth came down.

As Cottin and the others watched, Gus swung the long-handled sledge hammer in a great arc, from shoulder height straight down onto the end of the drill steel, and on around again and again. His solid eyes never left his target.

Alf, on one knee, held the steel upright with both hands, turning it half a turn between hammer blows, never flinching as the heavy sledge struck just inches from his hands and arms, just a foot in front of his face. His eyes seemed focused on nothing at all.

Then, in the maneuver that never failed to draw applause and murmurs of admiration from the on-lookers, the two men changed places without missing a beat. Caught in the middle, in a flash of time, as they could only be caught in a photograph, each had one hand on the hammer handle and one hand on the steel. One man moving upward, one moving down. And the blows never faltered, never lost their rhythm. Clanging. About every two seconds. And deeper went the hole.

Standing near the back of the crowd, Cottin had given his mind over to the Olsen brothers, dazed, his thoughts dulled by the rhythms of sound and motion, by the ring of steel-on-steel, by the blur of the hammer's arc. Consequently, when angry voices boiled out of the crowd only a few feet away, he was startled, shaken awake from a formless dream. Andrew jumped, and moved around to stand behind his father.

"No sumbitchin' company man touches my whiskey."

A slight red-headed miner named Skinner was standing there, clenched fists held down at his sides, glaring up at the big Polish mine foreman everybody knew as Alphabet. The miner's eyes were wide as quarters, his face flushed.

Then he opened his hand and slapped a bottle of liquor out of the bigger man's grasp.

"Poison as horse piss now that you've had your stinkin' hands on it," Skinner added.

"Why'd you hand it to me, then, little man?" Alphabet asked the question in a slow, even voice, but one tinged with ridicule.

"Thought you was somebody," Skinner replied, spitting out the words with a slight slur. "Figgered you company boys would be holed up countin' your money."

"Watch your mouth, Skinner, you little bastard," the foreman said, a little more ire rising in his voice. "I don't want to have to pound the shit out of you. Not right here in front of all these ladies."

The smaller man stepped forward, and the color of his eyes matched the hue of his wild hair.

"Yeah, that's your way, ain't it. Pushin' people around. Threatenin'. You boys in your pressed shirts is mighty tough."

"Go home, Skinner. Sleep it off."

The bigger man turned, and started to step away, but Skinner caught him by the shoulder and spun him around. Then he stuck his face right up against the foreman's chin.

"Your day's comin', Alphabet. We'll have a union in these mines any day now, and you company dogs ain't gonna bite so hard anymore."

Alphabet's face hardened, and he rammed a thick finger into the miner's chest, pushing him back.

"I'll tell you this once, Skinner, and once is all." His voice was low, deliberate, ominous. "If I hear that union shit coming out of your mouth just one more time, you can draw your pay and catch the train."

"You can't do that. I know my rights."

"Try me, you little bastard," Alphabet said, and he turned toward the men who had crowded around, but who had now grown mostly silent. "The rest of you. Get it out of your heads."

He turned and began to walk away.

"It won't be long, Pollock, when you'll be kissin' our asses." The voice had come from somewhere in the crowd.

Alphabet, whose real name was a combination of w's and y's and z's, turned back.

"I don't know who said that," he said, "but it doesn't matter. I don't care whether you've got John L. Lewis back there. A union card'll buy you only two things in this town. A busted ass and a one-way ticket out."

Over the mumbling, angry voices, Cottin could hear the rhythmic clanking, the metallic echo, as the hammer came down on the drill steel, again and again and again.

When he looked down at Andrew, the boy's eyes were wide and his face was drawn.

"Don't worry, son," he heard himself saying. "Just a couple of guys with a little too much to drink."

But Tom Cottin felt ill, and he wanted to move away from the crowd and the noise. Although he could see Anne Marie across the way with several of the miners' wives, he didn't approach her, didn't say anything at all, and instead sent Andrew off to find his friends.

Then he turned and walked down toward the river. There, he found a rock by the edge of the water, and sat watching the shifting reflections and shadows of the current, hearing nothing but the quiet roar.

He'd had only two beers, and his sickness couldn't be blamed on that. No, it went deeper, more toward the bone, and it had to do with dread.

He couldn't understand it. He felt like he'd been standing between Skinner and Alphabet, and each one had been yelling and jabbing their fingers at him. He felt a real nausea coming on, and he knelt in anticipation, in the rocks, by the water's edge.

5

"HELL, LET'S GO SIT OUT ON THE PORCH," ARVO BELKE WAS SAYING, AND he limped toward the door. "Might as well get us some sunshine and fresh air. Be winter again one of these days."

I was more than agreeable. I'd had about all the Prince Albert I could take: my head was starting to ache, and my eyes burned a little. I was surprised the old man had any lungs left at all, and I thought about rough bags made from deerskin, with the hair side turned in.

One chair sat on the porch, loose-legged and well-worn, and I insisted that he take it. If he got down on the porch and couldn't get up, I'd have to help him, and neither of us would have liked that.

"Most of us, we just wanted to threaten 'em with that union talk," he said after he'd made himself comfortable and pulled down his cap to block out part of the sun. "Aw, they was a few that was serious about it, I guess, and they'd wrote letters to the unions in Denver and such, but the rest of us, we just didn't know."

He stopped for a moment, thinking about what to say next. "Hell," he said suddenly. "Just thought of somethin'." He stood, slowly, and limped back inside the house.

While he was gone, which might have been as little as five minutes, or maybe as long as ten, I just sat quietly and eyed the rotting and the rusted, the mixed mess of castoffs that fought it out with the tumbleweeds in his yard: skeletons of two or three old pickups (it was hard to tell where one stopped and the next began); an old washing machine; a roll of chicken wire; a couple piles of grey and twisted boards. And I wondered how long Arvo Belke had lived there. I wondered if his life had been long enough to live through the heydays of Madero and collect all of this junk, too, or whether he had just moved in amongst it all, comfortable, a part of the assemblage.

But I wasn't going to ask. We had a chronology, a narrative going there, and I was more interested in that story than in his rusted farm tractor.

When he came back, he handed me a small, red button, the campaign type of button, as he sat down. Imprinted on it were four simple block letters: UMWA. United Mine Workers of America.

"Ran across that a week or so ago, diggin' through some old boxes, lookin' for somethin' else. And it reminded me. Just what we been talkin' about."

And he told me how somebody had passed a box of the buttons around in the equipment room at the mine, and how he wasn't certain he wanted to take one, and how he took one but wouldn't put it on. And how a lot of other miners did the same.

"Thought there's gonna be a fight right there," Arvo Belke said, "over who was or wasn't man enough to start wearin' that button around."

He paused.

"I put mine on," he said finally, "but there's a lot of married guys who wouldn't do it. I understood. Think most of us did."

He pulled his Prince Albert can and his papers out of his bib pocket, and started into the deliberate process one more time, watching his hands carefully as he worked.

"But then we had a bad accident. All of a sudden, them little red buttons sprang up all over town, like toadstools after a rain. There was a little red button on ever' black suit, ever' black dress. Even the preacher had one on."

———————

Like a near-sightless worm that lived far down in the ground, the Roma Tunnel mantrip worked its way deep into the mountain, its one headlight poking weakly into the blackness that lay thick and stubborn. Two stops from the end, a couple of miles in, Joe and Teddy Lazlo and four other miners got off the train and stood watching the light fade, then wink out. Inside the cloud of grey diesel smoke left hanging behind, each struck a match and lit the carbide light on his hard hat.

Then they walked away in twos, one pair going a short way further down the main tunnel, the other two pairs turning off in directions opposite each other, down lateral drifts.

"Give 'er hell, boys," was all they might say, and sometimes nothing at all.

The Lazlo brothers walked slowly, slogging along in their rubber suits and boots, pushing an empty ore car along a set of rusty rails deeper toward the core. Light from the burning carbide bounced off the peeled timbers—bleached wooden rib bones that lined the gut of the mountain, that held back the rock, that marked the way in and the way back out. All else was solid shadow.

"You muck and I timber," Teddy said after they'd walked about a quarter of a mile and come to the stack of spruce logs and the compressor that meant the rock face was just around the bend. Around there, a pile of loose and broken rubble lay at the end of the track, left from the drilling and blasting of the night shift. Left for them to clean up. "This is Wednesday, ain't it?"

They buttoned their rubber coats against the chill: water leaking out of the tunnels, running down both sides of the track in those trenches miners called the shit ditches, stayed at a constant thirty-three degrees, and the air was nearly as cold.

Joe blew on his hands and reached for a long-handled shovel.

"Better bar down before you start," Teddy said, looking up. "Big cracks."

"Sure as hell."

Joe picked up a long steel bar and walked up on top of the muck pile. Sticking the bar into a split in the rock, he jerked down hard and jumped away. With a warning that was little more than a faint groan, the overhead gave way, and a ton of loose rock crashed down on top of the muck pile, filling the air with a wet dust.

"Good idea," Joe said simply, "but now I got more shit to muck." Teddy half smiled at nothing that was funny at all.

———•·——

Day shift, night shift, the Lazlos or some other pair: it was a rock-and-water, hard-steel world. Cut into that headwall a foot or two at a time, gut that mountain, move that ore to the mill, just like yesterday, just like tomorrow.

Shovel the muck and strong-arm the boulders into the ore car. Drag the poles and the compressor from further down the drift. Lay track, if the company won't hire a track crew anymore. Notch and spike one or two new timber sets into place. Hook the air hoses— and water if you got it, or else drill dry—to the jackleg, and drill until the headwall is sieved with holes. Work blasting caps into the sticks of powder and tamp it all into the man-made pores. Run blasting wires and hook them into the main detonation line. Walk out, catch the 'trip, come back next turn and make sure there's still a zinc or a lead or a copper vein that's worth the ache in your legs at night.

———•·——

"Sunuvabitch! Holy shit, how can this be?"

Joe was stringing blasting wire when he heard his brother's agonized, almost shrieking, cry bouncing from wall to wall. Looking up, he saw Teddy standing dead still, staring at something in the palm of his hand, and even in the poor light, he could see eyes that were round and white, lips that moved and said nothing.

"What's the matter?"

"My watch," he said, struggling to finish a sentence. "Look at your watch, Joe. Look at your goddamned watch."

Joe ripped open his rubber pants and pulled the watch from his inside pants pocket, his own hands starting to shake.

3:55 p.m.

"Goddamn it!" he said. "We're in a helluva fix now. Got no time. Gotta run for it. Now! Run!"

With their lights bobbing wildly in the dark, the two began to run awkwardly down the drift, stumbling as they tripped on the rails and ties, fighting to keep their rubber boots from coming off.

"They won't blast will they?" Teddy asked, stopping to gasp and hold his stomach. "They'll know we're still in here."

"I don't know," Joe said, starting to run again. "I don't know. Maybe the mantrip's late. That's our only chance."

The mantrip was sometimes late, sometimes even this late, but when they reached the main tunnel, they could smell diesel smoke in the air.

"It's gone," Joe said flatly. "It's already gone."

"Let's cut the wires on our round," Teddy yelled, more panic creeping into his voice.

"Won't do no good, Teddy" Joe said, his voice growing suddenly more quiet and calm. "Everything else's gonna go."

Then they heard it: the first distant thump, then another and another. Closer. Louder

"Oh God," Teddy said, dropping to his knees. "Oh God, don't let this happen. We got families."

"Get down, kid," Joe said, pushing his younger brother lower, flatter, between the rails, then laying across the other's head and shoulders. "See you a little further down the road."

———•———

The miners who had come out were just filing into the dry room, starting to strip off their rubber jackets and pants and get ready for the walk back into town. The air was ripe with common talk: leaky air hoses, jammed chutes, drill steel stuck in the rock.

"Wait a minute," someone said suddenly, almost quietly. "Where's

Teddy and Joe? Where's the Lazlos?"

In an instant the room was taken over with the same question, over and over again, but almost in a scream.

"Where in the hell are the Lazlos?"

"Get to Monahan!" another yelled. "We got to get to Monahan!"

Some still dressed in rubber, others in old work shirts and Levis and some barefooted, the men ran as a mob out of the dry room, around the loading chutes and back toward the mouth of the main tunnel.

Pat Monahan, the shift foremen for the Roma day crew, stood next to a big red electrical box.

"Stop!" the first miner to see Monahan yelled. "Don't pull the round! We got guys . . ."

Then he saw that the lever was down. And as Monahan turned around to look their way, they felt the ground shake and dust stirred on the mountainside above.

"You son of a bitch," the first miner screamed, grabbing Monahan by the shirt. "You stupid son of a bitch. Why didn't you count? The Lazlo brothers are still in there."

Monahan looked at the miners, first with a look of shock at being screamed at and jerked around, then cooler, with only a hint of sorrow—or was it fear?—in the corners of his eyes.

"You boys sure? You sure they didn't just leg it for home?"

"Monahan, they never made it out! Can't you understand nothin?"

An abrupt silence, as every man stopped to look at another. For a moment, time didn't move, and they were stuck in place. Frozen.

"We'd better go back in then," Monahan said, shrugging his shoulders and turning toward the shed where the mantrip was stored. "But don't get your hopes up, boys. The whole round went. I seen this happen before."

Then he stopped and turned back around, facing the crowd.

"But just remember one thing, boys. Things like this, you got to learn to take care of your own. It ain't my fault, just like it ain't my job to count." He paused. "Cable Minerals pays you men to go in there. It's your job to see that you get out."

Teddy Lazlo was still alive, but the concussion that had killed his brother had blown them both against a stack of rails and broken Teddy's back. His hearing was gone, and flying rocks had embedded in his eyes. He mumbled something about his pocket watch. Two days later, he was dead as well.

6

"You got to take care of your own," Belke said. "That turned out to be the miners' call. Remember the Lazlos. You got to take care of your own."

As the old man's story unfolded, I almost forgot that I'd come to learn about my father, and his father, and the great grey links that seemed to connect us all. But I remembered, and I saw that it changed nothing, for I knew that Belke's labor story was indeed about Old Tom, about fate and time marching on. In some predetermined cadence. The way miners believed.

"We met in the fire house and we built big fires at the ball park and them United Mine Workers posters was nailed up on the telephone poles, though the company goons would rip 'em down damn neart as soon as they went up."

He stopped to cough harshly, then spit into the yard.

"But even after the Lazlos, some guys was still scared. 'Fraid of losin' their houses, bein' run outta town in the middle of winter. But we'd a got 'er done. We'd a had enough names, and we'd even called the law, I suppose, if that's what it took."

He leaned forward, his elbows on his knees.

"But that's when they brought the Navajos in."

The Navajos. *Did he tell you about his Navajos?* my father had asked me just two nights before. No. He'd said they hid, and that one day Madero would be left to the dog shit and Navajos. But had he told me about them, about who they were and what they'd been about? No.

"One day we thought we had 'er all figgered out. The next day, they was unloadin' Indians off a truck. Made no goddamned bones about it. Parked that big old army truck right there on the street and all them Indians came a-troopin' off. We might a stood a chance if we'd a grabbed our guns and marched them right back on again. But we didn't know what in the hell was a goin' on. We just stood around with our thumbs up our butts."

He stopped for a minute, and I sat quietly in the sun with him, just waiting for his thoughts.

"If Old Tom had a known what was a comin' for him," he said after a while, "he would a been the first guy there, puttin' them Navajos back on that truck."

As October petered out, and fall turned grey and lifeless and threatened winter, Madero took on a surly edge. The cold and ugly days strained tempers, and the wind gnawed at even the brighter attitudes. Like others, Anne Marie Cottin turned with the season: brooding, harsh, short. As the snowline made its first appearance high on the peaks surrounding town, Tom Cottin learned to keep his distance. Usually, he worked until the early dark and then, frequently but not always, stopped at the tavern on his short walk home.

"Tomasino, you know what I heard today?" The question came from Tony the Wop. Because he saw the old miner's name on bills and checks at the store, Cottin knew that his real name was Antonio Garabaldi. But to everyone else in town, he was Tony the Wop, and proud of it.

The two stood side-by-side, leaning against the bar and drinking beer. Their feet rested on a brass rail that had seen hundreds, no thousands, of miners' boots, and their coats were thrown across a chair nearby.

"What?" Tony always had something new to bring to the bar.

"I hear the company can't hire anybody with any brains anymore, because it's too fucking dangerous underground. So now they're going to bring in a bunch of them goddamned Indians to do the shit work. That's what I heard." He turned his head away and spat on the floor.

"I heard something like that, too, a couple of days ago. But I don't believe it." Actually, he had no reason not to believe it, but he disagreed with Tony out of habit. It was expected on both sides.

"I believe it. These cocksuckers won't pay an honest man an honest wage, so why wouldn't they go out and hire a bunch of Indians that don't know no better to work for less than day's wages?"

"I don't know. You could be right."

These kinds of conversations made Cottin a little uncomfortable. Despite the fact that he was a working man himself and saw the world as the miners saw the world, he was deeper inside the company, a company man. He'd worked for Cable Minerals for a long time, and though he had his complaints, plenty of them, he owed the company a vow of quiet support. In other words, he'd learned to keep his mouth shut. He knew the dangers of loose talk in the bar.

"There's going to be trouble, I betcha," Tony said. "These guys ain't going to sit around and watch their jobs get taken away from them by a tribe of *pellirossa*. There's going to be some blood on the fucking ground, I can tell you that for sure, *signore*."

The beer had quickly started to put a grating edge of Italian anger on Tony's voice. Cottin didn't say anything. He wanted to change the subject, or maybe just find a graceful route to the door.

"Joe and Teddy, they didn't die for nothin'. We'll have union, sure as hell's hotter'n this place, and then we'll see who cuts whose throats around here," Tony said loudly, as much to himself as to Cottin. "We'll just walk out and sit and wait. If the company don't pump some fresh air underground and fix the rotten timbers and stop telling us to drill dry, we don't go, and . . ."

Tired of listening to it, Cottin patted Tony on the back and said he had to get home to supper.

"Be seeing you, *amico*," the older man said as Cottin went out into the night.

———•———

More union talk. Tom Cottin didn't want to hear it. Others could stand on one side of the line or another, and that's where they were supposed to be. There, with their brothers. Management. Labor. Roles and costumes already drawn out. But how about him, the guy in the middle? Where were his brothers? Who was he supposed to serve, and how?

His bosses at Cable Minerals were already talking about cutting off credit to the loudest of the union sympathizers, telling him to get ready to get tough. But how could he say no to the wives and mothers who needed food? How could he tell the children to put the pencils back? How could he justify the unjustifiable?

That night, walking towards home in the cold, he wished he had someplace different and warmer and more comforting to go.

———•———

By the end of the week, twelve Navajo men were on the Cable Minerals payroll. A week later, six of the union's strongest agitators were called into the office after work and fired. They weren't told to get out of town. That wasn't needed. Without jobs, they had no choice, and most left within days.

Within two weeks, eight more Navajos had come from the reservation at Shiprock, and Pat Monahan had a list of three more white miners to fire. He told Skinner in the dry room, and Skinner had him down on the floor under a bench before the two of them could be pried apart by the other men. He called Bigelow at home, and he took the cursing for ten minutes before he quietly hung up the phone. To fire Arvo Belke, he had to go to the little miners' hospital, and see him lying there, in bandages.

———•———

Night shift at the Baltimore Tunnel. As the ore train lumbers by in the dark, a wall timber breaks way, falls between two moving cars, and a piece lodges across the coupling, sticking out on one side. The motorman can't see it, and nobody knows. When the ore train passes Arvo Belke and his mucking machine, the broken timber slams against the mucker, crushing Belke's left leg at the knee.

Two days later, Monahan hands him his last check and says that his rubber diggers and his lamp have already been turned in.

"I'd a waited, myself," Monahan explains. "But Alphabet says you'll be a bigger pain in the ass when you get out. Might as well get her done now, he says."

———·—·———

It was a tortured day in November, right at that bleak borderline with winter, when the sky and the wind and the ground had all turned metallic. Grey and hard. Flakes of snow, the remnants of leaves and dirt blew wildly up and down the streets, stinging the eyes. No sun, no heat, no promise of either.

As cold as it had turned, Tom Cottin was surprised to look out the store window and see that crowds had formed on both sides of the main street. An hour earlier, hardly a soul had moved against the nastiness of the day. White miners, Navajos, a few bundled-up women, children on their way home from school—all were knotted in fours and sixes, standing first on one foot and then the other, talking quietly and nervously, muttering, no laughter.

When Cottin stepped outside, he could feel a mood just as harsh, just as somber, as the color of the day. He saw Andrew, not far off, standing with books under his arm at the edge of the crowd. When he put his hand on the boy's shoulder, Andrew jumped.

"What's going on?" Tom Cottin asked.

Andrew said nothing. He just pointed out to the center of the street.

It was Arvo Belke. Belke was standing in the middle of the street, in front of the mining company offices, fixed at the center of what-ever was going on. With his left hand, he leaned on a brown wooden cane, propping himself up, while he held his right hand above his head in a fist, waving it. And he was bellowing over the wind, yelling toward the company doors.

As the wind shifted and swirled in the street, Cottin could hear some of the words: "Chicken shit . . . gutless bastards . . . thieving whores . . ." The insults seemed to be linked together in an endless string, and directed at someone inside.

Belke was drunk, Cottin was certain, but not merely drunk, for his eyes flashed with a rage that both twisted his face and graveled his voice. This was not the man Tom Cottin knew, not the man who came over with model planes for Andrew, with candy for Anne Marie. But everything was different, deformed and meaner, these days.

Finally, Alphabet walked out of the offices, into the wind, draw-ing the perfect counterpoint: Arvo in his dirty levis and flannel shirt with rolled up sleeves and sweatshirt sleeves sticking out, hair blow-ing wildly in the storm. And the man, in his light-colored, pressed khakis and matching shirt, a fedora-sort of hat, a sheaf of papers in his left hand.

He approached Belke, taking off his hat as he walked, gesturing, shaking the handful of papers at him, and Belke and his rage uncoiled like a breaking spring. With surprising quickness, Belke swung the wooden cane with both hands, hard, and hit the bigger man across the face with the sound of a breaking limb. Alphabet went down on his side as half the cane, the curled end, went spinning away in the air, and his papers and hat rode the wind down the middle of the street, unchased, tumbling.

Then Alphabet got up, wiping blood from his nose and mouth with his sleeve, and stood there, motionless. Arvo Belke balanced himself on his good leg, still holding on to half the cane, waiting. Alphabet stepped deliberately forward, and Belke swung again, but this time he hit only a pair of crossed arms, and the cane was swept aside. Then the street rang with a scream, a piercing scream, as Alphabet kicked Arvo Belke in his left leg, his heavily-bandaged leg, and the miner went down, trying to grab at his broken knee. The scream hung on the wind, stayed in the street, as Alphabet kicked the left leg again, and then again.

Four of the other miners took several steps forward, and Alphabet stepped back. He glared across at them from under his mass of black eyebrows, his jaw hardened, and they hesitated. And when he pointed his finger at them, a toy pistol, a warning, steady as steel, they froze. A half-smile crossed his face, and he turned and walked toward the office without a word, without looking back.

Andrew Cottin pulled away from his father, and with tears streaming down his cheeks and freezing in the wind, he ran as hard and fast as he could toward home. Barely able to hold on to his books, barely able to see. He locked the door to his room, and stayed there for the rest of the night.

Two night later, the family sat at dinner, and Tom Cottin told Anne Marie that he'd been called into the Cable Minerals office. She looked up, and he could see alarm in her eyes. But she didn't say anything. Andrew stared down at his plate.

"I thought maybe they were going to can me," he said. "How the hell would I know? I don't know anything anymore."

"Who was it?"

"Alphabet and Abrahams."

"What did they want?"

"They told me I was just doing a fine job for them. That I was loyal and that they appreciated that."

"That was all?"

"No," he said, his voice going a little flatter. "That wasn't all."

After they'd warmed him up, they told him that he was going to be responsible for dealing with the Navajos.

"This is going to be, well you know, tender," Abrahams started out. "There's likely to be some hard feelings against these people, and you, being over there and dealing with all these families day after day, well you can help smooth it out."

His right hand was busy, doodling nervously on a white tablet as they talked.

"But that's not the important thing," he went on. "It's the handling of their money. Some, we know, can't count. And those that can, well, we've come to understand that they don't take paying their bills very seriously. You follow me?"

Cottin followed easily enough, but he neither smiled nor nodded his head. He was not happy with this particular turn of events. The miners already saw him as a chickenshit company man, and only two days had passed since he'd been thrown against the meat counter by one of the men who'd been fired—a man who said the company could shove his store bill up its ass. And now Cable Minerals wanted to make him the company's Indian agent. He felt a tightness in his gut.

"From now on," Abrahams was saying, "Alphabet, er, Wyszyanski here, will bring the Indians' paychecks to you at the store. You take out what they owe the store, and give them what they have coming in cash."

Had the Navajos agreed to that? Cottin wondered, but then he knew it made no difference: they had no choice. They worked at the pleasure of the whites.

"There'll be other things," Alphabet added. "Charges for tools they lose or steal. Maybe rent, maybe not. Other things. You'll get a note from me with each packet of checks. You just go ahead and deduct whatever I say."

As Cottin was near the door, Abrahams spoke again.

"In case I didn't make myself clear, Cottin. It's your job to deal

with the Indians. They got a gripe, they'll come to you. You take
care of it." Then as an afterthought: "Maybe you should learn to speak
a little Navajo."

———·———

"What does it mean?" Anne Marie asked.

"I don't know," Tom Cottin answered. "But I don't think it's an
honor. I don't think it's an honor at all."

Anne Marie looked away, and Andrew got up and took his half-
emptied plate to the sink.

7

"I WAS TRYIN' TO GET SOMETHIN' BACK, I GUESS," ARVO BELKE SAID, followed by a small laugh that seemed to be filled with anger and sarcasm and self-ridicule. "But I guess I didn't get 'er done. Man ought not get drunk and pick a fight when he can't hardly stand up sober. She was broke bad already, and he broke her again worse."

In a strange way, his attitude seemed to have changed, as though he'd forgotten who was responsible for that leg.

"But that wasn't the only beatin' we took," he added, his voice turning flatter, more resigned. "We took 'em to court, and they whipped our asses there, too. They got a half-dozen of them Indians up there on the stand to testify that the union guys was bringin' whiskey underground to get 'em to join up with us. Company said we was fired for causin' unsafe workin' conditions." He snorted a half-laugh. "Now ain't that somethin'?"

Ironies. Even a judge should have been able to appreciate the contradictions.

"Were the whites taking liquor onto the job?" I asked.

"Why, hell no. If we'd a took whiskey underground, them Navajos woulda drank it and got drunker'n hell and passed out so everybody could see. Wouldn't a been no question."

He paused for a moment, and when he spoke again, it was almost as though he was telling me a secret, unveiling a mystery for the very first time.

"No, mister, them Navajos was bribed. Plain and simple. And probably threatened some, too."

We watched as a car pulled up to the end of his driveway and stopped. Then an arm reached out, opened and closed his mailbox, and the car moved on down the road.

"Anyhow, that was about it for me and Madero. By the time that there trial was over, my leg was healed up about as good as it was gonna get. So I went to Utah and went to buildin' railroad track. Got married and moved back over here, hell I don't know, sixteen, eighteen years ago. Wife's gone now, been four years next month. Couple a kids, workin' farms around here. That's about the way she goes."

He stood up and walked to the edge of the porch. I guessed that he was tired of talking to me, that he'd said about as much as we wanted to say.

"That's about what I know," he said, gazing off out into his yard. "Aw, I could talk about some other things. But I wasn't there, you see. I'd already give 'er up. And I ain't so sure what I remember any more, and what I mighta just dreamed up."

I thanked him for letting me come to his place, for the coffee, and for all the details he'd been able to fill in for me, and I walked down the steps, off the porch.

Then I turned and asked the one question I had to ask, the one that hadn't been answered.

"Tom Cottin," I said. "Did he kill a man?"

Arvo Belke took a long time to respond, thinking it all through as best he could.

"Ya know, I can't say for sure. I heard that he did, and I heard that he didn't. But I wasn't around. And him bein' a friend of mine, and your granddaddy to boot, why hell I wouldn't want to guess about somethin' like that."

"You don't remember who it was?"

He looked out toward the road. For at least a minute or two.

"No," he said slowly, shaking his head, looking down at the ground. "I guess I don't."

That's all right, I thought to myself. There's nothing wrong at all with a man grabbing the last opportunity he'll ever have to protect the honor and memory of an old friend. I respected that particular loss of memory, even if it did deny me something I thought I had to have.

"Ya know," he said as I started to step away, a little apology in his voice. "There'd be any number of people who know what happened to Tom Cottin in those next few years. But all I can think of are dead, or I just can't quite remember how the names and faces fit together anymore."

"That's okay," I said, and I told him that I thought his memory had been amazingly strong, and that he'd done me a great service. Then I turned to go.

"Son," I heard him say, and I looked back again. He came down the steps of the porch, slowly, painfully, one at a time, and limped up to me. "I'll tell ya what ya do."

I waited, not wanting to guess what he'd decided to add.

"You go down to Shiprock, and go see the Navajo police. Or go to the offices the tribe's got there. Somethin' like that. Ask 'em where you can find a fella by the name of Billy Yazzie. If he's still alive, they'll know."

I nodded my head, waiting in case there was more.

"That's all I got to say," he said, and he looked me straight in the eye.

———•·•———

But there was something else, something that I wanted to do. While we stood there in the yard, I told him about cleaning out Old Tom's shack, and about finding the wooden chains. I told him that I thought, somehow, that the chains ought to be used as a memorial to the old man. The best of what remained. And that one way to get that done would be for me to give them to people who had reasons to remember him, to talk about him, to regret his passing. People who were proof that he had lived.

"So I brought you this chain," I said simply, handing him a square box that had Canadian Club printed on all sides, and was taped across the top. And I watched while he opened it, unwrapped the torn-up sheet I'd packed it in, and removed the chain. It was light colored, with links big enough to have come from a two-by-four, with hooks at both ends.

"Why hell," he said seriously, almost quietly, "I can't take this." He half-tried, but only half-tried, to hand it back.

I assured him that he could, that he had to, that Tom Cottin would have wanted it that way, and that no one else would appreciate it as much. I asked only that he pass it on to his kids, and on down the line, and that they just remember where it came from.

It was an awkward moment, one in which neither of us wanted to say anything that might spill over or leak, that might make us go too soft. So we stood there, shifting our feet, keeping our eyes deliberately fixed on the chain. Then he handed me his red union button.

"It's a trade then," he said. "You'd be doin' me a favor if you'd just look at this here button from time to time, and remember me, too."

We parted with a handshake, and a mile or so down the road, I almost put my truck in the ditch, trying to drive and pin that button on my shirt at the same time.

PART FOUR

Billy Yazzie

1

"Who is Billy Yazzie?"

That question hits a nerve. I can see it in his eyes, can tell by the way he sits up straighter, more stiffened. But he doesn't answer, at least not for a while.

I camped not far from his mine last night, and I was there just after daybreak. I wanted to catch him fresh, maybe in the better mood that a sun-washed morning brings out in most people. Not that he responds like most people.

We've taken the morning coffee that he was just perking when I drove up, and walked out to the bench on the rim. The walk, the bench, the long stare: it's his ritual, and I fall into it, too. Maybe because broad horizons allow us the illusion of being far enough away from each other to be safe.

Spring has come to the desert while I've been gone. The sage and chamisa and rabbit brush have taken advantage of the little spring rains to jump higher out of the ground, and to throw a fresh lime-green cast across the land. Those broad green brush strokes that sweep back and forth across the floor below will not last, but fade and go grey-green and brown as the sun turns hotter and climbs higher in the sky.

But, for now, I can smell it. Can almost taste the sweet acid that sage and new juniper growth have left hanging in the air.

Below, little silvery flashes in the rocks. Water, little potholes of leftover rain, that will soon, too, give in to the sun.

How altered it looks in the morning light, how different from the evening terrain: like the same scene painted in different colors, and

yet more like a new landscape altogether. Where there were shadows, now crisp detail. And where a little spire had stood out so obviously in the evening light, now a background of homogeneous
browns, as though the rock had fallen and gone.

Time passes. A turkey vulture wobbles in the warming air above
us, circling ever more tightly, drawing a bead, wondering about our
health.

"How'd you come up with that?"

I look at him, and I see something that looks like a half-smile. But
pain and sarcasm and regret can produce that same look, too. I know
he's not happy. To see me. Or with my questions.

In the warming sun, I tell him about my long visit with the Finlander. I shorten and lengthen, as the story relates less or more to
him, the boy, and I draw him a picture of Madero in the late 1940s—
at least as filtered through the memory of Arvo Belke.

Oddly, my father nods his head more often, and seems more genu-
inely interested in this story, but without any great sense of pleasure.
Like bad news he's been expecting, and knows he has to listen to.
Like a quick trip through a scrapbook that hasn't been opened for a
long time.

Maybe he thinks I'll fill up on the unimportant, the little pictures,
and have to quit because my stomach can't hold any more.

"Who is Billy Yazzie?" I ask again.

"Some Navajo," he finally says.

"Is that all?"

"Ask old Belke."

"I did." It was a lie of sorts, but not really. I'd asked in my own
way.

"What'd he say?"

"He wouldn't."

He starts to say something, but then he doesn't. And by not speaking, he forces me to watch the desert in silence with him. I know

what he's trying to do: freeze me out, say nothing for so long that I give up and walk away and don't come back. Because it's no use.

"I guess I'll go down to the reservation and find out for myself," I say, standing up and looking down over the edge. It's easy to see patches and swatches of green now. The desert is moving into bloom.

"You do that," he says. "You do that."

I start to say something else, about having no choice, but he cuts me off.

"And when you do," he says, "you just make goddamned sure that he tells you about Sam Benally, too. That you get every sonofabitchin' piece of it."

Sam Benally. It rang a bell. It was one of those disconnected fragments that had fallen out of the mind of Old Tom.

"And when you've done that, you take it home and chew on it. And see how it tastes. And maybe it'll make you puke, like a peyote button, and you'll see lizards. And you'll see there ain't no reason in hell for you to come back here again."

He looks at his empty coffee cup.

"This time, Markus" he says, "get your goddamned gut full."

———•••———

Driving off the mesa again. Mid-morning, and the sagebrush seems even brighter, greener, when I'm down there inside it. The rich, sharp sweetness of its smell has climbed inside my truck and stayed there and rides with me as I drive along.

I smile a little to myself. Just a little. Despite the way things have gone. He doesn't want me to lose the trail, at least not quite yet. I can tell: the old bastard, for the first time, spoke my name.

2

I HEARD WILLIE NELSON SINGING FROM SOME PLACE OFF IN THE DISTANCE. I couldn't tell where it was coming from, but it didn't matter. Just something I heard.

Meanwhile, Billy Yazzie gripped his upper legs with his wrinkled and silver-ringed fingers, loosely, and talked about shooting sheep.

"One day, my father came home and started killing our sheep. He just kept pulling the trigger, until at least fifty were dead, and we thought his mind had deserted him. Then he burned them. He drug the bodies into a big pile and poured gasoline over them and set them on fire. All of us, even my father, were sickened by the smell.

"That night, as my mother cried, he told us that he was not crazy, there was a new government law, and he could only do what he had been told. My mother agreed. But she cried, too."

We sat on a wooden bench at the side of the old man's hogan, shaded but not saved from the hot afternoon sun. Even in springtime, the desert baked in heat coming out of a cloudless, windless sky. A half-dozen ewes and lambs grazed in the rabbit brush not far away. And an endless stream of pickup trucks flashed and roared along the reservation's main highway, leaving behind a floating cloud of country music.

I had asked the old man to talk about those earlier days in Madero, about Tom Cottin, and he talked about the shooting of the sheep, instead. Perhaps it's the Indian way, I thought, to surround the point, rather than attack it head-on. No matter. I was convinced that this story, added to Arvo Belke's labor stories, were necessary parts of the whole: the edge pieces of a puzzle that helped define the center and hold it in place.

Although Billy Yazzie spoke good English, he took his time, as though he had to weigh each of the Anglo words. He found the old story painful, he told me, and as he summoned up the old memories he had to also reach back for words and names he had not used for many, many years. He had to sort carefully, he said, for the dead, for the sake of the stories themselves.

As he spoke, his eyes were hidden in the shadows cast by an old broad-brimmed, sweat-crusted brown hat, one that had probably been used for everything from watering a horse to fanning a fire.

Meanwhile, I was fighting the heat, my forehead clammy, my palms wet, and my shirt sticking to my back like a plastic sandwich wrapper. The crippled sheepdog eyed me with suspicion, staring back at me over his shoulder. I eyed him, too, harder, until he turned and dropped into the shade under my truck.

"That was how it all really started, back when I was a young boy," the old man was saying, "when the government said the reservation had too many sheep for the small amount of grass and water. Many had to go, they said, so we burned up our food and our work and our lives.

"So we had nothing to sell. Little to eat. No wool to spin. Less goat's milk. Life on the reservation got very, very thin. What the Holy People had given us, the white people were taking away."

The soft tones of the old man's voice, a melody of little scraps and pieces of words rising and falling on the vocal wind, worked on me like a hypnotist's chant. I was listening as carefully as I could, but I looked skyward as he did, and I saw crows, shining in the relentless sun, and I wished that we could get on with the story.

"The thing is, the important thing, the men had to leave the reservation. For the first time ever in the history of the Dineh, many families had to leave their people. They had to go outside to find work."

"Some worked on ranches. Some went to the towns. Many from

here, me and Sam Benally and others, went to Madero to work in
the mines. Everybody said the best money was there."

Even in my mild stupor, I caught the mirthless, almost silent, laugh
that broke the rhythm of the old man's monologue.

"What price we paid for that good money."

I would hear it all, for I had plenty of time, and perhaps later in
the day the air would cool.

———————

Young Billy Yazzie sat behind the trading post counter, reading a
month-old *Saturday Evening Post*. It was a slow, feverishly hot, late
summer day. Only Ruth Benally was in the store, and she was taking
her time, moving her heavy body between the makeshift shelves,
examining jars and cans and packages as though there was much to
choose from. There wasn't. Just the necessities, and not even all of
those.

"I haven't seen Sam," Billy Yazzie said in Navajo as the older
woman finished her stack of canned beans, dried chili peppers, flour,
salt, and canned fruit. Sam Benally was a young man his own age,
twenty-two, who had grown up only a few miles from his own family's
hogan. However, since they'd both come back from trade school six
months before, he'd seen nothing of his friend.

"You know how it is. Every year we seem to have fewer sheep to
sell, less wool to take to market," she said, "so Sam left the reservation to make some money on his own." Then she laughed. "He
wanted to get away, anyway. You know how you young men are."

Yes, he knew. Restless. Tired, sometimes, of seeing nothing but
greasewood, sagebrush, and red rocks. Tired of watching his family
work so hard just to stay alive. Tired of the long, endless days that all
looked and felt the same.

"So he went away," Billy Yazzie said, a polite question, ringing up
her purchases on the ancient cash register.

"North," she said, digging into her change purse. "Up the Helado

River. He's working in a mine, in a town called Madero."

"I've heard of it," Billy Yazzie said. "I talked to the white man who came around looking for workers. Two of my cousins went up there."

"Yes, I'd forgotten," she said. "Well, at least they're able to do something. Better than herding goats you don't have." She laughed softly again.

Billy Yazzie piled her goods into the canvas bag she carried with her, and Ruth Benally opened the door and went out into the bright, hot, summer sun.

After she was gone, he sat on his stool, thumbing aimlessly through the magazine again. He wasn't happy with the thought that others had gone away and were at least making things happen, while he, who could speak fairly good English and who knew how to weld, was back on the reservation, selling beans and shovels for the trading post company.

But at least he could listen to the radio, which was a diversion he wouldn't have if he was sitting out next to some butte, watching sheep move across the broken rocks, waiting for the sun to get done with the wide, wide sky.

At the thought, he clicked on the old Philco that sat on a shelf to his right. Hank Williams. He liked Hank Williams. Or at least he liked Hank Williams better than that howling big band music they played on the only other station he could pickup. If one was country music, the other must be city music, and it sounded a lot like car horns, too, now that he thought about it.

Another customer pushed the door open, and the creaking sound startled him briefly. He hadn't heard the man ride up on his horse, because he'd been deep in thought, wondering what it might be like to work in a mine. It was old Charlie Nez, one of the oldest men on the reservation, come for a bag of oats. Billy Yazzie helped the bent old man tie a fifty-pound bag across his saddle and stood watching until Charlie Nez, leading his horse and walking slowly, disappeared through a hole in the juniper.

No other customers came that day.

———•———

That night, as they sat outside the hogan and watched the tips of the buttes glowing red in the last rays of the sun, Billy Yazzie told his mother that he thought he might be leaving in a week or so, that he might go to Madero, and that he thought maybe he could do well there. She said nothing, nor did she have to.

He knew that his mother, like most women, like most of the older people, felt that nothing good could come of a Navajo leaving his people, leaving his land, losing touch with the important things. She was sad, but like all Navajo women, she was strong, and she kept her sorrow to herself.

3

OLD BILLY YAZZIE SAT STIFFLY ERECT, HIS HANDS ON HIS THIGHS NOT quite covering the holes that had worn in the knees of his Levis. He stared off thoughtfully toward the horizon, and although he was talking to me, he looked mostly away. He could have been speaking to the sun.

"Maybe we wouldn't have gone to the mines at all," he says, "except that they sent this man to the reservation to find us, to make us promises. Good money, he said, and a place to live. This man, he had a new truck. Maybe we all thought we would have a new truck."

The old man looked over at me, but there was no expression in his eyes.

"We treated our goats better than the white men treated us in that place. Like animals, we were packed into those old houses. Sometimes we'd have to cook and eat out in the yard, even in winter. We had to nail our rugs and blankets up where there once were windows, just to keep out the snow and wind. We were so cold. All the time cold."

It was almost too warm to let me remember cold, much less regret it. I swatted a fly, a mean delta-shaped deer fly, off the back of my hand, and fell once again into a sort of sun-stupor.

"We were desert people. We were not made for the snow and cold, and many of us, the children mostly, got very, very sick. Some, a few anyway, died."

Between us and the highway, a single file of goats plodded along, pushed from behind by a young boy in high top tennis shoes and a red and white football jersey. If this lad practiced tribal tradition, it didn't show, but perhaps I was too quick to judge. After all, Billy Yazzie's plain grey workshirt might well have come from the same factory in Taiwan.

"Maybe we could have lived with the pay, and maybe we couldn't," the elder Yazzie said as he looked down at his clasped hands. "And maybe we could have learned to live in the cold, and maybe we couldn't. But the anger in the town—how could we live with that?"

He told me that he didn't know the words to say what it felt like to be hated for nothing. Even now, after all those years, he said he didn't understand why the whites didn't just shoot each other and leave the Navajos alone.

"One side hated us for being there," he said, "and the other side hated us for being Navajo."

When he seemed reluctant to go on, I asked him this: "Did you understand what labor unions were about, what some of the whites were trying to do?"

He pondered for awhile.

"I understood a little bit. And Sam Benally understood a little bit. We'd been away from the reservation, and we knew that white laws were many, and Indian laws were few. That white laws made things like companies. And we saw these unions as the workers' companies to fight against the owners' companies. But the rest, they only knew clans. And laws don't make clans. Blood makes clans."

———·•·———

Billy Yazzie rode the train from Three Rivers to Madero, herded into a single passenger car with a grey-brown collection of mining town commoners: white miners smelling of aftershave and looking anxiously out the windows, women who eyed him with an obvious distrust and clamped their jaws down tight, noisy children excited by the noise and a trip to anywhere at all. Although the coach, sandwiched in between empty and rattling ore cars, was crowded, the other passengers gave Billy Yazzie more than his share of room.

The cars swayed back and forth, almost in a rhythm, as the train rounded sharp turn after sharp turn, trying to stay with the course of the serpentine river. Rocked that way, sung to by the clicking of the wheels, some passengers slept. But Billy Yazzie could not.

He'd just gotten off the train, and was carrying his bag across the depot platform when he felt the heat of a stare that followed each of his steps. He looked up into the hard grey eyes of a young man, about his own age, dressed in high rubber boots, patched Levis, and a stained cotton shirt. His hair was red, and a hand-rolled cigarette hung out of one corner of his mouth.

"Just what we need. Another fuckin' Navajo," the white man said, though not as much to Billy Yazzie himself as to the smoke-filled cloud that hung there between them. Maybe, Billy Yazzie thought, this white man thinks that no Indian understands English.

He'd been cursed by white men before. It was a familiar part of leaving the reservation, doing business in the white men's towns. But he was dumb-struck here, in Madero, a town he thought had made a place for Navajos.

He said nothing and moved on, carrying his bag up the steep road that led to the main part of town. Once there, he sat on the edge of the wooden sidewalk and watched the trucks and cars, watched people coming and going along the street. The pattern of their behavior seemed to be no pattern. Sometimes they greeted each other warmly, sometimes they spoke grudgingly or not at all, and sometimes they turned away from one another in a clear pantomime of disrespect. No one, he noticed, spoke to the solitary Navajo.

Still, Billy Yazzie was hopeful, even during that night when he sat with Sam Benally and several of the others around a pot of mutton stew, and they told him that the whites were part coyote, that their promises were thick smoke that hid very small flames.

"They pay us all right," Sam Benally said, "and for awhile there was some to take to Shiprock. Some people moved back already, with enough for the winter. But they also make us pay. And then they make us pay more. Now we don't know. We work hard on these jobs, but the mountain gets further away."

"Payday comes," Billy Yazzie's cousin Nelson added, "and the whites walk away with their pockets full. For us, though, we're told, 'go to the store and see how much you have coming.' We go to the store, and they say, 'you made this much, and you took this many things from the store, and you don't have anything left.' Sometimes we have a little left over, enough for gasoline or a new hat. Some spend it on whiskey. But usually, it's a very little bit."

Sam Benally said that he himself made a little more money than most, since he already had a trade. He could fix trucks, and in this company, there were more trucks to fix than he could ever finish.

"But me," he said, "I don't have much either. Every time payday comes and I go to settle up, I get a little bit. Maybe next time my better pay will show up."

"And these houses," Nelson said after they'd paused to eat, "they're just boards and paper. They're freezing us to death. The doctor comes up from Three Rivers one day a week, and it's the Dineh who are always sick. Crying babies, shivering women wrapped up in blankets and rugs, strong men with great pain in their eyes. The long line goes out the door, and when they call names, it's Begay, Nez, Ahkeah, Manygoats, Benally, Nakai. I ask, where are the whites?"

It was not what Billy Yazzie wanted to hear, but he was a welder, he had a trade, and he still believed, despite what Sam Benally and Nelson said, that things would be different for him.

By night, Billy Yazzie slept under his blankets in one corner of a two-room house he shared with Nelson's family—his wife and three children—and two other single men. Crowded around the stove, they would sit and talk, mostly of the reservation, and sometimes pass a bottle of cheap Muscatel: contraband bought in the shadows around the back door of Madero's liquor store.

Other nights, sometimes as many as two or three a week, he and the others would sit through the movies shown free by the company in the old dance hall. The whites sat closer to the front, where the sound was better. The Indians didn't need the sound, and they could see the sword fights, horse chases and gunplay perfectly well from their chairs in the back.

By day, Billy Yazzie worked as hard as he'd ever worked in his life. He built tram buckets, he repaired the blades on old bulldozers, he put ore cars back together, he sealed cracks in the rod and ball mills. Like a medic on a battlefield, he moved from one critical situation to the next: patching, reconstructing, salvaging. Always in demand. Always behind.

Billy Yazzie was a valuable man. And for his skill, he was paid an extra dollar a day.

Because he moved around from the first whistle to the last—under ground, through the mills, around the dumps and the chutes—he heard things. And because he understood English better than the others, he could feel the thickening of the air, the simmering anger. To the others, he expressed it as a swelling, growing underneath an infected wound.

And the more he saw and heard, the wider grew the circles he made around the whites and their conflicts. The greater grew the distances he put between himself and the supercharged air. But he could not see in all directions at once.

"Yazzie, you're a smart Navajo."

Ed Ward, one of the more outspoken of the miners, had walked up behind him while he was picking up his tools in a deserted corner of the mill where a conveyor roller had broken loose.

Billy Yazzie said nothing. He didn't want to talk to Ward, about the union or anything else. The man was big and loud, and had a habit of calling Navajos gut-eaters.

"Why don't you and Benally and them other bucks help us out a little here?"

Billy Yazzie looked around at the man, still saying nothing. Silence was a tool, and he'd used it before to pry other white men off his back. The sooner he got out of this dark corner of the mill, the better.

"Ya know," Ward went on, "when the company brought you fellers in from the reservation, the one thing they never figgered on was you joinin' up with us. Now, if you Indians was to just sign up with us, why, it would be all over."

He took a wooden match out of the corner of his mouth.

"We could snap the company's back just like that."

He stuck the match up against Billy Yazzie's chest, and pushed down on it until it snapped.

Billy Yazzie looked down at the big hand only inches away from his face, and shook his head.

"You need to figger out who you're for and who you're against," Ward said. "You bucks come on over with us, and we'll all make a better livin' in the end. You understand more money, don'tcha, Yazzie?"

"More money, sure," Billy Yazzie said, smiling slightly, his eyes fixed on the other man's face. "But this fight is not for us. If you win, we work for you. If they win, we work for them. That's okay."

Then he picked up his tool bag and walked away, pulling his welding tanks along behind him. Even in the coolness of the mill, he could feel a heat at his back, and he knew it was a stare meant to hurt.

Two days later, just before the end of his shift, Billy Yazzie was called into the mill foreman's office. The foreman, Stankey, and another boss whose name was Alphabet, were sitting down, one behind a desk, the other next to it, when he walked in.

"Yazzie," Stankey said without any attempt at pleasantries, "we want to talk to you."

Yes, Billy Yazzie thought, or I wouldn't have been hauled in here. The air was heavy and thick, and smelled of cigars and sweat.

"We hear the union boys have been trying to sign you up."

Billy Yazzie said nothing, just stood there looking straight ahead at a calendar on the wall. A picture of a white woman in a bathing suit, almost naked. Something he'd never seen. The little pages with numbers had long-since been ripped away.

"They probably offered you whiskey, didn't they?"

They sounded tough, but in their eyes, the Navajo could see something else. Fear, maybe, and uncertainty. Why would they be afraid of him?

"No," Billy Yazzie said, shaking his head. "They offered me nothing, nothing but promises."

"You sure they didn't offer you a few bottles of hootch, firewater?" Both men looked at him intently, waiting for an answer.

"Nothing."

The men sat silently for a moment, each seeming to wait for the other to speak.

"Well, let's just say they did," the other man said finally. "Let's say they did, and you were willing to say so in court. Let's say Ward offered you, oh, a case of whiskey, and you told the judge about it. There'd be an extra fifty dollars in your next paycheck."

More than a week's wages, Billy Yazzie thought to himself, money he wanted about as much as anything. But as quickly as his mind flashed on the pickup truck he would like to buy, it also flashed on Ed Ward's face—a face, a set of eyes, a pair of hands he would not want waiting for him in the darkness of the mine.

"No, nothing," Billy Yazzie said. "They asked for help. I said no. Nothing more."

He shook his head again, harder this time.

"Better think about it, Yazzie," they said, frowning and waving him toward the door. "You better figure out who you're working for here."

———·•·———

That night, as he and the others sat around the stove, tired and almost ready for bed, Billy Yazzie told them about his conversation with the bosses.

"They wanted me to lie," he said in conclusion.

After a long break in the conversation, Nelson spoke up quietly.

"They talked to me, too," he said, "but I wasn't going to tell anybody."

He paused for a long time, and the others waited and watched the flame through the glass on the stove.

"I took the money," Nelson said finally. "My mother is very, very sick at home."

4

It was hot. Hot and dry. And even though I was not the one talking, I could feel the inside of my mouth going leathery, and I realized, suddenly, that there was no water out here. Few wells, dry springs, empty creeks. The water was all hauled in, in barrels and tanks.

Billy Yazzie tipped up a container of some kind—it looked like a bladder or a stomach out of some animal—and drank deeply. Water dribbled out of the corner of his mouth, and he wiped it off. Then he offered it to me. I was thirsty, yes, but I had to decline. Flies clustered on the outside of the water bag, and maybe it was just made out of hide, but I was not nearly that thirsty yet.

He said nothing, and fixed his eyes lazily on the sheep.

I had another question. I thought it might be too vague, too made-up and anxious, but I asked it anyway: "If the owners had their company, and the workers had their company, what about Tom Cottin? Where did he fit in?"

Again, he took time to answer. He crossed and recrossed his legs, and for the first time, I noticed his shoes. Old, faded-white basketball shoes.

"He had his own company. The company store."

Outside this other struggle, or above it? Was the old man saying that Tom Cottin wasn't in the middle of the labor fight? I doubted it.

"In the old days, the government would send out a white man to order us around, and they called him their Indian agent. Sometimes those men ran trading posts, too. What was the difference?"

Indian agent. I detected a hint of anger, or maybe sarcasm, in his voice.

"Tom Cottin had our money in his hands, all the time. He kept what he wanted, and we never knew how much that would be. Also, he told us: you live here, you live over here, you get this firewood, you can go visit your family, you can have this many bullets for hunting season. What was the difference?"

I didn't see a difference.

"He said new company rule this, new company rule that. We say okay, but outside, we laugh. We are not goats and cows."

He paused again, thinking probably about company rules.

"Every Sunday, the whites dress up in their best clothes and go to church. Bells ring. Much talk, shaking hands, singing. But they tell us we can have no ceremony. No Indian ceremony. Too much trouble."

He looked harder in my direction.

"We say, 'Tom Cottin, bullshit.'"

"You say?"

"Me? No. Sam Benally."

———————

Tom Cottin's office was on a raised platform that was really just a ceiling that went over the top of the meat lockers, maybe a half-story above the store's main and only floor. From his desk there, he saw Sam Benally come in and talk to a clerk, who gestured up the stairs toward the little unwalled office.

Cottin didn't know Sam Benally well. He was one of the quieter Navajos, though his English seemed better than that of all the others, excepting maybe Billy Yazzie. One of the married women, perhaps a cousin, did his shopping for him, and he didn't come into the store often.

Although Cottin pointed in invitation to a chair by his desk, Sam Benally remained standing, his Stetson held in his hands. About half the men still kept their black hair in traditional style, bound up with yarn in the back, but not Sam Benally. His was cut short, and his eyes were hidden behind a pair of dark glasses. His mouth was flat, tight, and mirthless.

"What can I do for you?" Cottin asked, smiling as broadly as he could. He never knew what the issue might be, or whether he might be facing a hot anger just barely beneath a cool and expressionless skin. With each passing month, he found it harder and harder to deal with the Indians, to look across the table at them as he doled out their pay: the measure of their worth—as workers and as human beings. Their faces said little, but he wondered when their masks might slip.

"Navajos want to dance," Sam Benally said. "Friday night Navajos want to dance. End of the ball field where fires are built."

"Well, Sam," Cottin began, "personally I'd think that's fine. But there's a company policy that says no Indian ceremonies. We're afraid it just might start trouble. People are, well, nervous, these days, you know." He had a hard time believing the sound of the words coming out of his own mouth.

Sam Benally's expression never changed, as though he was hearing exactly the words he expected to hear.

"Maybe the company don't understand," he said slowly. "Dances and songs are not for celebration. For worship, as you say. Church, like on Sunday."

"But there could be trouble."

"No peyote. Just dance and sing."

Cottin leaned back in his chair, his hands held with fingertips together, as in a children's game.

"No, that's not what I meant. It's the whites, maybe the ones with no jobs, that would cause the trouble. It just wouldn't be worth the risk."

"Maybe to you," the Navajo said flatly. "Every year, for most of our lives, we go to Shiprock or Window Rock to dance and sing the *Yeibichai*. That's what we do. Now you say, nine days no, you can't have that. We ask for Enemy Way time, and you say no, too many days too. Got to work, keep mines going. Okay, but *N'daa*, squaw dances, just one night sometimes. That's what we want."

How far can we stretch it, Cottin wondered to himself. How far can we bend the Indians to make them fit into this role we've designed for them? Those questions were with him most days, now, and in his nightmares, too: in those dreams, Navajos in hard hats were ringed around him everywhere, and his hands shook as he shuffled the little pieces of paper that represented the pay the Indians could never hope to collect.

And now this: how many of their traditions and freedoms can we take away? How long until the blood gets hot enough to boil over?

"I understand," he said, evenly, as pleasantly as he could. "But what if there's trouble? You and I will have broken the company law."

"Bullshit on the company law, Tom Cottin," Sam Benally said as he turned toward the stairs. "And bullshit on you."

Cottin looked down at his hands, and they were shaking.

———·—·———

Friday night's moon rose yellow, bright and full, big as a dollar and as hard around the edges. A little wind came up after sundown, putting small teeth into the autumn air, rustling the brittle leaves, making tree shadows dance. No clouds.

Just before dark, the Navajo men began hauling wood—big branches and stumps of spruce and aspen—onto the end of the ball field, where a circle of burned grass remembered earlier fires made for other reasons. Some wood they stacked high in a tepee shape; the rest, they laid off to the side. Away, dogs saw more of the moon, and clamored at it.

Then darkness closed in, until there was only the moon, and hints of edges, and movement. Near silence.

The drums and fire broke the nightspell together: the hollow pounding began softly at first, weak like the spark at the heart of the woodpile, then stronger, with greater power, just as the flame began to spread and climb.

Leather-bound sticks came down again and again, together, on the drums: one made of sheepskin stretched over a hollowed cottonwood trunk, the other made of hide stretched over a small rusted barrel. The beat did not echo, but was instead absorbed by the night.

Light from the growing fire probed deeper and deeper into the fading circle of darkness: coppery faces, dark eyes, muted colors, here and there a flash of silver. Everything that moved, moved with the drums.

Then the rattles: sharp coughs coming from dried gourds filled with corn kernels and squash seeds, with pieces of turquoise and grains of sand. With the drums, sometimes, and at other times rasping against the drum beat.

Voices: barely heard at first, an almost-timid crying-out solo, then louder as they all joined in the songs. Simple melodies, one note or few notes, repetitions, that anguished pleading sound that comes from prayer in song.

Then the men, and a fewer number of women, stood and began to dance.

————•——

Other eyes were watching. Beyond the reach of the fire light, back in the deep shadows cast by the stone schoolhouse, white men and women stood in clusters, uneasy on their feet. Most watched in silence; others growled and grumbled, but quietly, to themselves and those closest by.

Off to one side, Tom Cottin stood beside his wife, frowning, shaking his head in short, slow arcs. His hands rested on the shoulders of his son Andrew, who was silent as well. The boy stepped nervously from foot to foot, and his eyes were wide and reflected the colors and movement of the flames.

————•——

Hay aa yah, hay aa yah, hay aa yah . . .

Like a snake that fights to uncoil but cannot, the men danced. Some in hats, some with kerchiefs around their heads, some in moccasins, some with rattles, they shuffled around the fire, leaving little billows of dust that followed their feet. Singing, chanting, circling, eyes unfocused: seeing things on the ground, out there in the darkness, up in the sky, that no one else could see.

Minutes passed, then an hour, and the rhythms went on. The moon worked its way steadily across the sky.

———•———

Suddenly, the drums hushed, the voices trailed off and the men circling the fire stopped, held almost as if on puppet strings. Sound, movement, thought: all hung suspended in the air.

Inside the circle of light, only a few feet from the track of the dancers, a white had stepped into the ceremony. It was the man called Alphabet. The man who'd offered Billy Yazzie money to lie.

Near silence. The ticking of the clock. The beating of the heart. Little more.

The big man's tan cotton clothes were washed in orange by the fire, and his silver hair, drawing light from everywhere, thrashed in the wind like wild grass. Reflections of the flame danced off the length of iron pipe he held in one hand.

He looked from one fact to another, slowly, searchingly.

"Break it up," he shouted out suddenly. "Put this fire out and get back to your houses."

He paused, as if to allow a reply, but there was none.

"You were told not to gather here. You've had your fun, now break it down and get out of here."

No other sound, no movement.

"Can't you people hear? Get moving, or every damned one of you will be looking for a job tomorrow morning."

Sam Benally, a faded red bandana tied around his head, separated himself from the crowd of Navajos, and stepped forward into the brighter light. He said nothing.

"Is that you, Benally? You understand plain English. Tell them to get the hell out of here."

Sam Benally did not answer, but instead began a measured walk toward the white man. His face without expression and rigid, his hands hanging loosely at his sides.

As the Indian closed in on Alphabet, the white man raised his iron pipe and balled his other fist, ready, tensed.

Sam Benally walked on, straight ahead, his own hair stirred by the breeze, until his chest nearly touched that of the white man. And for a moment, neither moved.

Then Sam Benally began to sing. One voice, one tremulous melody reaching out into the night. Neither strong nor weak, but clear, vibrating with emotion, piercing.

. . . and the snake said, come with me, and I will show you high places your enemies can never reach . . .

Then another voice, Billy Yazzie's voice.

. . . and the raven shall be your bow and your arrows and fly through the air straight and true . . .

Nelson and his cousin. Ben Begay. Robert Lee. Others, until all the Navajos were lending their voices, not praying, but answering their own prayers.

Then the drums began again, pounding, louder than before, with a rhythm more definite than before. And the gourds, rasping with more crispness now, and louder too.

Alphabet took one step back, and spoke words that only he and Sam Benally could hear.

"So that's how it is, is it? Well, singing won't get you a goddamned thing."

He turned and walked out of the circle of light, carrying his piece of pipe like a spear, back stiff and shoulders square. He walked west, off toward the far end of the field, where the backstop and home plate would be.

Though no men resumed the dance, the Navajos still stood and sang, repeating the choruses over and over again, singing about high places and ravens and snakes.

Over near the stone schoolhouse, the whites watched and listened, huddled and quiet like accidental participants in the funeral of a stranger, sensing without understanding that they had reason to grieve. Somehow, for them too, something unfortunate was happening here.

They heard parts of Alphabet's words, the harshness and boldness in what he had to say. And they could hear the song, sounding at first like a lonely and fitting dirge, then sounding more like an angry, and thus unsettling, chant.

Then they heard sounds the Indians could not. The hard slamming of a metal door. The grinding of a starter. The roar of a punished engine.

And they saw the lights go on.

Billy Yazzie was still singing and looking at Sam Benally when he saw the headlights. He turned, they all turned, as the lights grew closer and closer and they could hear the engine revving, whining higher in a lower gear.

Still they sang, until they saw that the dump truck—an old truck that both Billy Yazzie and Sam Benally had worked on numerous times before—was picking up speed.

And the song faded away, had weakened to a few scattered voices, when the truck hit the bonfire.

Flames seemed to slide up and over the hood of the truck, and pieces of fire and smoke spun off into the night like rockets and flares. Going in three directions at once. Blowing waves of sparks and coals away from the churning wheels. Spreading orange and yellow light everywhere.

The Indians cowered and ran, shielding themselves and each other from the hot debris.

Then the truck was gone, and the field was silent, except for the popping of the burning wood. The solid darkness was accented by the clouds of grey, rolling smoke.

Without words, almost without any sound, mechanically, the Navajos picked up their blankets and their amulets and their drums and their gourds and walked away, back toward their houses, back into a night grown strangely quiet.

———

The whites walked away, too, until only the three Cottins were left, standing alone like stone posts. Anne Marie had turned away, was watching others of their type fade down the moonlit street. Tom stared straight ahead, his jaws hardened, his fingers unconsciously clenched into the shoulders of his son.

Andrew stared toward the smoldering remains of the fire, too, fighting back tears, afraid for what he felt through his father's fingertips. Afraid of fear. And angry. Angry in a way that he didn't understand, that one man, one white man, could bend and break the spirit and will of so many other people. People whose only crime had been to dance, and to sing.

The face of that man, lit up as though by the devil's own fire, crowned by a mane of white hair that blew wildly in the wind, would come back to him in the night for a long, long time.

5

BILLY YAZZIE'S VOICE GREW HARDER AND FLATTER AS HE TALKED. Perhaps he had forgotten some of what he had known for so long, only to be reminded by my questions, as we sat watching the sheep and goats and the spring heat that swept across the desert.

Some of the serenity, the grace, was gone from his eyes.

"Angry, you ask? Oh yes, very angry. Even that night, and for many nights after, some of the younger men wanted to fight back. Wanted to burn something, hurt somebody. They talked of burning down the company store."

Why not? The story made me angry, and I was no fool. I knew better than to try to judge right and wrong over such a long distance in time.

"Some of us—me, Sam Benally, some of the older men—we held them down. We knew things could only get worse."

It was about power, I knew he was saying. The Navajos had learned the same lesson Arvo Belke and the white miners had learned. Money, influence, guns, a truck in the night: Cable Minerals had all the tools it took to squeeze, pry, and hammer the town and its people into good little miners, and good little Indians.

"Besides, ever'thing was not lost. We still had one other link with the old ways, more important to some than dances and songs. But we knew that if we caused more trouble, that too could be easily taken away."

The sun was lower in the sky, now, and while I watched shadows begin to form at the base of the buttes, Billy Yazzie told me in detail about how his people had built a sweat lodge of some size along a timbered little creek that fed the Helado River. Using ironwood saplings they'd cut and hauled from much further down the river, the tribe had fashioned a lattice-work dome over which they could spread sheep skins and blankets to hold in the smoke and steam. There, they could go for the heat, the private driving out of the impurities that blocked the way to the other world.

Then he grew silent.

"But then, we lost that, too. Not torn down, not run over, but left more useless to us than if it had been torn apart stick by stick and thrown into the river to wash away to the sea."

———•———

They called it the Helado Art and Garden Society, and it met once a month, on a Saturday, for lunch and cards. Of its seven members, one was the storekeeper's wife, three were wives of mining company officials, one was a single schoolteacher, one was a railroader's wife and the seventh was a miner's wife who'd stopped coming early in the spring.

The naming of the group, done more for its initials than for any real meaning, was their secret joke. To each other, but only to each other, they were simply the HAGS. Still, they liked the name, like what it suggested, so they played it out. They worried over their flowers and the few green vegetables they could coax out of the cold, rocky ground. They arranged their columbines and poppies with a fine eye, and served up their lettuce and radishes with great fanfare.

At the same time, they painted and drew, but for amusement, for a chance to praise and laugh at each other, and seldom would they tack anything to the wall. There were definitely no showings, no hangings, no money wasted on frames.

Mostly they sipped tea, sometimes a little wine, and talked about other women in town.

In the two months that followed the Navajo ceremonies and their violent end, the society members were not talking about it. They were not crusaders, nor did they get together to look very deeply into the politics and conflicts that swirled around them. Each month, when the miner's wife failed to appear, they pretended at surprise and let the matter drop. As they didn't talk Indians, they didn't talk unions either.

This day, the content of the meeting had been driven by the season: it was fall, and time to put food by for the winter. Each year at that time, a steady stream of peddlers' trucks brought fresh fruits and vegetables up the valley, setting off a frenzy of canning and drying in Madero. Society members were always looking for new ways to preserve some of this produce from the farms along the fringe of the desert.

After the session had broken up and three of the women had gone back out through the gate, Anne Marie Cottin opened a bottle of wine for herself, Sarah Hogan and Madeline Swain, and they sprawled in the backyard, as they often did after the Saturday lunches. There, they could take off their shoes, talk a little less politely about their friends and neighbors, and tell jokes. During these backyard sessions, Madeline Swain, who sat quietly and contributed least to the arts and garden efforts, would usually erupt like a balloon overinflated with rank gas. Loud, profane and raucous, she would have been an ill fit in the Helado Arts and Garden Society, except that she said nothing during the meetings, and amused the younger women so well in the after-sessions. They loaned her a little social legitimacy, and she traded them back spices and salt. Their game: she pretended to be embarrassed by her own nastiness, and they pretended to be shocked.

Seldom did they ask where the jokes and accounts came from. With her husband often away on railroad business, Madeline Swain enjoyed more freedom than they did, and they didn't want to get too close to the lines she crossed. Things she could get away with, they could not. But she had a way of luring them, leading them, and sometimes she got them closer to the edge.

She was telling an Indian joke: " . . . we name our babies after the first thing we see when we step out of the tepee. That's where you got your name, Two Dogs Screwing."

After the usual laughter, the false embarrassment, the three grew silent, sipping their wine. Sarah Hogan was chewing at her nails. Anne Marie Cottin was peeling paint off an old chair.

"Maybe we shouldn't make Indian jokes," Sarah Hogan said eventually, and stopped at that.

"Yeah, you're right," Madeline Swain said. "Want to hear another one? The one about these two old squaws washing in the creek?"

The three grew silent again.

"Did you ever wonder what they do in those sweat houses?" Madeline Swain asked, strong tones of nastiness and curiosity mixing in her voice.

"Who?"

"The Navajo men, for chrissakes. Who did you think I was talking about?"

"They sweat," Anne Marie Cottin said. "They build fires and they sweat. What's mysterious about that?"

"I don't know. What else? I mean do they chant, or dance inside there? Walk on coals? Maybe they play with their peters."

"I guess you could ask."

Madeline Swain took another drink of wine, stretched her legs out straight in front of her, and looked at the brightly polished toenails sticking out from her sandals. Then she unbuttoned a couple of the buttons that held her sweater tight across her chest.

"I want to know. Maybe just for the hell of it. But the more you can find out about men's little secrets, the more you can lead them around. Particularly if their secrets involve those little things between their legs."

"Well, you be sure and report back. We can hardly wait."

"We'll see," Madeline Swain said. "We'll just see."

———•••———

Andrew Cottin, lying on his bed and reading *Tom Sawyer*, next to an open window, had no difficulty hearing all of this. In fact, he'd heard conversations like this before, twice, and he was in his room with the window open because he'd planned it that way.

The fourteen-year-old boy was fascinated by Madeline Swain: by her dirty talk, her swagger, her womanness. He didn't understand what was awakening in him, but he knew that she had something that the other women did not. And he wanted to know more about it. Where it came from, and how else it lived.

So, from time to time, when he could be certain that no one knew, he would follow Madeline Swain. To the post office. Home from the store. Down to the depot. Sauntering along behind her, or in the willows off to the side, or across the street. Careful to look the other way.

Most often, it was in the daylight, and nothing happened, usually, nothing he could see. Usually. Sometimes, it was at night, when he had excuses to be out, and she nearly always lost him in the dark. Nearly always.

———•••———

Charlie Joes wanted a sweat. His bones were aching from work-ing in the cold water inside the mine, his shoulders were always sore from swinging a pick, and his breathing was clogged up. But more than that, he felt out of touch with the rhythm of things, like days and nights were mixed up and storms were coming at the wrong times.

Consequently, midway through Sunday afternoon, he rolled up his blankets and crossed the river on the low railroad trestle. He fol-lowed the rails downriver until he came to the canyon they'd named Dripping Creek, then climbed a path through the narrow draw.

The sweat lodge was built on a rocky bar next to the creek, and showed signs of heavy use. Sheep skins partly covered the wooden frame, a shovel was leaning against the stump of a spruce tree, and a metal bucket hung from a broken limb. Trails were worn distinctly through the tall grass.

Charlie Joes spent a half-hour gathering wood from the thick timber further up the draw, then broke it up into small pieces and stacked it next to the lodge. Inside, he removed the dozen round rocks, about the size of bread loafs, that were crowded into a small pit.

Then he built his fire in a bigger hole next to the lodge, and sat on the ground to wait, watching the banks of clouds moving across the sky and seeing faces and animals in the boiling shapes. He kept the fire well stoked, until all of the wood was gone and a deep bed of red coals filled most of the pit. Then he mounded the round rocks on top of the coals.

When the stones began to take on a varnished, almost glass-like look, glowing with a vague redness of their own, he carried each one carefully inside the lodge with the shovel, and piled them atop each other in the small hole. Next, he covered over the gaps and holes in the sides and top of the dome with his blankets, and filled the bucket with water.

Then he took off his clothes and hung them on a limb, splashed creek water over his naked body, and sprinkled fresh dirt on the roof of the lodge to drive away poverty. Aloud, then, he asked the Holy People to join in his bath. Finally, he carried the bucket inside with him, and closed off the door.

He sat cross-legged next to the pit, and began to slowly lave water over the shimmering rocks with an old tin cup. A sharp hiss, and the water turned instantly to a stinging, purifying steam. Charlie Joes bent closer to catch every wave of the wet heat, to absorb every drop of the moisture, to let himself edge deeper inside the mystical vapor.

Then he began to chant quietly to himself: a song of creation, of the special place of the Dineh in the workings of the earth. And he could see the reservation, and his mother, and the evening sun capping the tops of the red towers with a fiery glow . . . and he could hear the sheep and the wind and the songs of the elders and he could remember the rest that came from sleeping out on the ground, watching the stars appear, one by one.

Automatically, almost unconsciously, Charlie Joes poured water over the rocks, building a thicker and thicker blanket of steam around him, causing salt-tinged water to run into his eyes and to flood his skin. Then he could take no more. The cloud seemed to have sucked all the air out of the dimness, and his body was inside out, and he needed to breathe.

He moved the cover back and stepped out into the sunlight. Water poured from his naked body, streaming down his torso and limbs, and as he began to cool, he reached to embrace the air. With his legs and arms spread wide, he threw his head far back and looked up into the sky, letting mother sun burn down on his chest.

That's when Charlie Joes heard the laughter.

Partially blinded from looking up toward the sun, and from the sweat in his eyes, he had to strain to focus, to locate the source of the sound. But then he saw her: a shapeless form at first, but then one that sharpened into a white woman as his vision cleared further, standing in the trees twenty yards away. She was laughing, and seemed to be pointing down at his genitals, which had shrunken from the shock of the cooler air.

He turned to reach for his clothes, to cover himself against the ridicule, but they were gone.

Charlie Joes stepped forward, toward the woman, not thinking clearly, but responding more to an instinct to fight for his dignity. But she turned and began to run, crashing through the brush. Then she stopped. And began to walk back toward him.

"What are you going to do, Indian man?" Madeline Swain asked, her voice edged with daring, sounding like contempt. "Rape me?"

The Navajo stopped and said nothing.

"Not with that little thing, you're not. You got to have a war stick if you're going to war."

Then she reached into the brush next to her and held Charlie Joes' clothes up so he could see.

"Want these? You'll have to catch me."

The Navajo took a step forward and then a second. She just stood there. Two more steps. She didn't move. Just a little further, and he'd be able to lunge, be able to grab his clothes and hold on, even if she tried to run.

Then a man stepped out from behind a tree next to her, and stood at her side. A big man. A familiar man.

"Give old Charlie back his clothes, now, Madeline," the man said in a voice that Charlie Joes knew well. "I can't have him running around like that. He might take sick."

The white woman tossed his clothes into the air, and they snagged and caught on limbs before they drifted to the ground. Then the two whites turned and walked away. Disappeared into the thick trees, leaving a loud ghost of laughter in their wake.

———·•·———

Up the hill forty yards or so, Andrew Cottin sat in the deep green foliage, the ferns and waist-high grasses, and watched Alphabet and Madeline Swain fade off into the aspen. He watched Charlie Joes put on his clothes slowly, roll up his blankets slowly, and walk slowly, slump-shouldered, down the mountainside. He watched a little plume of smoke curl up from the remains of the Indian's fire.

Then, after everyone was gone, he walked down, picked up the old bucket, and put the fire out. He could still smell the sweetness of sweat and the sourness of humiliation in the air.

6

"So far as I know, no Indian ever went back to that place."

Billy Yazzie gripped both his knees and stared out into the empty spaces, a man whose voice vibrated with pain, but who knew the wisdom of self-control.

"And the talk about revenge, about fighting back, grew louder every day. Some were willing to just pack up and go home. Some were not."

As we'd sat there through the hours, I'd had the feeling that the old man's stories had been little more than random memories, a sort of mapless wandering through whatever came to mind. Then I came to know the opposite. With a kind of dread, I understood that he'd been setting up the last act all along. That his choice of tales had been calculated, both for meaning and for the light they cast. And that he hadn't forgotten at all that I'd come to learn about the Cottins.

I saw, too, that the old man was beginning to tire. He took off his beaten old hat and ran his fingers through his short grey hair, then rubbed his eyes and held the bridge of his nose between forefinger and thumb.

"Then winter set in. Heavy winter. Snows started in early November and nearly every day brought more, until the roads were closed much of the time. Then we were back to trying to stay alive again, trying to stay warm, trying to make it through until spring."

In this heat, the weight of the Madero winter was not so easy for me to recall, but the dread still lingered, if I thought about it long enough.

"The memories of the last squaw dance, of the ruined sweat lodge began to fade as we fought again against the snow and cold. And things would have calmed down . . ."

He paused to look over at me, to make sure I understood.

"If it had not been for Sam Benally's rubber boots."

———·•·———

It was the week before Christmas, and snow had been falling for several days in a row, leaving the town buried in its own white shroud. Snowplows had left a high crusty ridge down the middle of main street, and some of the side streets were still drifted in, marked only by meandering footpaths, knee-deep ditches in the snow.

It was also payday—ugly and clumsy as usual, but more so for Tom Cottin when he sat alone in his little office and thought about the brutal contrast between the condition of the Indians and the fantasy of these holidays. Blinking red and green lights only cast the Navajo shanties, their whole Madero lives, in a greyer and more dismal glow. Laughter only left the absence of laughter louder, echoing with more emptiness. Where were their gifts and blessings? Where was their silly-looking Santa Claus?

At the end of the work day, he sat behind a wooden table with a box of Cable Mercantile charge slips on one side of him, and a cash box on the other. Each Navajo, in turn, would be shown his sheaf of yellow charge slips, wrapped in a piece of adding machine tape with a big dollar figure written in colored ink on the outside. Cottin would take each Indian's paycheck, underline the net pay figure on the stub, do the subtraction on a machine, show the results to the man standing there, and dole out the balance in cash.

Rarely did any of the Navajos ask to see their charge slips, to review their store purchases in any detail. But that day, that last payday before Christmas, Sam Benally wanted to see his yellow slips.

Cottin started to say something to dissuade the Navajo, to suggest that he was wasting time for everyone in line, but he remembered his last encounter with Sam Benally, over the dances, and he said nothing. Instead, he could feel his stomach starting to turn on him, that familiar churn, and he could see the tremor in his own hands as he handed the sheaf over.

Sam Benally thumbed through the pieces of paper, pausing three times to make notes to himself, using a blunt pencil and a piece of brown cardboard his took from his shirt pocket.

He handed the slips back, and said nothing.

Cottin went on with his calculations as though problems were practically out of the question, trying to let the actions of his hands project a confidence that his eyes, had they turned upward from the table, would have betrayed.

Sam Benally took his money, turned without a word, and walked out of the company store.

———·—·———

After he left the store, the Navajo walked south, to the edge of town, to an old tin building that had once been a livery stable, but had sat empty for a decade or more.

Several miners had pooled their labor and a small bit of money to fix the building up into a shop where they could work on their cars and trucks, where they could build a fire in an old barrel stove and work even on snowy days.

Jack Elton, a young miner still in his teens who'd come to Madero from a ranch just outside of the reservation, was inside, working on his old truck. Perhaps because they'd both come from the desert country at about the same time, started with Cable Minerals at the same time, Sam Benally and Jack Elton had gotten in the habit of speaking, short words but amiable when they met each other in the mines or on the street.

The Navajo watched the white youth for awhile, watched him loosening bolts on a starter motor that had ceased to work. Then he walked over, tapped Elton on the shoulder, and pointed to the truck's battery cables.

"Unhook," he said simply. Otherwise, hot sparks would soon be flying in every direction.

"Oh, yeah, thanks," Elton said, and started removing the screws that held the positive cable tight.

The Navajo let a minute go by, then asked, "Them boots. How much you pay for them boots?"

The white youth paused for a moment.

"I think it was fourteen dollars. Yeah, that's what it was, fourteen dollars at the company store."

Sam Benally walked away without another word.

———

After he'd turned on the Christmas lights in the front window and locked the store for the night, Tom Cottin crossed the street to the bar where the working men hung out.

A few of the single miners were still there, spending their paychecks and glad enough, squeezing all the life they could out of those late December days when they went under ground in the half-light of dawn, and came out again just as the world was going dark. The married men in the payday crowd had already paid their tabs and gone home for the night. "She's deep enough for me," they'd routinely say, and pack their lunch buckets on toward the flickering kitchen lights down the road.

In the easy company, Cottin found every reason to stay far later than usual, just listening and drinking, blunting the edges of his nerves. They talked about nothing that bothered him—no union, no politics, no company, no Navajos—none of those matters of the spleen that on another night might have brought the room to a boil. It was the season, certainly, and the easy payday hooch: they all stuck to the common ground where elk and fish and crazy women lived, where jokes were all funny and legends believed. And the beer and whiskey slid down, glass after glass, and the smoke grew thick and ripe.

Cottin was not used to the pace, but he kept up, and every thought of leaving was just a flash that was washed away in laughter and noise and more beer. He slipped into a comfortable daze, a disconnection from the real world that he hadn't felt in a considerable time.

He didn't know what time it was, a little after ten perhaps, when he gradually admitted to himself that he could hold no more. Despite the demands that he stay put, that he get back to his beer, that he make a bigger sacrifice to the holidays—"Set your ass down and have one more for old Saint Nick"—Cottin found his coat and slipped unsteadily out the door.

As he stepped into the winter night, he realized that someone else was standing with him in the recessed doorway. It was Sam Benally.

"Tom Cottin, I want to talk to you." Cottin was startled, but not by the man's use of English. By now, everybody knew that next to Billy Yazzie, San Benally could speak the best English among the tribe. Instead, he was jerked up short by the unusually hard tone in the young man's voice.

"Tomorrow," Cottin heard himself mumbling. "I'll talk to you tomorrow."

He knew that he was barely in shape to talk to anybody at all, about anything, and the thought of facing Navajo problems, his Navajo problems, terrified his stomach, and it began its familiar roll.

The young Indian looked at him steadily, coldly.

"Not tomorrow. Tonight. Now."

The sky had clouded over while Cottin was inside the tavern, and though a light snow had started to fall, the night air was mostly still and mild. Inside his heavy parka, Cottin was growing overly warm, starting to sweat.

"Look," he said, "whatever it is, we can discuss it better tomorrow, inside. Only crazy people stand outside and talk in the middle of a snowstorm at night."

As soon as he said it, he wished he had not.

"Crazy?"

Real hostility raised the pitch of Sam Benally's voice, and for the first time it occurred to Cottin that the young Indian might have been drinking, too.

"You think Indians crazy. Dumb, too," he went on.

"What is it you think you want? What's so goddamned important that we have to stand out here and talk about it?"

As fearful as he was, the alcohol in his system allowed him to feign, if not actually feel, some ragged edge of indignation. He was not being accorded his usual respect.

Sam Benally hesitated before he spoke, and when the words came, they were quieter, more measured.

"You been cheatin' the Navajo. You been stealin' from Indians."

Once again, he felt nausea creeping in, turmoil in his mind. He'd never been able to prepare himself for accusations such as these, even though he'd seen them in his nightmares.

"I don't know what the hell you're talking about, and neither do you."

His protests were lame, and he knew it.

"You lie, Cottin," the Navajo said flatly. "I count. I know how much things cost."

Cottin said nothing, staring out toward the Christmas lights across the street.

"I counted numbers tonight," the Indian continued. "I went home and counted my bills. You charged me too much, way too much."

"You're wrong . . ." Cottin started to say, but he was interrupted.

"Worse, you charge me for things I don't buy."

"You've lost your mind," Cottin said, careful not to use the word crazy again. "You signed for everything you were charged for. If not, it was a simple mistake. I've got the receipts to prove it."

Cottin felt himself sobering a little, but not enough to tell him what to do next. He didn't know what was coming, where it was going. He just wanted to get away and go home, so he could prepare for a world he knew would never be quite the same.

"Worse thing," Sam Benally was saying. "You charge us more than you charge whites for same things."

"Now why in the hell would I do that?" The storekeeper was trying to force a note of reconciliation into his voice. "What difference would it make to me?"

"Indians dumb." The Indian was once again sounding angry. "These boots . . ." He pointed toward his feet, to the black rubber boots that came nearly to his knees. "Eighteen dollars. Jack's boots, same boots, fourteen dollars. You cheatin' the Navajo."

For an instant, Cottin thought the younger man was going to swing at him, the way he stood with fists clenched and eyes blazing.

"Look, I can settle this," Cottin said. "You come to the store in the morning and I'll get out the paper work and show you where you're wrong. If we've made a mistake, I'll make it good to you, give you the money you've got coming back and more."

He felt certain that would mollify the angry Indian. But he was wrong.

"Now," he said. "I want to see now. You got 'em, you show 'em to me."

Somehow, Cottin felt like he'd trapped himself. On the morrow, he could have gathered up, conjured up if necessary, whatever paper work he needed to make his case. But what could he come up with now? What if there was nothing?

He knew it would do no good to refuse. Sam Benally wasn't going to relent, even if it meant neither would sleep that night.

"Come on. Let's go look."

They walked out into the street, and through a narrow slit that had been shoveled through the snow bank in the center.

Cottin's hands were shaking as he tried to fit a key into the door. After a couple of tries, he made it work.

The light switches were all in the rear of the store, where Cottin usually let himself out, so they made their way through the aisles in the dark. For Cottin, navigating the passageways, around sharp corners, past piles of boxes, around the meat counter to the stairs that led up to the balcony office was easy. For the Indian, it meant groping and stumbling and running into things. He fell a ways behind.

Cottin felt himself moving faster, faster than he needed to, faster than he ever moved through the store. If he got far enough ahead, maybe the Indian would give up and go away. His head was starting to pound from the alcohol and the exertion.

As Cottin sat down at his desk, he heard the Indian muttering and cursing, banging around below.

Cottin opened his upper righthand drawer, and his hand fell on the butt of a .38 special he kept there as protection, but from what he was never quite sure.

As Sam Benally's head cleared the top step, as the two men could look clearly into each other's eyes, Tom Cottin killed Sam Benally. The storekeeper heard a deafening roar, and he felt the pistol jerk and rise in his hand. And he saw the Indian collapse instantly, and roll quietly to the bottom of the stairs.

Tom Cottin sat bewildered, his heart pounding, looking down at the gun in his hand. He turned the barrel toward his own head, watching the red, green, and yellow lights blink and reflect off the polished steel, watching his own hand with a sort of stupid fascination, watching his finger tighten on the trigger, then relax. A furious trembling ratcheted through every nerve and muscle in his body, and he was cold, suddenly oh so cold. The gun slipped from his hand to the floor, and he put his head down on his desk and began, in great spasms, to cry.

7

THE DAY HAD ENDED. I'D LEFT THE OLD NAVAJO IN THE LATE-DAY SUN OF the reservation, and driven the ninety-or-so miles back up the Helado River in the kind of stupor that comes with shock. Did I see the trees, wet and brilliant after an afternoon rain? I couldn't remember. Was there traffic, and were there fishermen along the way? I didn't know. Perhaps I talked to myself.

Perhaps I did not.

I sat out on my porch in the end of the day's light, and my first conscious thought about the present, about anything going on before my eyes, was that the street lights should be coming on soon. The eight or ten or twelve bulbs should suddenly wink on.

A dog barked. Had he been barking all this time?

Had I eaten? No, I guessed I hadn't. Perhaps I should have. Maybe after the street lights came on. Maybe after I'd had more time to think.

I'd driven back to Madero only the day before, on a whim, and taken the key back from the postmaster, again. And I'd left for the reservation only that morning, but it seemed as though years had passed since my father had told me to get a gut full. To find out about Sam Benally.

I had a gut full. I'd digested large plates full of several people's lives. Said grace over their miseries. Drank their blood. Boiled their bones.

And I felt sick.

———•———

The old Indian had finally wound down. He had nothing more to tell, he'd said. Within a few months after the shooting, all the

Navajos had left Madero and returned to Shiprock and other parts of the reservation.

Yes, he'd said, there had been some kind of legal proceeding, but he hadn't understood it. He only knew, had heard later from others in the tribe, that Tom Cottin had not been punished.

Killing a Navajo was okay, he'd said, like running through a ceremonial fire with an old dump truck. Like desecrating a sweat lodge.

That was just the way it was.

—— • ——

I couldn't sleep. I wondered if I would ever sleep again. And I wondered if the balled-up, confused tangle of the old man carving wooden chains and Navajos in rubber boots and the frowning boy next to the rack of bull elk antlers and my father perched on a canyon rim would ever sort themselves out.

I wondered how much of this Neal had understood, or foreseen, or just sensed. I wondered if, somehow, on that rainy night in Las Vegas, he'd felt like he was just giving back something our grandfather had taken away.

But how could he have known? I needed rest. I needed sleep.

—— • ——

Old Billy Yazzie had walked with me to my truck.

Always in such battles, he'd said, the Navajos tried to carry some symbol of victory back to camp. Even in defeat, there could, then, always be stories of courage or skill or cunning to sustain and to re-arm the people.

And they hadn't left Madero without one small contribution to the tribal lore.

"The whites made a big show of burying Sam Benally there. A great display of their sorrow, with long faces and tears. And they thought that even in death they still owned the Indian man."

He stopped as a passing pickup drowned out his voice.

"We could not allow that."

He waited, as though casting a new scene in his mind.

"We went to the only white we trusted. We had no choice. We asked for help. And by the little light of a new moon, they went with their shovels, and they took Sam Benally away. He is buried here now…" And he nods toward the land off to the west. "Somewhere in here."

He stopped, looking for words I could understand.

"Better the vultures and coyotes of this place," he said, "than the flowers and tears of people who know so little shame."

His head tilted back, slightly, but with a noticeable gesture of pride.

"Whites still think he is buried there," he said. "But you know what they'd find if they dug up his box?"

I didn't answer. I was still stuck on the image of white men digging up a Navajo grave, under the faint light of a cold December moon. Of whites stealing away in the night with the body of a Navajo man.

"Only a pair of black rubber boots."

A tiny smile crossed his lips, and he turned away in good-bye.

On the floor of my pickup as I drove away: a cardboard box, with a wooden chain wrapped up inside. I'd thought maybe . . . but, no. Tom Cottin would not have wanted to be remembered by the Navajos, and they would do well to forget him, too. Sometimes, memories are best left to fade. To fade away.

PART FIVE

Claire Sadler

I DON'T GO BACK TO SEE HIM THIS TIME. DON'T HAVE TO TELL HIM WHAT I've found out. He already knows. My old man already knows what tales the reservation ghosts had to tell. He saw the stories being woven through his own eyes.

Instead, I want a few days off. A few days to walk the streets of Madero and think. A few days to sort through this shuffled deck, trying to put the cards back into believable sequences, and to matchup the colors.

———•·•———

The Helado is running full to its banks, with a power and a relentlessness that merely seems to rumble in the daylight hours. But after dark, swollen by the day's quota of melted snow, it turns to a louder thunder, and those who live along the river eye its banks and sleep poorly.

Meanwhile, the town stays mostly empty. Windows stay mostly boarded-up. The streets stay mostly wet, draining the snowmelt from the east-most side of town, leaving puddles in the middle and ditches running fast and red.

I walk down the street toward the river, glad to be out in the warmth of the sun, and pass a dozen or so old houses, some whole, some not. Pass a couple of tin buildings, stained, with hasps and locks. Locking who or what in or out? Pass a massive old concrete foundation, a maze of connected rectangles and squares, all that is left of the old Stanley mill. Pass a crumbled old stone building, gutted, no doors or windows, empty—an old assay office, I think.

On the edge of town, it's the ghost-houses and shacks where the

Navajos used to live. Some still stand, but more have collapsed into piles of rotten boards and fragments of glass and corroded old tin.

If I'm looking for something to turn over in my hand, to grasp, I don't find it. Other generations of the poor—long-haired earth dwellers with their plain-faced wives and Volkswagen buses—have wintered over in these mean old buildings, too, covering the walls with tie-dyed tapestries and the windows with clear plastic to keep out the winds and the drifts. They've left nothing of use or beauty behind. The floors are bare, or littered with old papers and bottles.

Still, just by sitting here in the fading light, alone, on a collapsed porch or an old stump, I can in fact coax a faint vapor of the past up out of the ground. Part comes from Billy Yazzie. Part comes from the pages of long-forgotten books. Part comes from imagination. And part is just there: stored echoes, energy that has been unwilling to leave the place.

Images of the women sitting outside with their battered old pans, shelling beans and mixing breads. The quick and sure movements of practiced hands. The rise and fall of melodic voices. Teasing, consoling, laughing.

Flickering pictures of gathered men, home from a successful late-fall hunt, moving rapidly and following old rules. Hanging a deer or an elk high by its back legs, catching the blood in a bucket, later to be used in a much-prized blood sausage.

Wide-eyed earth urchins, laughing always, wrestling and rolling in the dirt and the grass. Clothes too small and too large. Playing out Indians and cowboys.

I'm not yet able to be my father or my grandfather, or even to keep their faces in my mind, but some ghosts of old Madero come creeping back to me on wet feet during those solitary afternoons. The steps are small, but they are steps.

———•———

I find an old book on mining. *Hardrock Mining and Milling in the San Juan Mountains*, by an engineer named Robert Hollander, printed in 1932. It comes from a box under the bed of this scarred old cabin. Who knows how it got here. Someone else's name is written inside, with a flourish and thick and thin lines like old ink pens used to make. Sturgeon or something similar. Fancy, but hard to make out.

I don't read every line, nor even read on every yellowed, fragile page for that matter. But I do read in every chapter, some in detail, and I do look closely at every one of the old diagrams and drawings. Veins and water courses. Methods of timbering. How ore was assayed. Explosives. And such.

Why do I read it, that book with its dull green cover and cracking spine? Partly, I suppose, in an effort to make up for lost time, for connections never made, for stories never told.

If I understand the work that men did, perhaps I can understand how they thought. If I understand the tools they used, perhaps I can understand their acts. If I understand the economics, perhaps I can understand the fears.

But I can only stand so many ghosts. I've got a job to do, and I can't just wander the streets, listening to them talk. I'll lose touch. Momentum. I'm already daydreaming when I should be prying boards off of windows. Regretting when I should be using the days. Pondering when I should be catching fish.

If nothing else, I should be turning over a few more rocks.

2

I WENT BACK TO IKE'S PLACE. THE TAVERN. THE PLACE WHERE, ON A SNOWY Sunday only weeks before, it had all began to ball up and start rolling downhill.

Ike's had its regulars. I'd seen them in there before: two state highway department drivers, a wood sculptor, an alcoholic old silver miner, a couple of others without labels.

They all bitched in cadence about the weather and their ailments, but all that small talk was foreplay, just a batch of key words used to cue and call up old stories. Each man, it seemed, had his fables that stretched back and forth between today and yesterday and back again, like a piece of high quality rubber, being pulled and tugged from all sides.

Hunting stories became homicide stories and back to tales about women. Politics somehow led back to earlier mining days and on to myths of men who were men. Fishing stories started out as jokes and then became odes to bootleg whiskey. Every one, though, in its way, proved that there was an unbroken band of life, a process that let the past write the future.

Those connections were music to me, and I waited patiently for the name Tom Cottin to come up. But, at least in my presence, it never did.

Richert, the owner of the general store, was another of the regulars. Perhaps the most regular, since he could cross the street from his business or his apartment in the back during any hour of the day or night. It was said that on some afternoons, Richert left his door unlocked and his "open" sign out, and ran his store from the window table in Ike's, crossing the street only when a customer approached. Time management.

It was this shopkeeper I zeroed in on, not because he was either so old or so wise. But because his general store and the old company store were one and the same. Under new management, that's all.

I sat down with him at that table nearest the window, early in the afternoon. Before the highway crew, and after the lunch hour. A spread of brown beer bottles, roughly in the shape of Africa, suggested that Richert might have indeed been tending his counter from a more comfortable seat that day.

"Yeah, I heard the story about the killing," he said after I'd bought us both a beer and edged into the subject. "At least some of it, but I don't remember much. There's an old woman in town. Claire Sadler. You probably don't know her since she don't get out much. I take her groceries to her. She's tried to tell me the story two or three times, but somehow we never get it all done."

More than once, I'd stared into the faces of the people I met on the streets of Madero, wondering who would know. But those faces had all been too young, or too fresh out of Phoenix, or too blank-eyed for me to risk my own peace of mind by having to explain myself. Richert, it seemed, had stumbled across what I'd been looking for.

"What does she know about it?" I asked.

"Well, at least the way she tells it, she was the old man's chief clerk. But she's old, and sometimes I wonder if she remembers things, or just makes them up and starts believing them. She's got a way . . ."

He paused for a moment, as though measuring his words.

"She's a little different. And as I understand it, she's always been that way. Some people who live in this town don't even know she's around."

Like me. I didn't know she was around. But there were many old secrets of Madero that I would never learn. I liked it better that way.

"She might give you some real information about Tom Cottin, or she might just confuse you. I don't know."

I asked where she lived, and whether I could go and pay a call.

"The last house on the west side of Aspen," he said. Aspen was the street highest on the slope of the town, and the west side dead-ended in the trees. "But I don't think I'd just walk up there and knock on the door if I was you. I know she's got a shotgun. She's showed it to me at least a dozen times."

Then he laughed, a hearty booming kind of laugh meant to tell me that being subtly threatened by Claire Sadler was a special distinction not everyone in Madero had enjoyed.

"Day after tomorrow, I take her groceries. Or I should say, their groceries. You can come along and I'll introduce you, and let you do what you want after that."

———•———

"She's never been married, this old lady," Richert said as we walked up the hill. He balanced the small box of food on his shoulder. "And when I first came here, people always kind of talked about her with a smirk. Never wore dresses. Lived alone. That kind of thing."

He stopped to catch his breath.

"Must have lived alone here for thirty-five years, anyway. Then, about five years ago, this friend of hers from back East came out to live. They're quite a couple, those two. Take care of each other. That's good."

He stopped to shift the box.

"But I'll tell you one thing. At one time, maybe even still today, she was the most educated person in this town. Somebody told me that once she'd run some kind of a school back East. You'll see."

He paused.

"Guess she went to work in the store for the same reason I did. Nothin' better to do."

Her house must have once been owned by one of Madero's more prosperous merchants. Not large, but with Victorian lines and details that were designed, in contrast to the accidental look of most of the town's cabins and shacks. Tidy was the word that came to my mind, although paint had begun to chip and peel, and the iron fence showed signs of rust. Still, the flower garden was free of weeds, the porch was swept clean, and the iron gate opened without a sound. A small brass doorknob gleamed in the morning sun.

There was no answer at first, when Richert knocked.

Then the door opened slowly, and a pair of small grey eyes looked up at us, set deep among a network of wrinkles, through a tiny pair of glasses. Her hair, like the premises, was kept up—a skull cap of short white curls, precisely made and placed. She was a foot shorter than either of us, and looked to be quite thin.

"Ah, it's you, you old reprobate," she said, half-smiling as she shuffled backward to open the door. Her voice was strong, surprising, coming from such an elfin look. Then she stopped, as though she'd just realized that another shadow meant another person.

"And who's your friend?"

"Tom Cottin's grandson," he said. "He wants to meet you. He's interested in that story about the shooting of the Navajo in the company store."

She looked up at me inquisitively, as though something must be wrong with one of the two of us, if not both.

"Well, come on in, then." She stepped further back, and I could see that she was dressed in old bib overalls, and a faded flannel shirt with the sleeves rolled up to her elbows.

Then she turned to follow Richert back toward the kitchen, and I could see that she used two canes to walk.

"Barbara," I heard her say. "The food man cometh. Looks like we'll have to go ahead and live another week."

———•———

"What do you want to know about this for? Just curious maybe?"

We sat on the south side of their living room, the sunny side, each with a cup of coffee balanced on the arm of a chair. This was the part of the room they lived in, I could tell. On this side, two chairs and a small table, a wall full of bookshelves that had been dusted, and had seen books removed and replaced. On the other side, the darker side, another full wall of shelves contained musty books that might well have been outdated encyclopedias or works by old poets, describing a world that didn't count anymore. A couch and piano were covered over with sheets, and a cabinet full of glassware looked as though it hadn't seen real light in a number of years.

Had I walked across the invisible line, I knew, my footprints would have shown on the rugs.

"No," I said. "It's not just curiosity." But then I wasn't sure what else I wanted to say. "I'm just trying to find out the truth about my family, that's all." And I told her, briefly, about my conversations with Arvo Belke and Billy Yazzie.

"That's not always wise, you know." Then she bent forward in her chair, leaning toward me in a very knowing way, and kindly. "Left alone, imagination will always give families the benefit of the doubt."

The benefit of the doubt about what? The truth?

"I'm not certain I follow you."

"No, of course not. I often make no sense whatsoever. At least, that's what Barbara says. I mean, our clever little minds think the best of families, smiling around the Thanksgiving table, holding hands, you know. That's often much nicer than the truth. Don't you think?"

What a strange idea, I thought. And how mostly true.

"So the less you know, the more free you are to paint whatever picture you like," she added, nodding her head in agreement with herself. "My own family, for example, likes their painted pictures of me very much."

"What do you mean?"

"It's not important," she said, and dismissed the subject by waving it away with her hands. Then she looked around her, both ways, as if she was suddenly a little confused. Then settled back.

"Now what is it you wanted to know?"

I didn't know whether that signaled that we were starting back on square one or not.

"Tom Cottin," I said. "I'd like to know if he really shot Sam Benally." And what that meant to my father. And what role Cable Minerals played.

She didn't answer for a minute.

"That poor old man," she said finally. "The wrong place at the wrong time, as they always say. That's a movie line. I'm sure it is."

———•••———

Claire Sadler had a routine. She would rise at daybreak, no matter what the season, and devote the first hour of every day to what she came to think of as her private life. By the standards of others, her entire life was private. But this hour was more so. Claire Sadler would not have answered the door or the telephone, nor would she have ventured outside for anything except perhaps a serious fire in her house, and then only after she'd tried to put it out alone.

During this hour, she wrote long letters to friends of hers that she'd left behind in Pennsylvania, read poetry, and entered long and thoughtful passages into a journal she was keeping on her life. What the journal would come to, she did not know, but the internal dialogue that it represented came to be the most vital conversation she would have on any given day. On the few instances when she failed to write, she suffered through an edginess that stayed with her throughout the following hours.

That done, she would dress, open her blinds, and, if the day was not Sunday or Monday, she would walk down to the center of town and open the company store.

She entered through the back door, the way she always did on those mornings when she opened up. She turned on the lights there, hung up her coat, and turned the furnace fan on. She made a pot of fresh coffee on a table behind the meat counter, and washed the cups. Then she went to the front door and started to turn the heavy lock. But it was already turned. The door was unlocked.

Slightly alarmed, her first reaction then was to check the cash register, but all the change left over from the day before was there. Then she turned toward the office, upstairs, where the safe was kept, and the real money locked away for the night. That's when she saw the body at the bottom of the stairs: a crumpled mess of work clothes and straight black hair and dark skin. The pool of blood. The drying remains of brain matter. An Indian that had been thrown away, she thought, her mind faltering, starting to spin off and defend itself against what her eyes saw.

Other scrambled thoughts: Now, what to do? Clean this up. I've got to clean this up. Dead people can't be lying around here at opening time. Doesn't look good. Where's the mop?

Somebody else knows about this, I'm sure. Andrew? Has he been here yet? Who else? Who had already been here and gone to call the police? Who is taking care of that job?

But maybe not. The telephone is upstairs. I'll call someone? Who?

That's when she saw Tom Cottin, sitting at his desk, his head on his arms, breathing but not moving, not responding to the noises that she made. She started to step to him, to touch him, to ask him what horrible thing had happened there, but she couldn't. She just stood frozen, with her arm outstretched, a sound somewhere between and sob and a scream caught in her throat. Then she started to back away, and when she felt a stair railing behind her, she turned and ran down the steps, across the store, and out into the street.

It was early, cold and snowy, and Claire Sadler was the only person moving, though down the street she could see the exhaust cloud as a car was started. She was cold and shaking, but she sat on the edge of the sidewalk, hardly feeling the sting of the ice, waiting numbly for someone, anyone, to come along.

3

"WHY DID HE DO IT?" I ASKED.

She didn't answer. Forty years floated in the air between us, and she was digging around in there, like she'd misplaced something in a file drawer. Her eyes seemed to have no focus, yet they moved, and her lips slid back and forth over each other.

I asked the question again, and she came back to me, with a slight, almost apologetic smile.

"Why does anyone do anything?" she said. "In those days, I guess everything was out of necessity. That's the way it seemed."

"I don't know what that means."

"Of course not. You weren't there. But even the people who were there were didn't understand it all. I was confused then, and I'm confused now."

"By what?"

Even that simple question seemed to bother her a little, make her pause.

"We say we'll never look back, but then we always do, sooner or later. And when we do, a lot of the details are gone and the reasons don't seem to make much sense. Isn't that sad?"

I didn't quite know how to push the conversation more toward the particular, the specific, so I just sat there, sipping my coffee and watching the small, old woman decide whether she had anything to tell me or not. Richert had been right. The woman had an unusual mind.

"I know it seems important to you," she said finally, "but to me, it was, in many ways, just another thing. Those were some of the sorriest years of my life, and for many other people in this town, too. Everything was going wrong. Why not have a shooting, a killing, too? It seemed to be a natural part of the process."

She pulled herself onto her feet using the arms of her chair, and as she reached around for her canes, I feared that our conversation had come to a quick and, for me, disappointing end.

"Excuse me," she said. "I'll be back in a moment."

She disappeared, and I heard her talking in the kitchen.

"Barbara, would you please offer the gentleman more coffee? We brew a pretty pathetic pot, but maybe he'd like to try to gag down another cup."

The woman who entered with coffee pot in hand was taller by far than Claire Sadler, and just as slim. Her hair was white, and a fuller mass of curls, and a bright smile creased her longish face as she shuffled into the living room. A perfectly matched pair of caricatures, I thought to myself.

"Hello," she said. "I'm Barbara. Just plain Barbara. Don't get up and waste all that energy. You'll need it later. Claire thought we might be able to pawn some more of this coffee off on you. It's last month's, and we thought we might never get rid of it. Good thing you came along."

She chuckled to herself, quite happy with her joke. She filled both cups, and stood for a moment.

"I'd offer you some cookies," she said, "but Claire can't bake worth a damn."

She laughed again, and ambled back to the kitchen.

A book of Georgia O'Keeffe's paintings sat on a table near her chair, and I picked it up and thumbed through it while I waited for Claire Sadler to return. The pages looked well worn, and the spine was loose.

"One of my favorites," she said, as she walked back in. "Especially the New Mexico paintings. I'm fond of skulls, you see."

I put the book back in its place, feeling a little like I'd been caught peeking, although I wasn't sure why. It was just a book. And it was there in plain sight, asking to be read.

"Anyway, yes, Tom shot the Navajo," she said as she sat back down. "And I suppose you could say it was because the Indian had caught Tom cheating. Over some tools or something or other."

"Rubber boots."

"Boots. Yes. As I say, it's been awhile."

"But as I understand it," I said, "the Navajos must have believed they were getting cheated over a lot more than Sam Benally's boots."

She took awhile before she answered.

"Of course," she finally said. "And they were damned well right."

———·——

Claire Sadler had never been asked to join the Helado Art and Garden Society, nor did she expect to be. And she would have turned them down. They ridiculed her odd and solitary ways, and she detested their need to prop each other up. They bought and traded dress patterns, and she cut her own firewood. But worse: they gossiped without mercy, and she knew gossip to be the cruelest enemy she had ever faced. Of the countless defects of the human heart, she considered that to be the worst.

If she needed socializing, she found it at the store. There she had a chance to talk to every man, woman, and child in town, if she chose, though she often let the chances go by. She knew what they bought, how they paid, and what their special needs might be. Secrets, of sorts. And she kept those matters to herself.

For instance, she knew that Jay Rogers bought women's underwear. For himself. Once or twice a year, and just as the store was closing for the night, when she was there alone. And out of that knowledge grew a relationship that came as close as anything Claire Sadler had to friendship in Madero. They never spoke about anything so private, but they both knew what they both knew. It showed in their eyes, and generated a silent sense of trust.

Jay Rogers played the piano, and his boogie-woogie hands might have taken him wherever he wanted to go. But he came back to Madero after his Navy hitch was done, and like his uncle before him, he chose to work the old family gold claim and live alone in the old family house in town. He was a big man, and his hands, though thin and long-fingered, were hard and calloused. There was no mining machine he couldn't run, or fix.

But nearly every Saturday night, he'd walk clean-shaven and silent into the Eureka Tavern and have a few whiskeys at the bar. Some nights he would talk quietly to those around, then slip away without good-byes and plod solemnly toward home. Other nights, he'd drift to the back room, where the old upright piano stood. He'd pull the bench up close, light up an old crusty pipe that would sit untouched in an ash tray throughout most of the night, and begin to play with his eyes half closed. The back room would fill with people, and the house rushed to keep Jay in drinks.

Around midnight, though, his repertoire would change, and the beat would come down. As the miners and their wives headed for home, Jay Rogers closed his eyes further still and played blues chords, bits and pieces of the classics. Ivory Joe Walker. Chopin.

And that's when Claire Sadler liked to come in, to listen, to drink, and to talk.

———•—•———

"You know, Jay, I would like to have your opinion on something." There was a notable seriousness in her voice.

It was not yet midnight, but only the two of them were left in the back room. A cold rain had fallen all day and well into the night, and despite the fact that Jay Rogers felt like playing, few customers had stayed around to hear. He would have kept on playing anyway: he played for himself, not them, and to vent a passion that they could never understand.

But Claire Sadler wanted to talk. And he was always better for their conversations. She could put life into words in a way he could not. She could better explain why things happened. And she always had an example out of history to show how things were neither better nor worse, nor much different at all.

"I seldom have an opinion, unless you've already worked it up for me." Playing and whiskey left him more comfortable, more able to cast little jibes at himself, or the two of them.

"No, seriously," she said, her voice a little rasped by the two drinks she'd had to warm herself from the walk downtown in the rain. "There are some things going on at the store, under the table, in the dark, that sort of thing. I'd like to know what you think."

"Okay, Clarabelle," he said, putting his elbow on the table and resting the side of his face on his big hand. "You've got me hooked now."

She took a drink, and drew circles on the table with a straw.

"A couple of weeks ago, I was going through the bills at the end of the month, filing them upstairs. And I just happened to look at one. It was a charge to Mary Lee. You know, that nice Navajo woman who cleans at the school. It was for two twenty-five pound sacks of Bluebird flour, you know the kind they use for bread."

Jay Rogers knew he wasn't supposed to speak yet, so he just sipped his drink and watched her talk.

"It wouldn't have meant anything, I guess." She paused. "Except that I remember ordering that flour for Mary Lee, and it was just one sack, not two."

Another pause.

"As I say, it wasn't anything particularly unusual. When I asked Tom about it, he just said he'd forgotten to charge her for the bag she ordered the month before. Okay, I said, and forgot about it. But then, just for the hell of it, I looked through old bills a few days later, and there it was. She clearly had been charged for flour the month before."

"Old Tom can make mistakes just like anybody else," Jay Rogers said. "He's an honest man."

"One would suppose," she said slowly. "Then why, when I asked him about it again, did he just glare at me and walk away?"

"Maybe he just doesn't like being called to explain by people who work for him."

"Maybe."

He noticed how quiet she had become. In fact, he noticed how quiet the whole world had become. From the front room, just a couple of voices, the occasional rattle of ice. Above, the night rain still tapping on the high window glass.

"There's more."

"I thought there must be."

"Such as the figure one on an original bill turned into a seven, when the bills were totalled up at the end of the month."

"How do you know that?"

"The one was in my handwriting. Somebody else had very neatly changed it to a seven."

Jay Rogers thought for some time before he spoke.

"You know, Claire, those kind of things look bad, sure enough. But they're little things. If it happened to Hockersmith's widow, say, then maybe that would be something."

"Just because they're Navajos?"

"That's not what I meant. Hockersmith's widow's about starved out, that's all. Ever' penny counts."

Claire Sadler thought about that for a moment, then leaned closer to the big man.

"Well," she said, "let me tell you something that's not a little thing."

———•••———

Tom Cottin had aroused her suspicions, surely enough. Not that she wanted to cause him trouble. She didn't. She liked and respected the man, and she knew that he had plenty of troubles without any contribution from her. But, as only Jay Rogers knew, in the festering conflict between Navajo and white, Claire Sadler had very quietly chosen to help the Indians whenever she could.

Why? She resented their treatment, as a matter of fact, and it was not easy to sit quietly and watch their simplicity being turned back against them, used like a subtle prod to nudge them into a kind of mining-town slavery. They would never have come to Madero, she thought, had they known how numbers and language would be combined into some kind of potion that would take away so much of their strength.

Another reason: she didn't like the way she'd been treated either, and she didn't mind the opportunity of wiping the smug looks off the faces of Madero whites, to see them worry and regret and doubt. She smiled, sometimes, when she thought about a few of the tender ladies who might have to pay their Navajo floor scrubbers a decent wage. A couple of shopkeepers who might have to stop doubling their prices to the Indians. The hootch man, who might have to give up his big trade in cheap, watered-down wine.

So she waited and watched, lending a small hand wherever she could. But the stakes had gotten a little higher, and her efforts a little less benign, until she found herself, one night, sitting on the floor of the store office flinging papers around like the enraged store clerk she had temporarily become.

It was Mary Lee, again, or more correctly, her husband Curtis Lee. One of the hardest working and most dependable of the Navajo work force, and a man particularly skilled at running a tram. His week's pay had totalled eighty dollars, and his store charges nearly seventy-one. But receipts marked with the Lee's X and attached to Tom Cottin's adding machine tape totaled only sixty-three. A full ten percent of Curtis Lee's pay was unaccounted for, lost somewhere as undocumented store charges.

She'd hoped it could be explained, but as she and Jay Rogers sat there on a cold Saturday night, she'd been unable and afraid to ask, unsure about opening that particular box.

"You know, Clarabelle," he started again after a long pause and a fresh round of drinks. "I can see your point. Me, I don't know what the deal is between the company and the Indians, and the less I know, the better I like it. See, you'd be better off if you knew less, too."

"But I don't know less. That's the problem."

"So what do you think you can do about it?"

"Probably nothing. That's what makes me so damnably mad."

Neither said anything for a long while, but just sat listening to the little sounds. Faint laughter. The ticking of an old clock. Their own breathing. Rain.

"Here's the deal, Claire," Jay said after several minutes had passed. "You like the Navajos. Just try to think like one. Be patient and let good and bad sort themselves out here, and don't make a lot of unnecessary noise. This can't last, not even for another year. I see things. I hear things. Something is going to happen."

"And what might that be?" she asked, a hint of disbelief in her voice.

"It's hard to tell. Trouble. Maybe somebody'll blow old Alphabet's head off and throw his ass in the river. But something."

She thought about that for awhile.

"Okay," she said. "But answer another question for me."

He looked at her, waiting.

"Where do you suppose the money is going?"

He reached down and patted her hand.

"Who knows," he said, and breathed deeply. "Maybe Andrew needs his teeth fixed." He paused. "Maybe Anne Marie just needs new underwear."

They drank up and went home.

4

"Looking for anything special? A little Henry Miller, perhaps?"

The strong voice again, startling me a little, bringing me back out of my solitary cloud.

"Excuse me?" Where were we? Had she added more?

"You were staring so intently at my books," she said. "At the expatriate section. I thought maybe I could give you some help."

I said no, nothing, that I hadn't really been seeing the books at all. That I had been away, down a shadowy little side road.

"Jay was right, of course," she said, as though she hadn't interrupted her own monologue. "It couldn't go on, and it didn't. I just wished it could have happened the other way around."

"You would have preferred that it had been the Indians that did the shooting." I was not offended. I could see a kind of justice working there.

Her face wrinkled up further and she squinted her eyes, in kind of an impatient scowl.

"No, don't get the wrong idea. I wasn't just talking about that. I was talking about winners and losers and how easy it was for one side to rig the game. No, I just meant . . ."

She stopped.

"I don't know what I meant. Nobody ought to have died. We ought to have had better sense."

After I'd thought for a moment, I told her how I felt: I was pained by her story. Her memory was very convincing to me, and her earlier words about the imagination painting a prettier picture of families than the truth does was still ringing in my ears, like a fire bell.

"Well, I don't know whether my memory is convincing or not," she answered. "But it's all that's left. In fact, there was never much more than that. Ever. Now isn't that something?"

"What do you mean?"

"I burned everything."

I was jolted by her answer: the words, and matter of factness with which she laid them out. Burned everything. What was everything?

"Before the trial, I went down to the store one Sunday night and burned every damned receipt and bill and check stub in the entire establishment. Poof. Up in smoke."

A little smile sneaked across her lips, then was just as quickly wiped away.

"But why? You weren't going to do the Navajos any good by burning up all the, the . . . the evidence." I was having a difficult time getting the words out.

"I told you it was a confusing time, didn't I? Didn't I say that? Didn't I say I was confused? I thought so."

"Now I'm confused. Why protect the old man?"

She bowed her head for a moment and took off her glasses, pulling the wires loose from her ears, one at a time. She held the bridge of her nose between her thumb and forefinger, resting her eyes and mind from the strain of looking back.

"Despite Jay's advice, I was going to take it upon myself to see that justice was done. Particularly after what Tom had done to the Benally boy. I guess I was a little out of my head. I don't know."

She seemed reluctant to go on.

"So I went to see Wizzy, Wizzy . . . oh hell, I can't remember his name. I never could. Mr. Alphabet. I just felt like things might get even worse, if something serious wasn't done."

Mr. Alphabet had listened with great interest to her story, she said, and had made notes. He'd said that it was all such a shame, such a dreadful shame, but that Tom Cottin had acted in a way that nobody could condone. Undoubtedly, he would have to pay a high, high price. If she had the kind of information that she claimed to have, she had to come forth. Immediately. Otherwise, she herself could be guilty of a crime. Tom Cottin would pay, and she would not. Jozef Wyszyanski would see to that.

All Mr. Alphabet wanted her to do was gather up whatever documents she could find, bundle them up and summarize them for him, in writing. He would take it from there.

"I was rather proud of myself," she said, "for stepping forward. And that warm feeling lasted all of about eight hours. Then I discovered that Mr. Alphabet was interested in seeing Tom Cottin put away, all right, but not for merely shooting a Navajo. He had other reasons, and I came stumbling, bumbling along at just about the perfect time."

I didn't know what to say, or what to ask. So I just sat there like the student I'd become.

"So I gathered everything together, all right. Just as he asked me to. And then I burned every single solitary scrap."

As I'd said before, I was confused. What was she trying to tell me?

"You don't know about this particular situation, do you?" she asked. I shook my head.

"I guess I shouldn't be surprised."

———

Claire Sadler had been putting in long days. With Tom Cottin in jail, she was left to mind the store alone, except for help from a couple of miners' wives who came in during the busy hour when the day shift came off the mountain. She opened, not long after first light, and she closed, often well after dark.

The day she'd gone to see Alphabet was the longest of all. She'd awakened before daylight even, and paced the floor. During her private hour, she'd done nothing but list reasons in her journal why she should just leave things alone, and be patient. Let the process work.

But she couldn't. In her mind, cheating the Navajos and the shooting at the store were one and the same thing, tied together as positively as links in a chain. And to say nothing was to be . . . just another white. She had never been just another white.

Her nerve would not last. She knew that. There would be Anne Marie and the boy: she'd have to face them. There would be her own memories of Tom Cottin's kindnesses: they would come back, again and again. There would be nagging suspicions that she was just out to get his job: the rumors would start. Once her first foot went forward, she had to march on briskly, and get it done.

So at eight-thirty that night, she was still in the store, pawing through files, stacking bills, making notes. However, to make sense out of it, she had to keep reaching back, trying to remember what transactions had amounted to, or should have amounted to, and it was a task. She was too tired, her mind too crammed with faces and figures and doubts. Tomorrow, perhaps, she could finish.

As she began to turn off lights downstairs, she noticed that the light was still on in the Cable Minerals office across the street, and one of the company's orange-yellow pickups was still parked out front. It was Alphabet's. She was sure of it. And she wanted to talk to him, suddenly. Maybe to be patted on the head and to be propped up again, by words. That it was right. That it would be all right. She'd tell him that it would take another day. At least another day.

But by the time she went back upstairs and turned the lights off, then fetched her coat from the back and put it on and started out the front door, the light across the street had gone off. The pickup hadn't moved, and she didn't see anybody on the street. But the light was out, so she went back inside, checked the back door and the safe as she always did at the end of the day, locked up, and headed for home.

It was a January night, but not a cold one. The sky had clouded over and wood and coal smoke hovered close to the ground, promising snow by morning. Light from windows and street lights broke out onto piled snow, but couldn't reflect, or travel very far.

Ahead of Claire Sadler, crossing the street toward the light at the corner, she could see another form, another face. A few more steps, and she could see that it was Andrew Cottin. A flash of pain went through her, then. A hurting in the soul. She liked the boy. Liked him a lot. He seemed to be a loner, much like herself, and serious and studied in a way that young boys mostly were not. She wanted to do him no harm, to leave him untouched, somehow, by all of this.

They met at the light, spoke, and she fell in beside him. The Cottins' house was neither on her way, nor out of her way. Just a different route from the one she normally took. Same distance. So she walked along with him, saying little. Listening to their footsteps squeak in the frozen snow. Thinking about how they were linked together by harsh circumstance.

After a time, she asked the boy what brought him out on the street at that time of night.

Old Mrs. Jakoby's husband had gone to the hospital, he said, and his mother had sent him over to her house to haul in a few bucket-fuls of coal and some wood. That was easy, he said. Took maybe twenty minutes. But then she'd made him stay and eat cookies that he didn't really want, and drink hot chocolate that he didn't want either. And listen to her stories. Now he was going home.

At his gate, they said their good nights, and each took another step. Maybe two.

Then the scream. A loud and desperate scream.

They could both hear it. And they could both rush through the gate, to the door, and see Alphabet standing there, looming, with Anne Marie Cottin's underclothes in his hand.

———•—

She was washing up for bed, in her robe in the bathroom, when she heard the front door open and close. Good, she thought, the boy is home. Late, but finally here. She needed him those days.

But when she stepped out to ask him how Mrs. Jakoby was do-ing, she found that her voice didn't work, and that her arms and legs were frozen, couldn't move, not her own. She was confused, for part of a second, about the time and the place.

Jozef Wyszyanski was standing in the middle of the living room, teetering a little left and right, with the half-grin of an idiot on his face. His big hands hung loosely, limply, down at his sides, as though he'd forgotten that he'd brought them along. His hair was wild. Alphabet was drunk.

She ordered him out, but he said nothing, and he didn't move. She threatened him, but that only seemed to make his eyes open wider and shine brighter. She turned to run, but then she knew: barefoot and in her robe, almost naked, she had no place to go.

"Just bringin' you the news," he said finally, his voice stale and harsh as the whiskey that he'd been drinking. "You don't have to be afraid of me." His words were slurred, a little, but distinct enough.

"Just thought you oughta know. Your old man's finished. Screwed. Kaput." That last word brought a mist of spit from his lips.

"No," she said. "You're drunk. You're, you're . . ."

"Won't do you no good," he went on. "His chief bottlewasher, she's no damned fool. She knows what's been goin' on in that place. Old Sadler's got him by the short hairs now. In writin'. Facts and figures. You cheat Indians, you shoot one, shit, even a white man can't get away with that."

"No," she said again, unable to think of anything else. Just want-ing short words, words that would send him toward the door, so all of this could end.

"Oh, yeah, sweetheart," he said. "Receipts. Bills. The works."

"You lie."

"That's not polite, pretty woman. That's not the way to talk to a poor man who's just tryin' to help you out."

"What do you want?" Her voice was loud, and high pitched.

"Why, nothin'. Nothin'." But his eyes deceived him. They were hot, and edged in red. "Just a friend of the family. That's all. Just stoppin' by."

"You're not a friend of the family," she said, sounding tougher, more accusing. "You've never even been here before."

"Maybe I'll be comin' by more often, now," he said, a twisted grin working across his face. "Now that you'll be needin' help from time to time."

"You're a liar and a, a . . . maggot." She shouted out the word, and as she did, she felt herself going forward, leaping at him, pushing him in the chest and shoving him backwards a couple of steps. And she knew, in the middle of the act, that she'd made the wrong move.

His eyes seemed to drift in and out of focus, and they glowed with the devil's fire, and the grin deepened and froze itself on his face.

"Maggot, is it?" he asked, and he reached out, grabbed her robe at the neck and jerked down, quick and hard, ripping the front out of it, all the way to her knees. "Maggot, she says."

She grabbed the little that remained of her robe front, and tried to pull the torn edges closed, across her naked breasts. They wouldn't reach.

"I was tryin' to be nice," he said, his voice climbing up in pitch, his eyes nailed to her chest. "But you won't let me."

He reached out with one hand, and she thought he was going to pull her hands away, to bare her even more, but instead he pushed her backwards onto the couch, and she couldn't fight back or catch herself.

Then Alphabet moved forward, quickly, and jerked the fabric out of her hands, tore the rest of her robe open. She tried to fight him, tried to kick at him, but there was little she could do. He held her down with one hand, clamped her legs closed with his, and grabbed her panties by the elastic and pulled them down, over her legs, over her bare feet. Her best underwear, she thought oddly, looking in from somewhere out in space. Blue, with the embroidered initials. AMC. Something she'd done herself, on a long winter's night.

For a moment, all time slowed. Alphabet just stood there, in front of her, now holding her legs spread with his own, looking at her.

"Stop!" she screamed. Once. Twice. As loud as she could.

He said nothing. Stood there, breathing deeply. Smile gone from his face.

"I just came to bring you the news," he said. With his right hand, he began to unbutton the front of his pants.

That was as far as he got.

"Noooo!" Andrew Cottin screamed as loudly as he could as he threw himself through the front door, slamming it back against the wall with a crash.

The scene froze up, then, like a photograph taken at a thousandth of a second. Nothing moved. Eyes looked at eyes looked at eyes. Muscles tensed and locked themselves up. Breathing stopped.

Then Anne Marie rolled over on her side, and began to sob. Loudly. Mournfully. Alphabet turned and walked toward the door, panties still in one hand, buttons still unbuttoned.

"Little shit," he said, pushing Andrew aside. "And you, you don't know shit, either," pushing Claire Sadler aside, and he walked out into the street.

Out there, he began to cough. He wiped his mouth with the panties, the blue ones, the ones monogrammed AMC, and crammed them into his back pocket. Then he walked off into the winter night, down to his office, and to his truck.

Claire Sadler moved forward, tried to help the other woman to her feet, help her to cover herself. But she was stopped cold.

"How could you?" Anne Marie Cottin asked through her sobs. "How could you turn against Tom? How could you help that bastard? How?"

———·•·———

She walked slowly along the edge of the street, taking the long way home. Words hurting her ears, images burning her eyes. She could never see it through now. Not after tonight. Even if it might help the Navajos in some small way, it would lay so much else to waste. And it wouldn't, couldn't bring back the dead.

And it came to her, then, that she couldn't help them now, not any of them. If she told everything she knew, if she were forced by an oath in a court to lay it out there, everyone would pay. Tom. Anne Marie. The boy. The whole town. Herself. And the Navajos would still be played as pawns, no matter how the white games-within-games turned out. No, she couldn't help any of them. Everything was in ruins now.

Jay Rogers had been right. She never should have interfered with whatever forces were at work. The unknown was far too much bigger than the understood.

The next day, a Sunday, she asked Jay Rogers to watch her house for a few months, perhaps even live in it a day or two each week. Then she went to the store and systematically burned all the paperwork she could find, hauling it to the coal furnace downstairs. She wrote a letter of resignation to Cable Minerals and slipped it under the office door. Then she caught a ride down the valley, and, in Three Rivers, bought a train ticket for the long ride east.

5

WHEN THINKING ABOUT THEIR ANCESTORS, EVERYBODY HOPES, IF NOT assumes, that a hero lurks back in there someplace. If not a hero, at least someone whose bad acts have been so outrageous that they can be bent around by myth, through time, to resemble heroics. Would we still look back, I was wondering, if all we could hope for was petty theft and a grandmother lying with her legs forced open by a man like Alphabet? Maybe not. Probably not.

I must have been staring out the window, or down at my shoes, or into my cup, because Claire Sadler coughed to catch my ear, rubbed her hands together to catch my eye.

"Ah yes," she said, "I can see that you've never heard this part. As I said, I'm not surprised. Families don't talk about those kinds of things. Those things of sex, and humiliation. Of powerlessness. But people know. They know because they see it, they do it, behind their own locked doors."

She frowned that tight-lipped, kind of sympathetic, frown.

"I guess I'm sorry that you had to hear the story from me, but I'm under the impression that we're mostly interested in good history, you and I."

Yes, that's true, I remind myself. Sometimes I forget that I ignored my father's warnings, and now I have to be willing and ready to own whatever I dig up.

"You look a little pale around the gills, young man. Can I order you a little brandy or something, something to pep up your blood?"

"No," I said, "I'm fine. It's just one unexpected thing, one ugly thing after another. That's all."

"Yes," she said, looking at an old railroad clock on a lower shelf. "I guess it might be a bit early, after all. Even for us in the leisure class."

She pulled one of her canes out from beside her chair, and clasped both hands on top, as though she might be ready to stand up and usher me to the door. But then she began to talk again.

"I stayed away until the middle part of the summer, and when I came back the whole thing was pretty much over. They'd had a trial, but I'd escaped it. No summons, no nothing."

"How did the trial go?"

"I'm a poor source for information of that sort. I didn't want to think about it, and I didn't want to hear about it, so I asked no questions. What little I did hear made it sound like a bunch of lawyers' tomfoolery that just sort of confused and disappointed everyone in the end. Typical, I guess."

Yes, I supposed so. But still, there were people involved, people whose lives must have taken sharp, and perhaps tragic, turns. And I wanted to know about them.

"Most of the Navajos had gone back to the reservation. They'd seen about all of white man's justice that they could take. Anne Marie and the boy were gone, too, but I never knew where, or when. And Tom was off in a hospital somewhere, already beyond recovery, almost like a punch-drunk fighter, so it turned out."

"Mr. Alphabet, as you call him?"

"Oh, he stayed around for a few more months, I think. I'm not sure when he left. But the mines were closing down one after another, and pretty soon he was gone, too. Is he still alive? I don't know. I am, so I guess he might very well be, too."

What more could I ask Claire Sadler? What else didn't I know? In a couple of hours, a woman I had not even heard of two days earlier had laid the guts of Madero out on the store counter, a collection of innards that gave off a heat and a smell that made me want to turn away in despair.

But sitting there in the woman's parlor on a mid-spring day, I'd finally begun to understand a couple of things. I could see where some of Andrew Cottin's angers were born. And I could see why he wanted to leave the past alone, to let it mildew and rot by itself, in the dim, out of the light.

"Ah, but I'm afraid I've overlooked something," she was saying, with a look on her face that was both somber, but yet slightly amused. "Something I should have thought of earlier, perhaps. And it might be of interest to you."

I waited. Somehow I had the feeling that she hadn't forgotten anything at all, that this arrangement of events was her reward to herself for going through these motions.

"They never found a gun."

A gun? I'd never thought about it, even in the telling of Billy Yazzie's tale. I'd just assumed that it had gone to that place where misused weapons go.

"Sam Benally was shot with a gun, unquestionably," she said in an almost analytical tone. "The bullet hole was a pretty clear indication of that. And presumably Tom Cottin would have admitted to firing the shot. But the sheriff never found a weapon. And I've thought about it considerably since then. I never saw it either."

"Strange," I said. "Where could it have gone?"

"It was obvious. Nobody in town had any real doubts. But for some reason, the sheriff, no matter how hard he tried, could never come up with it. I guess with Tom babbling hysterically about what he'd done, they decided they wouldn't need it after all. Or perhaps they liked the confusion, the doubt, the complication of having no gun to wave about."

———

By the time Andrew Cottin had turned fifteen, his mother wasn't getting him up on winter mornings any more. Every winter seemed to bother her more, and when she did roll out on those dim grey mornings when snow blew and whistled through the air outside, she was often sullen, angry almost. He didn't want to see that frown, those pained eyes, and he was glad to let her sleep. His father surely must have felt the same way.

She balanced out her days by adding to the other end: her light was always on late, sometimes well past twelve. She read, listened to the radio, and wrote letters home.

Andrew wasn't crazy about seeing his father in the mornings, either. He always looked like he'd just had a bad dream, and had spent the night running away from big animals, or down into a hole full of snakes. His hands shook. Consequently, Andrew was always the first up, school day or not, and frequently out the door without seeing either of the others. He liked it that way. Besides, he'd always had his job to do.

In the fall of each year, two big dump trucks would pull into the alley behind Cable Mercantile, filled with a dirt-like form of coal the locals called stoker coal. Furnaces in the bigger buildings in town all burned it. Using a heavy metal chute stuck down through little ground-level windows, the truckers would fill two basement rooms under the store with the winter's supply of fuel.

Ever since he'd been old enough to move a shovel, Andrew had been responsible for loading that coal into the furnace, and for seeing that the ashes and clinkers were hauled to the pile out back. If the fire ever went out, and particularly if the pipes froze, Andrew would have serious hell to pay.

He tended other fires, too, but the store was his first stop. Because coal dust usually drifted up through the heating grates while he was down there shoveling, his old man wanted the job done before he or Claire Sadler opened up, so they could sweep around the grates before the public came in.

So Andrew would open the back door, stumble down the dark steps just inside, tend his furnace and move on. The only time he even ventured into the rest of the store was when he felt like helping himself to a Pepsi or a Snickers before he went off to school. Once he'd taken a box of .22 shells, and once he'd taken fifty cents out of the cash register. But that felt like stealing from his father, and it bothered him. So he kept his pilfering in the nickel and dime range.

———

As always, the house was quiet when he left, and the streets were empty. Daylight was breaking, the packed snow squeaked underneath his feet, and some of the night's Christmas lights were still on. He unlocked the back door of the store, banged his way down the steps, took off his coat, and began to shovel.

Christmas was coming, he thought, but he didn't want anything in particular. Last year, he'd gotten his big wish—a .30-06, and he'd shot his first bull elk with the rifle that fall—so this year promised to be kind of flat. Besides, the spirit just wasn't there. A record player would be good.

Then he felt something on his neck, wet, and he thought a cooler upstairs, or maybe the pop machine, had sprung a leak. But when he wiped it off, it was sticky, not like water, and he walked over under the bare light bulb to look at it. Dark red. Blood. It was dripping down through the heat grate over his head.

He dropped the shovel, and sprinted up the steps, taking them two at a time, not certain whether he wanted to look, or just run. But blood was blood, the reddest flag of distress, and not to be wiped away, ignored. So he went, and he had his look.

———

It had been a long, cold walk from town to the cemetery in the dark. There was no moon, and the night was spitting a little snow. Andrew Cottin walked alone, carrying a flashlight, and hoping that no one would come along. No car would force him to jump the bank and hide in the snow. None did.

———

He didn't know why he'd taken the gun. But when he couldn't rouse his father, couldn't make him move or talk or understand, he was angry. He had to change something, somehow. Make things different from how they seemed to be. So he took the gun and ran.

At first he hid it in the coal pile downstairs, but he knew they'd look there before too long. He couldn't throw it in the river. It was all frozen over. He didn't want to throw it out in the snow, just to get forgotten and turn up in the spring. He couldn't bury it . . . but yet he could. He knew where to find freshly turned dirt.

That next morning, when the crowd assembled to sob their sobs and lend their voices to "Nearer My God to Thee," to say their proper words, they lowered Sam Benally's cheap coffin into the ground and shoveled in the dirt. And with each shovelful of dirt, Sam Benally and the gun that killed him both went deeper into the earth.

6

So perhaps there was a heroic note in this dirge after all, a little fanfare that promised something more than gloom. Someone, my father, had been bolder, and taken a chance. And I liked him better for that, for at least playing a role, for doing something that contrasted with everything else that seemed so grey and sour. Perhaps he wanted to help the old man. Or maybe he'd had some other plan for the gun. But at least, or so it seemed, he'd done more than stand there and wipe his eyes.

"Odd, though," I said. "He was just a kid. One would think they would wring it out of him, or beat it out of him."

Claire raised her eyebrows at me, and half smiled.

"Just a kid? No, I don't think so. He was a little more than that. Intense, I think, is the word they use now. No, I don't think they felt too comfortable pushing him around. Besides . . ." She paused for a second and smiled. "As far as they knew, he had a gun. Ha!"

Then she smiled wryly, and posed for a moment, staring off into space.

"But it was all a charade, a big show. You see, did anybody really give a shilling whether Tom Cottin was sent to jail or not? No. He'd just killed a Navajo, you know, not a real person. Such things happen all the time around the edges of the reservations. And half the people in this town, more perhaps, wanted the Indian problem taken care of anyway."

"Alphabet wanted him gone. Didn't you tell me that?"

"I don't know. Maybe it was just one night of love. Maybe the bloom quickly faded from the rose."

"That's an ugly thought."

"I guess we'll never know," she said. "And except for you and your nose for good history, I'm quite certain that no one would give a tinker's damn about it now."

We sat there in silence for a minute or more. I was taking and using the story as only I could, shaping and fitting it in with all the other pieces. And I supposed the story, in its retelling, had somehow become new to her as well, seen through a finer filter of time. Images, pictures, feelings fading in and out.

A boy walking alone through the darkness of a cemetery. Had he just thrown the gun into the bottom of the hole and ran? Or had he thrown in a shovelful of dirt or two? Or had he crawled down into the hole and covered the pistol up with the cold, fresh earth?

Then the feel of that dirt and darkness, the pull of that blue-black hole in the ground, brought something else to my mind. Something I'd heard from Billy Yazzie.

"Strange things happened around the making of Sam Benally's grave," I said.

"What are you referring to?" she asked, with a look of new interest in her eyes, as though I might be about to tell her something she didn't already know.

"According to Billy Yazzie, somebody dug Sam Benally up."

She sat there for a moment, as though not hearing me. No surprise registered on her face. Her eyes barely flickered. She neither caught nor held her breath. But I saw the tops of her hands grow more pale as her fingers gripped harder around the head of her cane.

"Oh," she said, "they were bastards. Bastards." A new fire had come into her voice, and then into her eyes. "The whites of this town promoted that funeral as though it was the kindest, most generous thing they'd ever done. And all for an Indian. Grieving, black clothes, a mouthful of gentle Christian words. Wailing over the grave like a bunch of shameless fools."

She took a deeper breath, then, and her hands seemed to relax.

"Somehow they seemed to have conveniently forgotten that they were the ones who killed him."

It was clear to me then that I hadn't understood everything I'd already learned.

"Billy Yazzie came to see me. I was in the back of the store." Her voice had leveled and softened, as though she was simply trying to talk her way through an old dream. Maybe it had always seemed like a dream to her. "His face was tired and full of grief. And he said the whites could have their ceremony, but the Navajos could not leave the body there. He couldn't say why, exactly, but only that it was wrong to leave Sam Benally forever alone there, lost among the spirits and the bones of the whites."

She turned her eyes back on me, as though reminding herself that I, and she, were just sitting there, and that forty years had gone by.

"They needed help."

The night was cold and clear. Had the moon been bright, the three feet of snow on the ground would have reflected the glow from every angle. But the moon was new and small, a thin crescent, and not much help. So they placed kerosene lanterns at each end of the grave, and that was enough. If a car had come down the road, they could have easily hidden the light with the blankets they brought along. But it was 2 a.m. There would be no cars. Not that time of the year.

"Good thing this dirt ain't froze yet," Jay Rogers said as he sunk his shovel into the ground and piled a new mound of dirt up alongside the grave. "We'd have to pour some of that damned kerosene on the ground and set it on fire. They'd damned sure see us then."

"I guess their tears didn't soak the ground," Claire Sadler said, digging at the other end. "Otherwise, we'd be digging through a layer of ice." The words came out clipped and flat, almost sad.

They shoveled quickly, both to keep warm and to get the job done.

Jay Rogers, a strong man and used to the business end of a shovel, moved dirt briskly and in big bites. Claire Sadler worked as steadily, saying nothing. The great stillness of the night wrapped around them like a dark fog, and was eased only by their small grunts and the soft bang of metal against small rocks, and sometimes by the squeak of their boots against the frozen snow.

When the hole was three feet deep, Jay Rogers stopped and leaned on the handle of his shovel. A yellow light from the lantern played across his long, thin face. His shallow breathing sent clouds of vapor trailing off, disappearing into the still night.

"What am I supposed to do with him when we get him out of here?" he asked. "You never said."

"Just take him down on the reservation someplace and bury him."

"Where?"

"Maybe north of Shiprock. Or west. It doesn't matter."

"Then how will they know where in the hell he is?"

"They won't."

He started to ask another question, but she had gone back to digging. And he read that as a signal that he should do the same.

Sometime after three, Jay Rogers' shovel blade struck metal. And, scraping back dirt, they could see pieces of small gilded angels reflecting back the lantern light.

"Funny," he said after they'd taken a minute to look. "I thought it would be just a plywood box. I figured they'd bury him in whatever they could find around the carpenter shop. Or just stick him in a hole and go on."

"That would be too honest," she replied. "Painted angels and amens make a better show."

Laid out on the ground, partly on the freshly-dug earth and partly in the snow, the body of Sam Benally seemed strangely harmless and empty and still. He seemed more a reminder of a man, a token, and less the leftover parts of once-living flesh.

He was not going to sit up and speak. He was not going to tell them anything at all. The voice that had lived in there had gotten cleanly and easily away.

He was dressed just as he had been the night he was shot. Dirty denim overalls, worn cotton shirt, black rubber boots. Only his black hair seemed to have been slicked back, fixed up, for the occasion.

"Help me here," Claire Sadler said as she began to pull at one of the rubber boots.

"What in the hell are you doing?"

Perhaps he thought she wanted the boots for herself.

"We're leaving the boots in the casket."

He didn't say anything.

"It's something Billy Yazzie wanted done." She pulled harder. "And he's right."

Jay Rogers knelt in the snow to help her pull, and he said quietly, "There seems to be quite a lot here that I don't understand."

———·—·———

The moon would move closer to the center of the sky, and then cross to the other side. The sun would come up. And the light of a new day would shine down upon Sam Benally's grave. Nothing, it seemed, was different. Nor, somehow, did anything feel quite the same.

———·—·———

"Navajos don't willingly touch the dead," Claire Sadler said to me, no doubt reading questions that were written all across my face. "It brings the witches down."

A simple explanation. I nodded.

"Nor, for that same reason, do they often visit graves."

I nodded again.

"Well," she said, "I would think that even you have heard about enough."

She sat back in her chair, cane clasped between her knees, hands in her lap. She was plainly growing tired.

"What else is there?"

"Nothing. That's all I know. Or at least all that I know that I know. Memories fade. People die off, and those that don't can't think straight anyway. As they say in the old detective novels, Inspector Cottin, the trail has grown awfully cold by now."

"Is there no one else who knows?" I asked.

"Who else could there be? I guess there might still be Mr. Alphabet. Perhaps he could help you out."

I assumed she was merely being sarcastic, but I responded anyway. "Where would I find him?"

"Well, if there is a hell, that would be good place to start looking. Other than that, I guess I couldn't say."

Claire Sadler pulled her second cane out from beside the chair, and lifted herself to her feet. She said the time had arrived when she and Barbara had their early evening glass of brandy out on the back porch, and asked whether I wanted to stay for the occasion.

I thought about it for a moment, and declined. I was exhausted, and I wanted to lie down.

"It's probably just as well," she said as she headed toward the kitchen, moving briskly on her canes. "You probably couldn't keep pace with Barbara anyway."

———•———

I never saw Claire Sadler again. I didn't return to her house, and of course, I never saw her on the street. However, several days after I'd spoken with her, Richert gave me an envelope from her when I stopped by the store for some beer and bread.

I was surprised to see it, and didn't care to open it right there in the store. I put the groceries in my pickup and crossed the street to the bench in front of Ike's. I opened it there.

"Dear young fellow," it began, just as I would have expected, and it was written in a hand of straight up-and-down jagged lines, firm, spare, just as I would have expected, as well.

> *I enjoyed your visit, and I wish you well. I have a request of you, however. Please do nothing solely on the basis of what you've heard from me. I've told you what my memory believes to be true, but I have no proof. I have only impressions and a sense of how things came about. I have, perhaps, filtered out too much of the good and held on to too much of the bad. That's a flaw, indeed, but it's served me well.*
>
> *In exchange, I'll give you a gift of sorts. I've asked Barbara to make a copy of a page from my personal journal, dated November 8, 1951. She's done so, and I've scratched it up a bit and attached it to this letter. With any luck, it will perhaps accomplish two things: help you understand the tenor of the times, and give you a vague idea of where you might go from here.*
>
> *Families may be of value. They were certainly not to me. If things turn out differently for you, I will have been happy to have helped.*

Behind that sheet was a legal-sized piece of paper, a photocopy of a page removed from a loose-leaf lined book.

> *Weather grey and cloudy. Spitting snow. How could fall have gone so quickly? Waited too long to order coal, I'm sure. Now the price will be a dollar a ton higher. Somewhere along the way, I should have learned.*
>
> *Usually, we're not in a position to spot the end of one era and the beginning of another right when that happens. But I believe I see one today. Jozef Wyszyanski, the man they call Alphabet, is gone. Rumors have persisted for weeks that he was being reassigned by Cable Minerals, but I dared not believe them. At any rate, he's gone, I believe to some copper project along the San Juan River.*
>
> *Can I say that he was the single biggest cause of trouble in Madero*

for the past five years? I can say anything I want. He was. And with him gone, it will surely be a different place.

I just wish he would have gone before he got his dirty hands on Anne Marie Cottin.

Here, a long paragraph was covered over with correction fluid, coats and coats of it, so that I had no way of making out even one word. There might be ways, I thought, but I've got to respect this unique person's rights.

In his going, however, he performed perfectly true to character. He left in the night, not because he owed money or the such, but because he took with him Madeline Swain, wife of the chief railroad engineer. Not unexpected, to those who have been alert for the past year or so. Thus, Madero is relieved not only of its most troublesome man, but also of its most immoral woman. Two dirty birds with one stone. It was a good day, this one, all in all.

A day in the life of Claire Sadler, more than forty years ago. Let me read that book, or perhaps just a year of it, I thought. Let me use her sharp eye and her sharp words to frame a new picture of Madero, about 1950. Let me feel what she felt, for surely, no record would be more true, no nerves more raw, no comment more straight to the bone.

No, don't let me read it, no more of it than just this single page. Don't tell me more than I need to know. After all, her's was a life to which fate had not been particularly kind. I don't need, can't really stand, a sharper sense of her pain.

A gift, she'd said. Yes, it was a gift. And I felt honored by it. I folded the letter carefully, placed it back in its envelope, and carried it home with me. There, I packed it away in the box that held my old photographs. A valuable addition to my small, costly collection of Madero souvenirs.

And that night, I responded with a purpose, a sense of satisfaction, that I had not felt in a long, long time. Carefully, I wrapped another of Old Tom's chains in cotton rags and packed it in another small box. Inside, I enclosed a short note: I asked that the chain be admired in the memory of Tom Cottin, and that one day it be passed along to whoever would also get Claire Sadler's book of paintings by Georgia O'Keeffe. I saw an association there, I said, that I really couldn't explain. And I thanked her again for her help.

I asked Richert to deliver the little box the next time he climbed the hill with their food. Without a question, he agreed.

Where would the chain go from there? It didn't matter, so long as it moved link by link, memory by memory, through Claire Sadler's careful hands.

PART SIX

The Lady

1

MADERO COMES A LITTLE MORE TO LIFE IN THE LONGER DAYS THAT PROMISE summer. As shutters and boards disappear from the windows of the rough summer cabins, the old places seem to open their eyes, awake after a winter-long sleep. Vehicles with Arizona, California and Texas license plates are scattered along the usually empty streets, and the air in Ike's Place grows pungent and ripe with fishing stories. Newer, often louder, voices bounce and echo off the old wood.

More traffic snakes up the narrow river valley. Sometimes, several cars pass in an hour, almost all just moving through, bound for the pass at the headwaters, toward other towns. Sometimes they stop for gas, sometimes they never even slow below fifty.

———•◦•———

For some reason, I've wanted to write down all that I've learned. It has taken me a full week. The characters: I've colored their eyes and hair, and put words into their mouths. I've given them reasons for the things they did, and made them be cruel and bitter and dishonest, if that's what it takes. I've moved them around and lined them up and put them away. Through that, they've become more than mere wooden soldiers, and have started to march and move around on their own in the night. They've taken on flesh of their own, slipped their cardboard forms, started moving and breathing inside the world bounded by the old photographs.

Realizing that, I haul a box out from under my bed, and spread those yellowed and cracked photographs out on the table again. I can see more life in there now, and imagine more of the things I can not see.

The storekeeper and his family. Has that store already become their universe, the box within which most of the important events of their lives will be contained? Are words like "promise" and "someday" parts of their vocabulary, with words like "Navajo" and "union" yet to come?

The family on the train platform, ready for the Durango trip. Has each of them already started keeping secrets from the rest? Is this trip a quick escape, their good try at raising themselves above the anger and dark clouds building up around them? Who is she waving to?

The group pictures. Who among them is fighting for a union, growing lettuce, cheating the Indians? Have they heard Jay Rogers play? Or seen the Navajos dance? Who is holding hands just beyond the eye of the lens?

A father, his son, a trophy bull elk. What burdens have become so great as to suck the life out of this moment? What does the father fear? And the boy already know?

The answers are not here, of course. And will never be. But to be able to ask the questions suggests that I know more about their time on earth, their particular agonies, than I've ever known before. And it means that, for better or worse, I can comprehend that there were real people back there, with bad dreams and lost keys and wandering eyes and good marks in school. Common things. And that's something, at least to me.

When I drive up to the mine, to the little tin hovel that's been my old man's hide-out for so long, I see quickly that something has changed. And I can pick it out: his truck is gone.

My stomach aches, suddenly, and I feel just a little sick. He's pulled out, I think. Run for it. He's going to wait me out on some other pile of rocks on the edge of some other desert. Make me sweat for it, or quit.

Ten minutes pass, and I walk around. Everything else looks the same. I wonder if he's boarded up the mine.

Then I hear a truck, and then I see it, and it's him. Pulling his water tank behind him on an old two-wheel trailer. I'm glad, but I never know what he'll say, or what he'll do.

He backs it into place, and gets out. He looks at me without any expression, and I feel like he knew that I was here. Had time to get over it. Then I thought of my tracks. He would have seen my tracks in the road, and gotten out and studied them, and known they weren't his.

"Ran outta water," he says, flatly, almost as though I'd been here when he left. I wonder where he gets it. But then I remember an old ranch on the way up, and I figure they have a well. People share water in this part of the country. It's a common law.

——•—•——

On the bench, on the rim. Late morning. I've hauled out a couple of cold beers, and I can tell that he's happy to have one. Even if it does come from me.

The red spires look hot in the sun. They shimmer. The air is thick and still, and the heat has pulled the horizon in much closer, to where it seems almost within comprehension.

"I talked to Billy Yazzie," I say.

He looks at me and then looks away.

"He told me all about Sam Benally, just like you said."

He looks back at me, and the look on his face is almost that of a twisted smile. But I know there's no happiness or pleasure behind that hardened, weathered mask. More like a tired resignation, I think. An admission of something.

"Now don't ya think you've seen enough?"

I don't know how to answer that. But it's not so hard to understand where his venom comes from, now.

"I talked to an old woman, too. You would remember her. Claire Sadler."

Perhaps I should be surprised when his frown softens just a little, when a shade more easiness creeps into his eyes, but I'm not. He hasn't forgotten that he and the old woman had a bond, forged in the fires of a particular hell. It's the kind of thing I would expect to stick in his mind.

"I figgered she'd be long gone by now," he says, as though he might have sent me to talk to her, had he known. Maybe, but I doubt it.

Long gone. Out of Madero, or off the earth?

"She's not going anywhere," I say. "Maybe never."

His face has stiffened again now. He's had time to think about what Claire Sadler knows, and what she might have said.

"She told me some things," I add. "About how the store operated." I'm trying to pick my words carefully, here. "About how it was to live there then. About what happened with your mother and the guy they called Alphabet."

I've said too much, or said it in the wrong way. He gets up and walks off, toward the mine, without a word and without even looking my way.

I want to tell him that I'm beginning to see. That I know him better for knowing the storms that washed him up and then washed him away. But maybe he's guessed that. And it's not something he is willing to hear.

I want to ask him where I should look next. He's telling me that he has no answer for that.

———————

I let him get rid of me, at least for a few hours. I don't try to stop him when I see him trudging down the trail to the rim, toward the steps that lead down through the crack to his mine. I don't try to go with him, or follow him. Instead, I move away on my own.

By noon, I'm on the floor of the canyon below, and I can look up and see the spot on the skyline where the bench is located, where we sit and talk on some mornings and evenings.

From down here, we would be nothing but spots, no more than desert chickadees on a ledge. A coyote could lie in the shade of a rock here, and watch and wait, knowing that we would finally go away.

And I can see the dump of the mine where he's working, an inverted triangle of loose shale spilling down through the cliffs, topped off with a handful of tin-covered buildings. I watch it for a few minutes, and I see a solitary car crawl out onto the dump, probably to the end of a short set of tracks. I see it tip up, and rocks tumble into the air. Moments, seconds, later, I hear the sound of falling rock.

If he's dumping onto the dumps instead of into his loading chutes, he's not bringing out copper. At least not today.

Another three hours later, I'm climbing up the other side, nearing the rim across the canyon from the mine. I hear a soft thump and feel the earth move beneath me. I look across and see smoke and dust rolling out of the little portal cut into the hill. My father stands on the dump, watching. Then he turns and disappears into one of the buildings. Killing time, probably. Keeping away from the upper rim where he probably thinks I still sit and wait.

———·—·———

It's late afternoon, and I've rounded the head of the little canyon and made my way back to camp. My father has not come up from his mine under the rim. He could be drilling, but I can't hear his compressor running. He could be doing almost anything.

I'd like to leave him alone, but he has plenty of time to be alone. I'd like to let him rest, but he has plenty of time to do that, too. I've got to get this done. Get the rest of the story. Get it written, if only in the air. Get on with life.

Time passes. I walk out to the bench and look over. Nothing. What did I expect? Vultures? To see him standing down there in the bottom, where I stood before? To see myself down there?

I wonder what I should be making with this time. The distance between what I want and where I stand, now, still seems vast. Maybe too great to span.

That night: "Why did you just leave town, leaving your father sitting in jail?"

He just stares at me.

"Why didn't anyone stick around to help him?"

"I was fourteen goddamned years old, for chrissakes. I did what I was told."

"Why did your mother insist on leaving?"

"How in the hell do I know? She was sick inside, and he was crazy. I don't know. Do I need to draw you a picture?"

"You could have gone back."

"I could have done a lot of things."

Later that night: "I want to find Jozef Wyszyanski. Alphabet."

He's suddenly angrier. Hot. I can see it in the way his eyebrows pull down over the bridge of his nose. The little pulsing that happens at the top of his jaws.

"You want all kinds of shit," he says. His voice is harsh. "Well, I want somethin' too. Tomorrow, first light, I want you to throw your shit into the back of your truck and hit the road. And I don't want you comin' back. Ever. Not until you've got the decency to leave me and what belongs to me alone." He walks away in the dark. Stooped. Tired. Older now.

A whole pack of coyotes must have moved in during the day. I can hear them yapping and barking and howling just over the low ridge off to the west. I know they're not likely to come near me, but I don't like it anyway. Makes it hard to think.

A soft wind whooshes back and forth through the junipers. Stops. Starts up again. Stops.

I hear the trailer door slam shut, and I see a light moving off through the trees, over the ridge. The coyotes must be getting to him, too.

After ten minutes or so, I hear a shot. The sound washes away in the wind, and then I see the light again as he walks back. The trailer door slams, and it's dark.

The coyotes have grown silent, and I don't hear them again for the rest of the night.

2

It was a good enough time to be in the desert. The days were warm, hot sometimes, but the nights were still cool, inviting sleep. I could wander the banks of the San Juan, then, and be glad about it, even though the summer rains had started turning the Madero days a cool, wet, deep green, and I would have liked to have been in the middle of that ripeness, that richness. But I had no excuse for being there. My last chances lay in the desert.

For a few days, I tried what I hoped would be the quick and easy way. I went to courthouses and libraries in places like Farmington and Pagosa Springs and Blanding, looking at tax records and old newspapers and transfers of mining claims. Sifting through that lore was like opening old storybooks, over and over again. Like prying the lids off of old tombs. But there was no Cable Minerals. No Wyszyanski. There were Swains, but I wasn't ready, yet, to approach the task from such an oblique angle as that, with so little chance of hitting my mark.

So for awhile longer, I didn't ask anybody anything, thinking like a student of Zen that I might only catch it by looking away and letting it sneak up on me. So I just drove around, camped, studied faces, thumbed through thin telephone books, and walked the labyrinth of sandstone canyons, looking for pueblo ruins. I watched the tour busses come and go, and sat high above the goosenecks of the river watching little armadas of rubber rafts snake through the canyon. It was a small world of trading posts and gas stations and little cafés that served Navajo tacos. And I could have lived in it for a long time.

But, like a koan, it did come to me. Eventually. Not like a flash in the night, or even a flash flood. No, more simply. Like rain on the road.

———•———

I'd been hiking up Mule Creek, looking at ruins tucked high under the rim and urging the little cottonwoods in the creek bottom to keep up the fight, to stay green and alive, even though the water was gone and the sand bottom dry. Then the weather turned, almost before I realized what it was all about.

Moving with a speed unusual even for the desert, sharp-edged black clouds boiled across the sky, cracking with lightning and rolling with thunder, spilling water in sheets. Within minutes, the dry creek bed was dry no more as red water danced down through the rocks, creating instant pools of foam and floating sticks, then moving on. Above me, on both sides, water cascaded off the rim onto the benches of slick rock below, creating miniature waterfalls everywhere, bounding from ledge to ledge. The air was heavy with a rich, sweet smell, not different from that of garden dirt, and only a little cool.

I was soaked before I could find an overhang to crawl under, but I'd gone far enough up the canyon anyway, so I just turned back. I was concerned about my camera and annoyed with the water in my boots, but I was delighted, too, with the changing face of the red rock cliffs.

The rain was still coming down when I reached the road. I slid into my pickup seat and started to take off my boots, but a flash of metal, a color, caught my eye. Behind me, on the other side of the big culvert that formed a bridge over the creek, another pickup was partly off the road. For whatever reason—caved shoulder, slick clay mud, poor visibility—the rear end of the truck had skidded around and gone slightly over the hill. The angle was not steep, but the rear wheels had spun away their little bit of traction, and just barely touched the rocks.

As I approached, I could see through the water-blurred windows that someone was sitting inside. It was a man, I saw as I got closer still, and he was reading a newspaper. I tapped on the window and he jumped and tossed his paper onto the seat.

"*Ya te'eh,*" the man said as he rolled down his window, but he was no more Navajo than I was. His eyebrows were one long inter-connected bush of grey, and his jaw was grizzled and brown. He had on a beat up old cowboy hat, and a kitchen match drooped from the corner of his mouth.

"Need some help?" I asked, feeling odd about the question. After all, he was the one that was warm and dry. I was the one whose boots were still full of water.

"Why, hell yes I need help," he said. "But I wasn't about to go out walking in this shittin' rain to find it. Knew somebody'd come along sooner or later."

"Well, I'm already wet, so maybe I can just go ahead and give you a hand. Think I can pull you out?"

"That a four-wheel drive?"

"Yes."

"Well then," he said, opening his door and pulling his hat down over his eyes, "I think we're in business. I got a chain in the back."

My wheels dug four sizeable holes in the soft dirt road on my first try, and I could move his truck a little, but I couldn't get it out. I tried again, but this time I let my own back wheels slightly over the edge on the opposite side of the road, put rocks in front of my front wheels, and hooked my winch to his frame. Inch by inch, slowly and with the kind of groans that stressed metal makes, his pickup came up over the edge and out.

"Well, I owe you one," the other man said. "I was up checkin' my stock up on the flats, and I guess I just wasn't watchin' the goddamned road."

I told him that it was fine, that he could do the same for me some-day, that I always seemed to be needing help. I turned and started winding my winch cable in.

"Say," he said, turning back toward me. "You sleep in that thing?"

"Sometimes," I said. "Most times, just out on the ground."

"Thought so. On a night like this, you could do better in a motel room."

"Probably."

"Well," he said, "I own half interest in one in Bluff. The River Rapids. It ain't much, but I'd like to put you up for the night."

He pulled his billfold out of his rear pocket, and leaned inside the cab of his truck. I could see him writing.

"Here's a business card. Says one free night on the back. Just give it to 'em at the desk. I don't go around there much, but they still know who I am."

After he was gone and I had my own pickup on the road, I sat inside and took off my boots. And I looked at the card. On the back, in a barely decipherable scrawl, it did say "one free night," and carried a signature that looked like Shirley Duebue. On the front, it said River Rapids Motel, gave the address and the names of the proprietors: Shorty Durham and Madeline Wyszyanski.

Comb Ridge runs north and south, and you could climb over the steep red hogback in places. Even get a horse over it in other places, perhaps, if you were careful. But the smooth pillows of red sandstone that approach it from the west become, eventually, high, toothed cliffs, and if you're a Mormon wagon train, you stand no chance.

The San Juan River, coming out of the Colorado mountains of the same name, runs east and west in those parts. It's a wide river, and red/brown most of the time. It moves slowly, relentlessly, through the sagebrush country, and bends and clusters of cottonwood trees mark its route.

Comb Ridge and the San Juan River do battle at Bluff. The river wins. At Bluff, in the 1880s, the river let the tired Mormons through.

Like Madero, Bluff had withered with age. Some of the old stone houses had endured, and others were weeded-over piles of rock. If Bluff was bigger than Madero, it was only because it was flat, with more room to spread out away from the red buttes on the back edge of town. Like Madero, Bluff lived as best it could off the highway that cut the center of town.

There, off to the south between the highway and the river, crouched the River Rapids Motel. Brown, old, plain: one of those collections of boxes that sprung up out of the ground in the '50s, when Americans took to the highways and found they could sleep better if their cars were parked no more than fifty feet away. Cheap frame construction. A single string of small cubicles, all in a row. Metal doors. No pool.

Down the road a quarter mile was a brand new one. Multi-level. Bright colors. All the comforts. Brand name. It was easy to see where all the highway business had gone.

The young Navajo girl who checked me in kept her eyes down, focused on things behind the front desk, as though my face and my wet clothes were sights she was probably not supposed to see.

Only when I handed her the business card did she look up, and she did that only long enough to shrug, as though it didn't make a damned bit of difference to her if Shorty Durham was fool enough to give away lodging to the likes of me.

"Number five," she said, handing me a key and gesturing weakly off to her right.

Perhaps it was a boldness that came from being wet and dirty and parading ugly before the rest of the world, but as we turned away from each other, something inspired me to speak out, to waste no further time.

"Uh . . . is Mrs. Wyszyanski here? I mean, is she available?"

She looked at me without expression, studying me, and for a moment I thought perhaps I'd made no sense.

"The Lady?" It felt like a rhetorical question, one I didn't know I'd asked. "No," she said finally, "not tonight." She paused. "Unless it's something very important."

"No, not at all," I said. "When would she be around, you know, regularly?"

"Tomorrow. Most any time during the day."

I thanked her and pulled my pickup down to number five. Since mine was one of only two vehicles in the parking lot, I wondered why she hadn't given me one, or two, or three, or four. The unit on the far end appeared to be the only other one occupied.

———•———

Truck traffic seemed to pickup during the night. Maybe it had something to do with the oil fields just to the east. Maybe it was live-stock moving on and off the reservation across the river. Maybe it was only my imagination. But the roars and backfires and rattles seemed to never end, and a dozen times through the night I found myself staring at the little crack of light that came off the walkway and sneaked in under the bottom of my blind.

Come morning, I was groggy and still tired. I felt poorly prepared, as though I'd come to a test without ever opening the book. I was not ready for Madeline Wyszyanski.

Thinking that the young clerk might have mentioned my ques-tions to the woman, and that she might come bolting through the screen door as I walked by, demanding to know what in the hell I wanted, I detoured my way to breakfast. I walked around the far end of the motel building, past the two rooms marked 9A and 9B, back to the highway, and down the road to a little café. After breakfast, I walked back along the river, watching the slow-moving muddy wa-ter of the storied San Juan.

Do you just walk up and tip your hat and say I just stopped by to tell you how much I think you've screwed up my life? I walked through the rocks and sand, watching a pair of ducks master the current on the far side and glide into the peaceful water behind a half-sunk cottonwood log. And why would they even talk to me? If they wanted to confess, they could always find themselves a holy man.

Then there was this: I had to hate them. There was no choice. They'd tromped back and forth over my beginnings, the life that was handed down to me, and every time they'd left tracks and stains that wouldn't wear away and a rank smell that still seemed to cling to everything they'd ever touched. I knew them by their deeds, and that's the way it had to be.

But I needed them. Needed to find a way to wring their memories like an old dishrag, until the water of time and place and people ran out and I could bottle it up and carry it away.

So maybe I could play a coyote game. A game known only to me. Somehow, I'd pretend that those forty years had somehow eaten through some biological cord, and the Alphabet of today was different from the Alphabet of 1950. The sins of the young would, for the sake of this game, be temporarily forgiven of the old, and they'd be allowed to outgrow their own guilt.

I'd trick them, and hate them over my shoulder on my way out of their lives.

Looking neither right nor left, moving as smartly as if I didn't have a doubt or question in my mind, I walked into the office.

No one was behind the front desk. But after a couple of minutes had passed, the same young Navajo girl walked out from behind the curtain, from the office in the back.

"Can I help you?" she asked, with a raised sort of eyebrow and tone of voice that said I most certainly could not want a room at that hour of the day and must want something else.

I asked about the proprietor again.

"Doctor's appointment," she said simply. "Be here this afternoon."

I nodded and started to turn toward the door.

"I told The Lady you asked about her before," the girl said, "but then you didn't hang around. She wants to know if you're a cop, or a bill collector, or what."

"No, none of those," I said. "You could just tell her that I'm . . . well, tell her I'm a friend of an old friend."

She looked at me stoically.

"And I'll be back this afternoon."

She turned back toward the inner office.

The River Rapids didn't have a pool, but it did have a picnic table that sat out under an ancient spreading cottonwood, well in sight of the office. After I'd taken my lunch at the same café down the road, I sat there reading. I'd picked up a book on the cutting of the Mormon Hole-in-the-Rock Trail somewhere in my travels, and I was a little intrigued to be sitting almost precisely at one of the trail's key junctions while I read.

I heard the office screen door slam, not loudly, and looked up to see a woman walking toward me, walking with that labored gait of a person who spends no more time than necessary on her feet. Swaying, as though her knees ached.

The Lady. Madeline Wyszyanski. The first thing I noticed was her hair. A mass of bleached blond patches in a field of white, wild, that seemed to go in every direction at once. Underneath it, her face seemed as small as a doll's. A very wrinkled and tired doll, one that stays up too late and frowns a lot to keep the day at bay. Eyebrows drawn on, but eyes lost behind a puffy squint.

From the waist down, she was a slender woman, somewhat shapeless and hipless in the manner of people who have begun to age. Above the waist, she was bigger, top-heavy, stuffed into a blouse that had probably fit her once upon a time.

She waved a cigarette in her hand as she walked.

"Is there something I can do for you, mister?" she asked, her voice a little loud, a raspy growl that seemed to come naturally with the look. She stopped as soon as she could stand comfortably in the shade, turning slightly to look at me more out of the corners of her eyes. From that angle, I could see that her shirt gaped badly between button holes.

"Maybe," I said. "I didn't really want to bother you. I was mainly interested in finding Jozef Wyszyanski."

She didn't answer for a minute.

"I hope you didn't come a long ways, sonny," she said, then, "because it's going to be a pretty useless trip. Joe Wyszyanski has been dead for twenty years."

I was not surprised, and perhaps not even disappointed. A lot of time had passed. They could have both been dead, and I'd recognized that all along. So what now? It could be a long, long road that just petered out here in the rocks and sand. The end that wasn't an end, but just a slow fade to black.

Everything depended then on the woman, and what she knew.

"I'm sorry to hear that," I said, trying to sound truly sympathetic and friendly. I kept my voice low. "And I guess it could mean a lot of wasted time. I don't know. If you're interested in talking to me, well, maybe it will all work out."

She looked at me, squinting her eyes a little more, trying to see if she could figure me out.

"About what?"

"Well, first, let me tell you my name. It's Markus Cottin."

She would have said "so what?" if she'd known me better. I could see it in her eyes.

"I guess that doesn't ring any bells for you," I said. "But do you remember a man named Tom Cottin? Back in Madero?"

The Lady paused for a moment, and took a drag from her cigarette. Then she shook her head slowly from side to side.

"You got the wrong woman, mister," she said. "Tough luck. I don't remember much, and what I do remember sure as hell ain't anything I'm interested in tellin' to you."

Then she turned and started walking toward the motel office.

"Wait a minute," I said more loudly, to her back. "Shorty Durham said you'd talk to me." It was a lie, but worth a try.

She stopped, turned and stood there. I got up from the table and walked after her.

When I got close enough so that she didn't have to raise her voice, she said simply, "Piss on Shorty Durham."

Then she turned and resumed her walk back toward the office, back toward the sign that said River Rapids, and Vacancy.

3

I DROVE AROUND AWHILE, DOWN TOWARD MEXICAN HAT AND THE SPIRES of Monument Valley, then back again, over toward the settlements to the east, and then back another time. The solidness of the rock, and the sense that we, all of us, were just a passing fancy tolerated by the desert for its own amusement, settled me down.

Finally, I pulled up in front of the River Rapids and walked into the office, just as I'd done before. I rang the little bell and stood at the desk until The Lady came out from the back room.

I could see from the look in her squinted, puffy eyes that she was irritated and was about to tell me about that, but I didn't want her to set the tone.

"I'd like a room for the night, please," I said.

She pushed the registration card over the counter to me.

"I might even stay for a week. Maybe a month," I said as I started to write, making my marks deliberately quick and bold.

"Suit yourself," she said. "I don't mind the business. But let's get one thing clear. You're not buying time from me."

"Look," I said, my head still down, "everybody's dead. It makes no difference now. All I'm trying to do is find out what ever became of my grandfather." A small lie, maybe, but I couldn't say I wanted to know what had become of my father.

"Ask somebody else."

"Who?" I looked hard at her eyes.

"What the hell do you think I am? Your family album?"

"What will it take?" I handed her my credit card.

"More than you've got, sonny. More than you've got."

She finished with my credit card and handed it back. Then she handed me a key.

"Number four," she said.

"How about number nine?" I asked. "The one on the end?"

The Lady looked at me with an expression that was both puzzled and pained, the way a mother might look at a particularly difficult, if not stupid, child.

"No, sonny," she said. "That's where I sleep."

She turned and went into the back office, and I walked out.

———————

At five minutes after five, she walked past my room. I heard her steps on the board walkway, saw her shadow cross my window, and heard her steps grow more faint. Then the slamming of a door.

I waited for forty-five minutes, giving her some time, then walked down to number nine and knocked sharply.

When she opened the door, stale cigarette smoke boiled out, and maybe the smell of fried food. And of booze.

The eyes that looked out at me had already started to unfocus, and disappear.

"I knew it was you. Can't you take goddamned No for an answer?"

I just stood there. She opened the door wider and I could see that the tight blouse had been replaced by a white baggy tee shirt that said Madonna across the front. It was thin, and lace-like patterns showed through from under the first "a" and the second "n."

"No," she said. "Get it? N-O, no. Now get your ass out of here and leave me alone."

"I wish you'd . . ."

She didn't let me finish.

"I don't care what you wish, sonny." She was almost yelling at me. "You come in here trying to pry into my private affairs, trying to upset my life. Well, I only have one thing to say to you. Get the fuck out."

Maybe I was just tired: I hadn't slept that well the night before.

Maybe all the emotions that had surged and ebbed over the weeks had merely gone off to accumulate in some backwater pocket of my mind. Maybe I was still angry over the stories I'd heard. Something, whatever it was, caused me to break loose, and harshly.

"You sorry old bitch," I heard someone say, as though it wasn't really me. "You screw up other people's lives and whine about being left alone. Well, I'm not buying it."

She stepped back, and I stepped forward, still not knowing fully what I was up to, or capable of.

"If you'd shut your goddamned mouth for a minute and just listen, maybe you could do a little bit of good for once in your . . . your pathetic life."

She started to slam the heavy metal door in my face, and I responded by grabbing hold of the outside edge, stopping it before it closed. Then she must have thrown her entire body against the door, because it slammed shut. Or almost shut, but not quite. Because my hand was still wrapped around the outside edge.

Incredible pain shot up my arm and into my spine, and I must have screamed, for the door opened again. I dropped to my knees, and tried to squeeze the pain out of my mangled hand. I could see blood coming up through my fingers, dripping onto the floor. The world was swimming around me, and I could hardly see through the pain and tears that caught in my eyes. In the background, I could hear a voice, The Lady's voice, level and remarkably contained, talking on the telephone.

"Ruby? I think our only paying customer just broke his hand. You load him up and take him over to the clinic. I'll watch the desk until you get back."

It was dark by the time the straight-faced Navajo girl dropped me off in front of number four. A short cast held the two broken bones in my hand in place, and pills they'd given me had begun to separate me from the pain—as though only one of the several hands on the end of my arm was throbbing, and that wasn't so bad.

"I wouldn't mess with The Lady if I were you," she said, obviously a few hours late. "You're lucky she didn't pull a gun. It's happened before."

I mumbled a thanks and stumbled out of her car. I just wanted to rest, to lie down and let the medicine work. I took more of the pills and lay suspended, happy, floating over my bed, in and out of sleep. A couple of times, I could hear footsteps going to and fro, back and forth in front of number four.

——— · ———

The sun was shining when I woke up, and my hand throbbed. For a half-hour I just laid there, wondering what to do. My first instinct was to get my clothes on, leave the key, and get out of the motel and the town as soon as I could get behind the wheel of my truck. I needed to be somewhere else, but I didn't know where. I tried to label my feeling: embarrassment, shame, anger, resignation, confusion. It was all of those, I decided, plus perhaps a little fear.

I showered with my right hand held out to the side, away from the water, which brought on a nauseating wave of pain. I had to get out and sit on the toilet with my arm cradled across my chest, waiting for the throbbing to pass. Dressing with one hand took awhile, but I knew I'd get better at it soon, once my left hand learned and responded without being deliberately lifted and set in motion.

When I walked outside into the sunshine, she was sitting at the picnic table with a cup of coffee, smoking a cigarette and watching me. Somehow, I felt like a mouse who'd just looked up and seen an owl. Unconsciously, I stepped back.

She flipped her chin up, shortly and quickly, gesturing for me to come forward. I hesitated, then walked across the parking gravel, aware of each and every step I took.

"Sit down," she said, her expression blank, "before you fall down."

I did.

"How's the hand?"

I said it wasn't as bad as I'd expected it to be.

"You had it coming," she said. "But I'm sorry, anyway. Bad for business, roughin' up the paying customers."

I said I was checking out.

"Suit yourself," she said. "You're a threat to the peace and quiet around here, anyway."

I said nothing, and just sat looking down at the bright whiteness of the cast on my hand, at my battered fingers sticking out.

"But as far as your old grandfather is concerned," she said after awhile, "I had nothing to do with that. Nothing. My old man, maybe, but me, not a thing."

After what we'd already gone through, I was startled to hear her bring up the subject without cajoling from me.

"Why don't you just tell me?" I asked. "It might save me a lot of pain. And make me go away."

"Why? Why should I dig back though that old crap that I've forgotten on purpose, just for you? It's just not worth it to me."

"What do you want?"

"Like I said before. More than you've got."

"Try me."

The Lady sipped a little coffee, smoked a little, and watched traffic passing by on the highway.

"You know what I really want, sonny? I mean what I really want?" Her voice softened a little.

I just waited for her to go on.

"I don't know why I'm telling you this, but I'll tell you anyway. I just want to sell this goddamned rat-hole of a motel, get enough money to go back to East St. Louis, someplace with green grass, before I die out here in the sheep shit and the sagebrush. You do that for me, and I'll tell you any shit-assin' thing you want to know."

I still didn't say anything.

"Five years ago, I could have sold this place a dozen times over. Now . . ." She looked down the road to the sign that said Pool. Satellite TV. FAX. "Now I couldn't even give it away."

"You're right on one count," I said. "You want more than I've got."

"See? You want the goods, but you ain't got the price. You ain't no better than some of the winos I know."

"I don't know where you think the trouble is going to come from. You left the sheriff behind forty years ago, if that's what you're worried about. Like I said before, everybody's dead. Long gone. Nobody cares about any of this except me."

She was thinking.

"Besides," I added, looking down at my cast, "this may all turn out to be about as useless as a dog chasing its tail. I scream at you, you bust my hand, and you might not be able to help me anyway. Remember, I came here looking for Jozef Wyszyanski, not you."

"True enough," she said. "But he ain't here. And I am."

"But what do you know?" I let a little note of skepticism creep in.

"I'm not sure what I know, but know enough to keep my mouth shut."

"Just answer an easy question for me. One question."

"Which is?"

"How did you get here?"

She looked at me a long time through her squinted eyes.

"Goddamn you," she finally said, shaking her head slowly back and forth.

Before her name was Madeline Swain, it had been Madeline Conklin—that was the name the orphanage in East St. Louis had given her—and Madeline Conklin had a seared soul. Because down in there, the orphan's fire burned hot: she wanted more and she wanted out and she wanted to get even. She hated blacks and she hated poor people, and she hated East St. Louis because it had too much of both. So when Harold Swain, the railroad man, offered her a ticket to move on down the tracks, she didn't hesitate for a moment. She married him the same week he asked. It didn't have to last, not any longer than it took her to find another ticket that would take her further down the line. Life ahead looked to her like one whistle-stop after another, and she just wanted to make sure they led away. And weren't too far apart.

By the time she and the railroad man reached Madero, she was still young, not yet even twenty, and still reaching out, grasping. If a gathering or a movement or a man promised something she thought she ought to have, she'd give it a try, at least mess with it. She talked her way into the Helado Art and Garden Society, not because she knew anything about painting or gardening—she didn't—but because the women there seemed to have better dreams, and better chances of getting there. They seemed to lack that sense of being chased, one which she could never quite shake.

She even tried being a Republican, because she suspected that money was hidden in there somewhere. But that didn't work. When people asked her why she liked Dewey, she didn't know. And she wasn't geared right for tacking up political posters.

The thing she did best, she did nearly alone. Just the right lift to slightly-large breasts, just the right stretch of denim across a tight butt, and she found tools that matched her lack of regret and her way of stepping up and taking. Doors swung quietly open. With the railroad man out on the job much of the week, she had space and she had time, and she used both deliberately. The young miners were sport, mostly; the middle-aged merchants and banker-types, mostly investments. She worked quietly, after the public eye had closed for the night.

Her involvement with Jozef Wyszyanski had not been an accident.

Alphabet rented a couple of rooms in the back of the house next to the one occupied by the Swains, and she watched him. Watched the arrogance with which he operated. Watched his swagger and indifference. And she liked that. If he wasn't going places, he was making good use of where he was.

So every month or so, when the mood struck her, she would turn a lamp on in her bedroom and undress, strip herself naked, without pulling the curtains. And she'd dance. She never knew for sure whether Alphabet was there, perhaps standing in his bedroom in the dark, but on some nights she could sense a presence across the way. And she was almost certain that she could feel the heat of his eyes.

One night, Madeline Swain found out. It was after midnight, and she and a young miner were hooked up inside the mechanics' shop, their clothes off, on a couch of sorts made from an old truck seat, when Alphabet flipped on the light. The room seemed to explode, and there he stood. The young man scrambled, grabbing his clothes and trying to dress, and he hardly heard Alphabet telling him to draw his pay the next morning and catch the train out of town.

Madeline Swain just sat there, her arms across her chest and a defiant look in her eye, and waited. Alphabet loomed in front of her, and he told her things about the colors of her underwear, about the things she did with her body, about how she danced. She knew indeed that he had, at least once, been there in the dark.

Then he began to unbutton his pants, and he pushed her back, and he jammed himself into her with such strength and ferocity that her hip joints and knees hurt for several days.

———·•·———

She could overlook a meanness that seemed to run through his entire soul. She understood meanness, especially meanness born out of need, out of ambition, and it didn't bother her much at all. And the more he came to represent the mining company, the more she heard his name cursed in the streets, the more she felt the heat and the stirring, and the more she lured him on. She didn't care that they hated him, so long as they hated him for his strength.

She still found and used other men. He didn't care. And Madeline Swain was quite certain that Alphabet had other women. They both knew that sex, even though at times it felt so good, was a tool with many and varied uses, and neither wanted to stifle the other's opportunities to jab and lift and cut with that tool. So they stuck to their routine: she gave him window shows, and he found her when he was ready, when he decided that it was time for her to make good on her vulgar promises.

Still, she looked forward to the day when he'd leave Madero, when he'd have something different to offer, and she'd be able to attach herself to him, finally, or decide to cut him loose. She didn't know which it would be, but when the day came and he told her he was leaving for the San Juan River, she told him good-bye. She'd stay. If the choice had to be between Madero and Indians and sagebrush, she'd wait and hope. There was time, and there would be other men.

But she had been wrong. There was no time. Two days later, Swain the railroad man told her that the trains running through Madero were pulling empty cars, and service would be shut down by the end of the year. Before that happened, before they cut him off without a dime, he intended to take her and go back to the Illinois Southern, back home. In just a week or two. To Madeline Swain, that meant East St. Louis, and three nights later she left town with Alphabet, bound for the San Juan River.

Where had all her choices gone?

———————

Madeline Wyszyanski went inside for more coffee, and I wasn't certain she'd come back. But after a time she did, and brought me a cup as well.

"Big mistake, I guess," she said after she'd settled in again. "Hell, I don't know. You always think there's time, and then you look around, and it's time to get a new calendar."

She stared out toward the horizon, unfocused, the way people do when they start looking back.

"We hadn't been at that mine on the border more than about six months when Joe woke up and finally admitted to himself that it wasn't no goddamned mine at all. Just a petered-out old copper hole that barely paid enough to stay open. That's all he was doin', he finally admitted, just keepin' it open."

I listened, and tried to encourage her with small smiles.

"Cable Minerals didn't give a shit about that copper mine, he said. All they'd been tryin' to do was get him out of Madero and keep his mouth shut."

"About what?"

"Sonny, here's where our little one-question deal comes to an end. It ain't doin' me a damned bit of good, tellin' you my little stories. And with my luck, they'll just come back and bite me in the ass."

"But nobody cares, like I said. Tom Cottin and his wife are both dead. So's Alphabet. Even the town is dead, for chrissakes."

She thought about it for a minute or two, then went on as though she wasn't finished after all. The dead, I thought, keep going back and summoning the dead.

"So he raised some kind of hell. I don't know who he threatened, or what with, but he had his ways. He was just mean enough, and maybe crazy enough, and nobody wanted to find out the hard way just how deep that went. So, six months or so later, they moved us on. Over to Page, I think it was. Just another goddamned mine."

She stopped to light a cigarette and watch the smoke drift away on the slight wind.

"Me, I'd had enough of that shit by then. Rundown shacks. Pisshole little towns, if there was any at all. I could walk as far as I wanted in any direction, through the sand and rocks and brush, and where would I be? Nowhere. And if I had tried to leave, he would have probably just blacked my eyes anyway. And what would I do then? I didn't have a goddamned clue. So I stuck it out. Stuck it out with Joe Wyszyanski."

I wanted to ask her about marrying him, but she was talking, and I didn't want to give her a chance to stop.

"I cooked in some of them boarding houses. Waited tables some places. And we saved a dollar here and a dollar there. In the back of my mind, I think I always thought I was gonna clean it out some night, take it all and run like hell and never look back. But I never did."

She stopped, looking back.

"And I don't know why. I just don't know why."

Then she waved her hand, painting the front of her motel with one broad stroke.

"No," she said. "I let him talk me into buyin' this shit hole instead. Aw, it was all right then. Decent house, back there by the river. Until the Navvies burned it down."

"What do you mean? Burned it down?"

"Yeah, this hell hole was gonna be our retirement," she went on, ignoring my question. "An easy way to make a buck, someday. In the meantime, we took Shorty Durham in as a partner so he could run it, and we kept on chasin' them mines."

She went on about the ups and the downs, about the Globes and the Silver Citys, about the dreams that were always about to happen, but never quite came together. Then she stopped and just sat there, looking toward the buttes above town, but not seeing them.

"Then Joe had a stretch of bad luck. Dynamite blasts in a couple of the mills where he worked shut 'em down for quite awhile. Some kook with a hard-on for the company, he said. Anyway, he was out of work for two, three months at a time. Then he hurt his back, and was laid up for another couple a months. After that, he seemed to just kinda run outta gas. So we just said to hell with it, we put in enough goddamned time in these black holes. So we came back here."

Dynamite blasts in a couple of mills. I could almost hear the explosions. Smell the powder smoke. And see the man the deputies would be hauling away. It would be in the papers.

"Maybe we shoulda just stayed out there, though. Right on till the end. Things never worked out too good for Joe, here." She paused again, like she was looking her words over. "Maybe he had too much time on his hands. And too many Navvies around here to worry about. He got it in his head that they were out to get him. Maybe he was right. I don't know. He believed it for damned sure when they burned the house down."

Somehow a bunch of Navajo "bucks", as she called them, had got their hands on a couple of bottles of cheap whiskey. When they'd gotten too drunk to walk and too cold to lay around on the ground, they'd wandered around the end of the motel and broken into the last room. Then they'd started smashing up the furniture in the room, maybe to build a fire. Alphabet heard the noise, and he knew what was going on, so he went and threw them out. The next thing they knew, she said, the house was on fire.

I didn't have anything to say, so I just watched her as she lit another cigarette.

"Were they out to get him? Hell, I don't know. Maybe so. Maybe they got him. All I know is that about six months later, he disappeared."

It was a Saturday morning, she said, and hot. In the middle of August. The desert was fried dead in its own heat, and the highway laid out there through the rocks with no traffic at all. They hadn't had a paying customer in something like two weeks, and money was running low. Alphabet had paced the floor for several days, and they'd fought about everything in life that had never gone quite right.

Finally, he'd said that he was going to find work somewhere. That he was going to hire out on a labor job somewhere. Make a few bucks. Get the hell out of there before he went stir crazy. He'd put a few clothes in a bag, and said he'd call in a day or two. But she never heard from him again.

In May, a Navajo sheepherder found his jeep in the bottom of a gulch down around Copper Canyon. It was burned out, but there was no sign of a body. No way of knowing what had gone on.

———·+·———

"Guess it was gonna come to that," she concluded, "sooner or later. They hated his guts, and he knew it. And he just took it and threw it back at them."

"Who did it? Somebody who'd worked for him?"

"Maybe," she said, slowly. As though the thought had never come to her. "But who knows? Once they get down here on the reservation, they all look and act alike. They're lazy and they steal and they run in packs. But the one thing they don't do is talk. So nobody knows."

I thought of the stone-faced desk clerk.

"But you still hire them."

"Do I have some kinda choice? See any whites walkin' around here that will work for three bucks an hour? I have to watch 'em, though, or they'll steal me blind."

That didn't sound right to me. To me, Ruby the desk clerk had tried to cover up for The Lady. Showed her some respect. Loyalty. But I didn't push it. I wanted to get back to something else.

"You said Cable Minerals wanted to keep Alphabet's mouth shut." It was worth a try.

A hard set of lines wrinkled across her forehead.

"Don't keep pushin' that line," she said, chopping off the ends of her words. "Like I told you, that's where the story stops. I can't remember anymore. Try askin' somebody else."

"But dammit, lady, don't you understand?" I was getting a little tired, too, and starting to sound like it. "There isn't anybody else."

She said nothing.

"If it was your family, wouldn't you want to know?"

She gave me a hard, stony stare.

"That family shit don't cut much cake with me, sonny. The only family I got is under a rock around here someplace. Or down in a hole. We don't get together much anymore."

She'd beaten me. There was little more I could say, and little more I could ask. So I just sat there, staring at the highway, watching a truck driver hop down from his cab and check his tires out.

The Lady stood up, picked up her cigarettes, lighter and both cups, and started to walk away. Then she stopped and looked back.

"No more stories," she said.

"I'll be here," I replied. "I'll get a room for the night."

"It don't matter. It don't matter at all any more," she said, and walked away.

I thought about going out and buying a bottle of gin or vodka or whatever she drank, even if I had to drive all the way to the next town to get it, and getting her dead-ass drunk. But what good would that do? She might talk, all right. In fact, she might talk all night long. But how could I trust what she had to say? And if I was drinking right along with her, which was usually the way those things went, how could I trust anything I heard? Or remembered?

Besides, she seemed at times to be trying to hold on to that woman-ness thing. What if that got loose, and she couldn't be who she was? How would that work, when I hid my eyes? What kind of damage would that do to her ability to talk to me, to ever look me in the face again?

I walked up to the office, thinking I could at least get some ice and have a stiff drink of my own. The expressionless Navajo girl was behind the counter.

She asked about my hand, and I told her, and thanked her again for seeing me through the trip to the clinic.

"She tell you about how the Navajos murdered her old man?" she asked, surprising me.

"Yes, she told me."

"It's all bullshit."

I waited.

"No Navajo killed her old man."

"How about the house? Did it catch on fire?"

"Maybe."

"How did that happen?"

She shrugged.

"I don't know. But you can bet it was plenty well-insured."

----·----

Memory. I thought about it that night as I sat outside in the early evening, sipping my brandy. No matter how carefully we line it up and fasten it into place, it still slips a degree or two off. Not that I'd found so many inconsistencies. I hadn't. But it was getting easier to see little distortions in those mirrors that reflected back. So when was the truth not exactly the truth?

Then I thought of something Billy Yazzie had said: there will be many versions of the same story and all of them are true. How can that be? How do you arrive at the real truth? There is no such thing, he had said. The truth is merely what you choose to believe.

And me, I had something new to believe. Something that told me the two dynamite blasts that had put Alphabet out of work would coincide exactly with the two that had sent my father to jail. I didn't have to check places and dates. I didn't have to prove the obvious.

----·----

I waited, clinking the ice in my glass, thinking she might come out, but she never did. And as darkness crept in, I could feel the energy slipping out of me, as though I'd just sprung a vital leak, and I went inside for the night. A light was still on in her room.

4

THE PAINKILLERS AND BRANDY COMBINED TO DROP ME INTO A HEAVY SLEEP, one that was thick, like fog, with no hard edges and no sound. It was the sleep of the near-dead.

So I had a hard time fighting my way out of it when she started pounding on my door.

I heard it first as some far off noise, maybe the backfiring of trucks in my dreams, or the sound of distant dynamite, but it kept coming closer to me, until I realized someone was beating on the metal only yards away from my head.

I turned on the light and looked at my watch. It was ten fifty. I'd been asleep about an hour.

When I pulled my pants on and opened up, she was standing there, holding a drink in one hand, and a bottle of vodka in the other. Her eyes were streaked with red and shining, as though she'd been crying, and her hair was matted and pushed down in spots. She had her Madonna tee shirt on again, but now the front of it sagged and swung when she moved.

"It's the shits," she said abruptly, pushing her way through the door, "the way I've let you get to me. Life was not so fucking good before, but it's worse now. I want you out of here."

Her voice was a little raspier than before, but not slurred.

"Right now?" I asked, trying to wake up as far as possible as fast as possible. I pulled a sweatshirt on over my head.

"Tomorrow. In the morning. Just hit the road."

I held out my hands. I'll surrender, I'll go, they said.

"But I figure you're just gonna keep on until you squeeze

somethin' out of me. You may go, but you'll just keep comin' back, lurkin' around here like a goddamned vulture."

I thought I could see where she was headed, and I liked it. So I just nodded my head in agreement.

"Got a glass?" she asked.

I picked mine up off the table and held it out. She slopped it about half full.

"Here, drink this. I prefer to drink alone. It's cheaper. But then I get suspicious of sober people."

I checked my ice bucket in the sink. There were still a few pieces left. And I added a little water. A foul drink, but what choice did I have?

She took the only chair in the room, so I sat on the bed.

"Ask," she said.

"Excuse me?"

"I said fucking ask. Get this over with, so I can get some sleep."

I had to pause for a minute, trying to shake the fog out of my head, trying to decide what should come first, and where the curves might be too sharp for her to handle.

"Okay," I said finally. "Do you know anything about the store cheating the Navajos?"

She let her eyes widen, not directed at anything, vacant, and the trip back, into time, took some time.

"Alphabet liked to brag," she said finally, talking almost to herself. "Sometimes he'd get drunk and hunt me up in the night, and we'd do it until he'd worn himself out, and then he'd just lay there and talk, babbling."

She took a drink.

"That's the only way I know anything at all. It was from the braggin' he'd do after his ashes got hauled."

———————

Alphabet showed up at the store just at closing time one day early in the fall, not long after the company had made Tom Cottin their buffer against the Navajos. Cottin could see that the company man had something on his mind, but he didn't ask. He just went about his usual closing routine of totalling the day's business and putting money and receipts away. No one else was in the store, except for young Andrew, who was stocking shelves, a chore he took on from time to time when he wanted to make an extra dollar or two.

Alphabet was still there, leaning on the display case full of cheap watches and jewelry when Tom Cottin came back down from the office upstairs.

"Cottin," he began. "We've got kind of a serious problem, and we need you to help us fix it."

The storekeeper waited.

"We never counted on them Navajos going back to the reservation."

"What do you mean?"

"We never figured on them making a little bit of money then high-tailing it back down south to live off of it."

"There are plenty more where those came from, they say."

"That's not the point," Alphabet said, putting his hands in his back pockets and beginning to pace. "We put a bunch of time and money into training these Indians, and then they take off. We can't have it."

The storekeeper wasn't sure where this conversation was headed, but it made him uneasy anyway. His new responsibility for dealing with the Navajos had already become a headache. He'd had to have one thrown in jail for getting drunk and beating the windows out of the firehouse, trying to get in and turn on a siren.

"It's a goddamned joke. The more important the job, the more we train them. The more we train them, the more important they are to us. The more important they are, the better we pay them. And the better we pay them, the sooner they haul ass back to their squaws or the reservation or whatever the hell it is."

"I heard some good ones had quit."

"Last week we lost our best hoist operator. The week before, our best motor man."

"I've got to put some meat back in the locker," Tom Cottin said, and started walking toward the back of the store. He could hear the other man following along behind him. While he cleaned out the meat display case, Alphabet just stood and watched, as though he wanted the storekeeper's absolute attention.

"Now listen to me, Cottin," he said as the younger man was wiping his hands. "We've got the solution to this."

His voice had dropped, both in tone and in volume.

"But it all depends on you."

Cottin didn't like the sound of it.

"You've got to see to it that they don't get that money saved up. That they spend what they make."

He could see it coming. He could see now what must have been on their minds all along when they gave him the task of dealing with the Navajos. If the Indians are going to have somebody to focus their anger on, we'll toss the guy at the store out to them. Let them chew on his hide.

"What do you want me to do? Start charging them rent, like you said before?" He hoped that was it, but the pain in his belly told him that it wasn't.

"It's not that simple. We thought about it, but we figure they'll just camp along the river, like some of them did at first."

Cottin threw down his rag and started walking toward the front of the store.

"I don't like the sound of this," he said back over his shoulder.

Alphabet caught up with him, grabbed him by the shoulder, and spun him around.

"I don't give a shit whether you like the sound of it or not. I don't want your opinions. You're going to do it, or you're going to head down the road yourself."

They stood there, staring into each other's eyes, an invisible beam of anger connecting the two.

"Goddamn it, what do you want?"

"Look, Cottin, I'm not here to help you do your goddamned job. All I'm telling you is this. You make damned sure that when these Navajos get whatever money is left over after their store charges, there's not enough to let them get out of Madero."

Cottin let time pass, let the air fill up with his anger, let the store fill with the tension that was growing between the two men.

"You're telling me to cheat them."

"I'm not telling you any such thing. I'm telling you what we want to accomplish. You can raise prices. You can do whatever you want. Just don't lay it on the whites. We got problems enough with them and their wages as it is. We can't lose all of them, too."

Cottin walked angrily to the front of the store, went behind the main counter, and pulled out a small box with alphabetized tabs and copies of charge receipts. He grabbed a handful and flung them out on the counter top.

"Here, you bastard," he said, his voice loud, echoing through the building. "Let's practice a little. You show me just what I'm going to do."

Alphabet picked up one receipt. The named printed on top was Billy Yazzie. The receipt was for one sack of beans.

"Good example," Alphabet said evenly, his voice cool and under control. "Here's a man we can't lose."

He took a pencil out of his shirt pocket.

"It's easy," he said, marking the receipt. "Just change this here one to a four. Even your kid there . . ." and he jerked his head off toward where Andrew was shoving cans back onto the shelves, not looking up. " . . . could handle a simple little chore like that. Maybe we oughtta just hire him."

Tom Cottin walked the streets of Madero that night, well after dark. He'd finished his dinner, put on a jacket, and walked all the streets of the town, end to end. He'd wished they were longer, and that there were more of them.

He had to quit the store and move on, he told himself. He had to get out before things turned worse. This scheme couldn't last. But where would he go? What would he do? School had already started for the year, and he couldn't just pull the boy out.

He reached the bridge on the north edge of town, and stood looking down, barely seeing reflections off the water. He began feeling dizzy, and he clutched the steel railing of the bridge. For a moment, he couldn't remember where he was, or what he was doing. He thought about his childhood, and about a couple of kids he'd once known in school. One was a bully, an ugly and mean boy, and Tom Cottin wondered whose boss that boy had turned out to be. The other was a young girl, a pretty girl, who had moved away. He wondered where she'd gone.

Then his mind was pounding and rolling and tumbling with dozens of thoughts, all confused, all balled up together. His legs turned to rubber under him, and he fell to his knees. He couldn't breathe.

When his mind cleared, he was sitting in the dirt at the end of the bridge, still holding on to the steel, and his hands were nearly frozen. What part of this is a dream, he wondered. When will I wake up and be younger, and it will be summertime again? Summertime in Nevada?

As he walked toward home, he realized that tears were coming from his eyes, flowing in deep streams down his cheeks. Strange, he thought, looking at himself dispassionately, curiously, from a great distance out in space. I don't cry.

———·———

The next morning, he asked Alphabet to give him some time, to let him try to come up with some other way of handling the Indian

problem. Alphabet told him to get back to the store, to do as he was
told, or to start packing.

———————

That afternoon, an older woman named Mary Bluerock came into
Cable Mercantile. She spoke no English, and tended to go about her
store business slowly and silently.

She came to the front counter with an armload, and Tom Cottin
began to write it up, keeping his eyes down, glad that she was not
one of his customers who liked to laugh and try to make small talk.

Two pounds of bacon. One package of cookies. One box of salt.
One package of needles. Two cans of tomatoes. Four bars of soap.
Four pounds of potatoes.

She made her X, and after she'd gone out through the door, Tom
Cottin changed the one box of salt to two, and the price of the needles
from forty-nine cents to a dollar forty-nine. But his hand was shaking so badly that he couldn't make the changes cleanly, and his de-
ceit was obvious. He wadded up the ticket, threw it away, and made
a new one, this time showing two boxes of salt and needles at a dollar forty-nine. Her X was easy to duplicate. Then he went into the
bathroom at the back of the store and threw up.

5

"You got any cigarettes?"

I noticed that Madeline Wyszyanski's withered old hands were shaking, fluttering like big ugly butterflies.

"No, I'm sorry," I said. "Don't use them."

"I'll be back, then," she said, and went out the door in a rush, with just a little fumbling of the knob.

Her drink was about half gone, and I thought about sweetening it up a little. But again, I wasn't sure that this kind of truth serum was the best idea. If she passed out, or told me stories that came more out of delirium than history, I would have lost the best, and perhaps only, opportunity to pry open this critical lid. There would not be another night. I was certain of that.

I was still thinking about her drink when she came back in a cloud of smoke, carrying a glass full of ice. I was relieved to see that she'd put a sweater on over her Madonna shirt.

She must have followed my eyes, or caught some little sigh.

"My tits were cold," she said simply. "They were hot items once, but tonight they're just cold."

Then she laughed, a raspy cough that sounded to me like a combination of humor and bitterness. Her puffed-up eyes suggested both. She filled her own glass to the rim, and drank it down a half an inch.

"Alphabet was pretty damned proud of that plan," she went on, easily picking up where she'd left off. That raised my confidence.

"He'd laugh when he told me how he did it, how he trapped them with the store. You ever hear that song by Tennessee Ernie Ford? I owe my soul to the company store?"

"'Sixteen Tons'," I said. "I've heard it."

"Every time I hear it, I think about that. The Pollock and his trick store. And I see him layin' there, in my bed, playin' with himself and patting himself on the back, all at the same time."

It didn't make a pretty picture in my mind.

Then she tried to sing, but there was no tune. Only a howl sort of. For a second, I thought she was trying to make me laugh. But I knew better than that.

"I ooh-ooh my-ah so-oo-oo-ol to the company store."

When I didn't clap, she just sat there, sad-faced, shoulders slumping, staring down into her glass. Thinking about the song, perhaps.

"Of course, once that Navajo got shot right between the eyes, he didn't know a damned thing about it." She came back to the story, abruptly. "I mean, that's what he'd tell people. Couldn't figure out why that bastard the storekeeper would do such a thing. Must have a lot of money stashed away someplace, he'd tell people on the street."

She shook her head, and absent-mindedly ran her hand through her hair, messing it up even more.

"Yeah, he could be a mean, deceitful son of a bitch," she said woefully. "And people were afraid of him. That's why I liked to bait him and catch him. I liked to think that I had somethin' over on the whole damned town. I was screwin' the guy who was screwin' them."

It was a small victory, I thought, but who was I to say? "Could a got his ass hung, I guess. Maybe I would have been better off if he had. I'd a caught some other train to some other place."

"Why didn't he?"

"Didn't he what?"

"Get his ass hung. The town was small. People knew things. He couldn't have been fooling everybody."

"'Cause he was Alphabet, I guess." She took another long, hard drink. "Besides, it was just a wooden little Indian they shot. It wasn't like it was a serious crime or anything."

I couldn't tell whether she was being serious or sarcastic, but I had a sad feeling that she meant it just as it had come out of her mouth.

"But for another thing, you fuck with the bull, you get the horn."

———••———

Byron Teller, the district attorney, went to Madero to probe, to lay his ear down on the chest of the community, trying to weigh the odds for or against finding an impartial jury of Tom Cottin's peers. As a convenience, he'd planned to ride along with a deputy sheriff returning Tom Cottin to Madero, and to make certain that Cable Minerals understood the need to keep an eye on the man, if they hoped to reclaim the two thousand dollars they'd posted as bail. It wasn't the sort of errand he normally did, but it would cause no harm.

Besides, he thought, it would give him a chance to see Tom Cottin's behavior firsthand. According to the jail clerks, the storekeeper had acted the part of the low-key madman since he'd been behind bars: crying at times, sullen and silent at others, pacing and talking to himself. Other prisoners had complained about the noise he made at night.

However, when Teller and the deputy sheriff had arrived at the jail, Tom Cottin had refused to leave, holding onto the bars like a condemned man facing the final parade. He wouldn't go anywhere, he said. Too many people wanted him out of the way.

Nothing they could do would change his mind, and his fear—a very real fear that caused his wide-open eyes to dart from side to side— left Teller little choice. He dismissed the deputy sheriff and drove on to Madero alone, wishing he could figure out what Tom Cottin saw in the dark.

When the district attorney arrived at the Cable Minerals offices, J.J. Abrahams, the general manager, was there to greet him, to offer him a drink, to offer whatever help the company might provide. He took the news about Tom Cottin's refusal to leave the jail, and the bail money that would be returned, almost without comment, registering little surprise.

"Who knows what in the sam hell is going on in that guy's mind," was all he said.

Then he insisted that Teller take time for a little tour. The district attorney didn't like Abrahams' invitation to "go look around," and he said so, wanting to stay at arm's length, and wanting to get on with his work. But Abrahams was insistent, more than that, and twice he pointed out that the company was not a party in this particular matter, only trying to help.

After they'd driven past several of the bigger tunnels, Abrahams pulled up next to the door of the Demon Creek mill, and suggested they look inside.

Teller was startled by the noise of the place: rod and ball mills thundering and banging, machines throbbing, rock rattling as it fell from conveyor belts, water hissing and bubbling in a variety of tanks, voices shouting to be heard. It reminded him of movies he'd seen about steel mills, or some patriotic film clips made during the war, showing ship yards.

Their walk was more of a climb, up several flights of metal stairs to the mill foreman's office, high above the chaos of sounds and motions. As the metal door slammed closed, the world became instantly quiet, and Teller was startled at the volume of his own voice.

"It's sure as hell noisy enough out there," he said simply.

Abrahams motioned toward a chair and Teller, who was not a small man and thus a little winded, was glad to sit. Abrahams took a seat on the edge of a desk. He said nothing.

"Okay, J.J.," Teller said, not willing to let the silence hang there. "What the hell is on your mind?"

"Metals prices are on my mind, Byron," the smooth-jawed company man said after a moment. "Paying all those men down there, that's on my mind, too. And trying to keep the railroad running. I guess you might just say that I'm a worrier, Byron."

No answer.

"And sometimes when I'm worried, I have to look for ways to get those problems off my mind. Sometimes I tell myself stories. You like stories, Byron?"

"No, goddammit, J.J., I don't like stories," Teller said. "And I don't like wasting time either. I've got work to do, and I've got to get back down that canyon tonight. I suggest we get on back to town."

Abrahams got to his feet and walked over to the window, and he stood looking down on the little men running around below, saying nothing for a couple of minutes. Then he turned back toward Teller, and began to talk to him in a voice that was quiet, yet loud enough to be heard, and the words came out slowly.

"You know, Byron," he began, "I was going to tell you a little story. One about a small-time crook. Let's make him a store clerk. What do you think of that, Byron? And I was going to tell you that our clerk got caught with his hand in the till. And, instead of just taking his medicine like he should, our little crook did what little crooks usually do. He tried to blame somebody else. In fact, he caused so much trouble that the biggest employer in the county had to close down. Jobs were gone. Wages stopped. Children starved."

Abrahams stopped and turned back around toward Teller.

"And I was going to tell you about the story's happy ending. But I can see that you're not in the mood for stories, Byron. So I won't bother."

"Your story is bullshit, J.J. Why don't you make one up about killing a Navajo, instead?" Anger was creeping into the district attorney's voice.

"No, no more stories, Byron," Abrahams said in voice that was a little less calm, a little less smooth. "I'll just get to the moral, instead. It goes something like this. A district attorney who wants to stay in office finds a way to drop cases that do more harm than good."

"Don't threaten me, J.J. I'll have your ass."

"Let me try it another way. A district attorney who wants to avail himself of several thousands of dollars in campaign money, or maybe just expense money, finds a way to admit that he has no case when he has no gun, no witnesses, and no real harm done."

Teller stood and walked to the door. With his hand on the knob, he turned and spoke.

"Get me back to town, J.J. One more line of bullshit out of your mouth and I'll have you in a cell with your so-called little crook."

———•—•———

The ride back into Madero went without a word from either man. However, as Teller was opening his door to get out, Abrahams addressed him in that same quiet, controlled voice.

"Are you thinking my offer over, Byron?"

"That wasn't an offer, Mr. Abrahams. That was a threat."

"No, it was just an offer of help. And I'd think of it strictly in those terms if I were you."

———•—•———

Darkness had already settled into the Helado Canyon when the district attorney left Madero and headed back down toward Three Rivers. The moon was nearly full, and Teller could easily see the river glinting off to his right, then his left, then his right again. He was no more than four or five miles out of town when he noticed a set of headlights back in the cloud of dust that boiled up behind his car.

The headlights made him uneasy, so he slowed and pulled over onto the shoulder to let the other vehicle pass. But the other vehicle slowed, too, and pulled off onto the shoulder fifty yards behind him. Then its lights went out.

Teller pulled back onto the road and drove away, going considerably faster than he normally drove in the gravel and dirt. The other headlights came back on, and in just a couple of minutes the vehicle was on his tail again, keeping the same distance, no matter how fast or slowly he drove.

Sixteen miles below Madero, Teller rounded a sharp turn in the road, pulled off suddenly next to a set of loading pens, and cut his lights. As the trailing vehicle, a pickup, went by, the moonlight played off a distinctive color: Cable Minerals particular shade of orange-yellow. The pickup stopped a quarter-mile down the road, turned around, and came back. It slowed almost to a stop when its headlights washed over Teller's car, but then moved on back up the canyon. At the curve, the pickup turned around again, and its lights went out.

Teller pulled back on the road, driving at his normal speed, and the other vehicle followed. And it was still there behind him when he approached the outskirts of Three Rivers. Only when Teller reached the bright lights on Main Street did the other vehicle turn around and head back, presumably, toward Madero.

Three days later, Teller received a two thousand dollar check in the mail. The check was made out to him personally, and came from Cable Minerals. A note, written on Abrahams' personal letterhead, said, "Campaign donation, or to be used as needed for any expenses."

He held the top center of the check between his thumbs and forefingers, poised to rip it into shreds. They can't compromise me like this, he thought angrily. They can't play these games of push-and-shove. But then he stopped. He would always have that option, the option of throwing it back in their faces. Besides, he might want the check for evidence.

For now, he could sleep on it. He could dream about his chances in the next election. He could worry about the fact that he was fifty-six years old, and not well-off. He could wonder about being followed, and wonder why. No, perhaps he wouldn't be able to sleep on it at all.

Then he rose from his desk, walked over to his shelf of books, and put the check in his antique volume of old water law. He slid the dusty book back into its dusty place, and left the office for the rest of the day.

———•———

Madeline Swain danced that night. Taking off her clothes piece by piece, she swayed easily back and forth in the half-light of the lamp. She hummed to herself, the tune to Eddy Arnold's latest song, as she stripped. Lifted her breasts with her hands. Ran her palms up the insides of her legs.

Are you out there, Alphabet? I'll bet you are. I'll bet you're watching me right now. I saw your truck parked out there. You're watching me, aren't you?

Her lights had been off for five minutes or less, when she heard his sharp knock at the door. He'd never come to her on the same night that she'd danced before. She wondered about that.

When they had used each other enough, had twisted the bed sheets nearly to pieces, he just laid there, cooling down and breathing deeply, letting the tension drain from his muscles. Then he began to talk, as he often did, about things she recognized and things she did not. There was no theme, no train of thought, just little vignettes out of his life. He often just babbled, as if he'd talked to no one in years.

Then he stopped, short, and grew silent. She just waited, watching him watch the streaks from a near-full moon coming in under the window blind. She herself had nothing to say.

"I might want you to do something for me," he said finally.

"Why don't you try asking?" she answered. "That way, I could turn you down."

"If I could get John Beard, you know, the judge, drunk some night, which ain't hard to do, and talk him into coming over to my apartment for one last good one, I might just want you to do your little show."

She sat up in the bed.

"What in the hell for?"

"I got a little worry on my mind, that's all," he said, throwing back the covers and sitting on the edge of the bed. "Abrahams thinks the DA will have to back off, and this Navajo shooting ain't goin' to amount to nothing." And he told her about Abrahams and Teller in the mill.

"But I'm not sure that's enough. I'd like to have something on the judge."

The room grew silent.

"So you get him over there in the dark and I do this little dance for him and he gets all swollen up, and then what?"

"I don't know. I was just thinking."

"Well, maybe you and him will just have to figure something out. I don't lay down for men whose bellies stick out further than their peters do. I've never been that hard up."

He didn't answer.

"I'll think of something," he said finally, and got up to dress.

6

"You want to see my little dance?"

She looked at me as she took another sip of her vodka.

I was afraid to answer.

"Never mind," she said. "I don't think your old heart could take it." Then she unleashed another of those raucous, raspy laughs, the kind you hear in alleys, maybe, or along the waterfront.

She stood up, and for a moment, I was afraid she might do it, but instead she walked into the bathroom and closed the door. Through the thin door, I could hear the drizzle and the flush.

"Never got to do my little dance for the judge," she said when she came back. Was that a ring of disappointment in her voice? "Not sure why. Maybe they gave him a new pencil and pen set, hell, I don't know. Set him up with some young Navajo girl, maybe."

She was filling my room with a choking cigarette smoke again, and I opened the window. I just hoped she didn't give singing another try. Dogs would howl.

A thought as I sat there: if she never said another meaningful word, I'd really, finally, made it to what Arvo Belke had called the innards of the whole sad story. Of all of the dozens of people who would have known how this all came about, it had taken me two months to find just one. But one was all it took, really, if Madeline Wyszyanski was telling me the truth. And why should I believe otherwise? Sitting here at the River Rapids Motel, she should be glad for her one turn in the confessional.

"So they had the old judge taken care of, and mister district attorney, and who knows who else. If there had been a jury, they would have had them all by the balls, too."

"No jury?"

"Nah. It was sort of like they all got together and voted to forget the whole damned thing."

"You mean there wasn't even a trial?"

"Oh hell, there was something. They got together. Spent some money. I don't know. That part's just all kind of a blur."

Her face had started to sag, and her eyes seemed to be closing up from both the top and bottom. I was afraid she might pass out on me, and that I might have to carry her down to number nine. I didn't want to embrace, to shoulder, that kind of load, even when I didn't have a cast on one hand.

"I remember, though, there was just one thing old Alphabet was still worried about. What the goofy storekeeper was gonna say."

She leaned forward, elbows on her knees, and stared into her glass, as though the ice cubes there were crystal balls, the kind that looked into the past and future as well, with equal clarity. Or lack of it.

"What in the hell was he gonna say, standing up there, not sure whether they were gonna hang him or not?" she asked. "Was he just gonna fall down on the floor bawlin' like a baby and say he did it? Or was he gonna start workin' his way around the room, pointin' fingers and callin' out names? They were scared shitless that he might do that, ya know."

She tried to take another drink, but the ice fell against her lips, slopping the liquid until it ran down the corners of her mouth. She choked a little, wiped it off with her sleeve, and went on.

"But . . . ah shit, how can I say this nice? But then your grandmomma dropped her drawers. Is that nice? Sure it is. Anyway, you know what happens when a woman has to go crawlin' to a man like Joe Wyszyanski, beggin' for a little help? You know how much that help's gonna cost? Why hell yes you do."

So that was how he'd told it to her. That was how he'd explained, maybe, the monogrammed panties that had showed up in his back pocket. Of course. Why would he tell one woman that he'd had to pry another woman's legs apart?

She was starting to sound drunk now, and suddenly I felt a little stab of reluctance, an urge to call time out. Did we really have to drag this old piece of soiled fabric out into the light, along with everything else?

"Them proper sorts . . . but I really kinda liked her, really, your grandmomma . . . Alphabet said they liked it like that. He said she liked it a lot. Wanted more. Why hell, he was a bull of a man."

How different the same scene looked through different eyes. Claire Sadler's eyes. Madeline Swain's eyes. Many versions of the same story, all of them true. And there was plenty of room in there for me to build my own version, pick the parts that I wanted to believe.

"But don't get the wrong idea, sonny," she said, letting her head fall back and roll off to the side, looking up at the ceiling. "He didn't even want the extra little nooky. He didn't really go in for nothin' like the normal kind. It was just another one of those little tricks he dreamt up at night. His manners was so bad."

———————

The little conference room with bars on the windows served a single purpose on most days: the place where the deputies and jail staff ate their lunches. On other days, though, it was put to official use. Lawyers met their clients there, and inmates sometimes went in there to hold hands with the old lady and try to maintain some kind of weak touch with the outside. Shelves of law books lined one wall, there for those who wanted to try reading themselves out of jail.

This day, Jozef Wyszyanski was talking to Tom Cottin.

It was a monologue: Alphabet did all the talking. And it was friendly enough at first. The company was worried about Tom, he said, and wanted to make certain he was being taken care of. Don't worry about legal expenses, either, he said. We've got that taken care of. We'll have bail hearing next Monday, he said, and the company will put up all the money, and by Tuesday, Tom would be back with his family in Madero.

Through all of that, Tom Cottin just sat and stared at the other man, sometimes blankly, at other times with a frown or the gritting of his teeth or the clenching of his jaw.

Finally, he spoke.

"You're nothing but a stinking liar."

"Now, you just . . ."

"You don't want me out of here. Unless it's to go to the chair. Or maybe the pen. And you know why? Because you're afraid of me, aren't you? You, the Navajos, the company, the whole damned town, everybody wants me locked up, don't you? Well, too damned bad. I'm going to get you, just the way you got me."

His voice was soft, and his hands were shaking badly, uncontrollably. Alphabet could see tears starting to form up in the corners of his eyes.

"You need me, Cottin. I can get the charges reduced to some kind of manslaughter. You probably won't even serve any more time. But not unless you cooperate."

He paused to let the words sink in.

"You've got to do what I say. I'm your boss. You do what I say."

Tom Cottin said nothing, but shook his head back and forth, over and again, with his eyes closed, as though keeping the rhythm of a song only he could hear.

"You say nothin'. Plead guilty. They fine you. We pay it. That's all. But you've got to say nothin'. About me. The company. Anyone."

Time stopped for a full minute or two, as both men stared at each other across the scarred wooden table.

Then Tom Cottin gave Alphabet the bird, the digit, the finger. Shaking his hand as he did it, but not saying a word.

"Okay, you simple son of a bitch," Alphabet said, anger building quickly in his voice. "I'm going to tell you a little story. That cute little wife of yours, well she's got no use for you anymore. What she needs, she gets from me."

Tom Cottin stared at him, his eyes wide, like he was seeing and hearing nothing. Not there. Not anywhere.

"You think not? You think I'm shittin' you? Here, try these on for size."

Alphabet pulled the blue panties out of his back pocket. The monogrammed ones. With the letter AMC. And he tossed them on the table.

"How's that suit you, huh?"

No answer. Just that fixed, unfocused, gaping stare.

"And that ain't all. She wants to run away. She wants me to take her and that kid of yours and head for California. Tonight. Tomorrow. She's ready any time."

Alphabet paused, letting the words sink in.

"Next time she comes around, you just ask her. Ask her what's puttin' a smile on her face since her piss poor excuse for a husband's been gone."

Had the table not been bolted down, Tom Cottin would have overturned it on Alphabet. As it was, he lunged over the table at the bigger man, only to sprawl on top, helpless as Alphabet laid down on top of him.

"Listen, you stupid son of a bitch," he hissed in the storekeeper's ear, "I'm not through talking to you. I don't want the goddamned guard to come busting in here and haul you away. Not yet. Not before we make a deal."

He shoved Tom Cottin, then, and the smaller man slid back across the table, caught himself before he fell, and held on to his chair for support. Tears of anger were running down his cheeks, and his face was a flaming apple red.

"Now listen. You bring my name up in court, I've got to leave town. And if I do, I'm taking your wife and kid with me. She'll go. She's crazy about me. Just ask her. She likes my hammer better'n yours."

He paused to wipe his mouth with his sleeve.

"You say nothin' and I give her back. I leave town one of these days, she doesn't go, and you never see me again. Everything's even. You understand?"

No answer.

"I get your charges reduced. I protect you from the Navajos. I give you back your old lady. You need me, Cottin. Fuck with me and you're going to lose everything you've got."

Alphabet stood up to leave.

"Do we have a deal?"

Still no answer.

"Have it your way," he said. "I guess I'll just have to tell your attorney that you want to stand trial for murder. As for the other things, well I guess we'll just see."

As he left, Tom Cottin was sitting at the table, tears streaming down his face, pounding the palms of his hands on the flat surface over and over again, rocking in his chair.

Although he didn't have a handshake on it, Alphabet felt reasonably certain that he and Tom Cottin had struck a deal.

———•·•———

Judge John Beard had a terrible hangover. How he'd let himself get entangled in a late-night drinking escapade with Byron Teller was a question he couldn't answer. But it sometimes happened when he traveled to the county seat for trials and hearings. The two of them liked to talk about the old days.

He couldn't remember everything from the night before, but what he could remember was important. Somewhere between the fourth and eighth round of drinks, Teller had convinced him that the state had no case against Tom Cottin. They had no weapon, all the documents that might have shown a motive had been destroyed, and the only person that might know anything—the store clerk Claire Sadler—was hiding out back East. All that was left was Cottin's confession, they concluded, and his craziness, real or not, threw a hazy light even on that.

Beard argued at first.

"A man is dead," he said. "Somebody has got to be tried for it."

"Well let me put it to you this way," Teller said. "I'm not inclined to spend thousands of taxpayer dollars to try this case, send a deputy out after Sadler, and try to wring some kind of testimony out of a mental case all over a dead . . ."

"Navajo."

"You said it, I didn't."

They drank for awhile in silence, each man looking for wisdom in his own glass.

"What do you want to do?"

"They say manslaughter. Cottin goes to a hospital. I'd take it."

Several more minutes go by.

"Byron, is there something here I don't understand?"

"Nah. You understand it. You just don't want to face it."

"What do you mean?"

"We'd be prosecuting the wrong goddamned man, that's all. Trying to convict a scapegoat. And if you and I weren't such good old boys, if we didn't owe a favor or two here and there, we'd get mean. We'd find a way to file charges against that company. Maybe against the whole damned town. But we ain't got the guts."

"You're drunk."

"I suppose. But I know dirty hands when I see 'em. Let me see yours."

The judge laid his hands on the table, palms up. The district attorney did the same.

"John," Teller said, his voice growing more somber. "Maybe we ought to go wash."

———•·•———

The day after the verdict was read, Byron Teller sat alone in his office. After a time, he walked over to his bookshelf and pulled out his volume of old water law. He removed the check, studied it for awhile, then systematically tore it to shreds.

The next day, he announced that he would not be seeking a seventh term. He was moving to a lower, milder climate.

7

"WELL, SONNY," SHE SAID, HER VOICE NOTICEABLY THICKER AND EVEN raspier now. "You wanted to know how it was. That's how it was."

Then neither of us spoke. We were looking back on the same things, but not seeing the same things at all. If this part of history was an old trunk, she knew the inside—the darkness and confinement and smell of it. From the outside, I could see the scars and the rust, and be glad I'd stumbled upon a key.

"Y'know," she said after awhile, barely seeing me through half-closed eyes. "I think about those days a lot. Try not to, but I do. They may seem like the shits to you, stories you hear and such. But to me . . . to me, those were the best days of my whole goddamned life. Now who would have ever expected that?"

I didn't say anything.

"It's true," she said. "I had men. A little bit of money. Things to look forward to."

She drained her glass and stood up, holding onto the table for a moment for support.

"Now, I've got the goddamned edge of the Indian reservation and you know what I do for excitement? Nothin'. I wash pillow cases and wait for the spooks to catch up with me."

She just stood there, looking in my direction, but with eyes that could probably only see vague shapes.

"Not goin' to think about those days again. Ever. You take 'em. You carry the sunsabitches around for a while."

She lost her balance for a second, and hit the edge of the table. Her empty bottle tipped over with a bang, rolled against the ashtray, spun around and stopped. She grabbed the neck of it in her hand.

"Shit," she said, and disappeared out the door.

I just sat and stared for a long time, close to an hour, well after I'd heard the bottle crash in the parking lot, well after I heard the door on number nine slam shut.

I left the River Rapids shortly after daylight. For some reason, I felt like I'd just gotten up from a drunken one night stand, and I wanted to get as far away as I could before the sun hit and I was forced to say or do something to make it seem prettier than it really was. Just as important, I knew that she would never come out into the light until she knew I was gone. So I left the key on the table, and closed my door with a bang.

The office was dark, and no traffic moved on the highway. Still, I sat there for a moment anyway, and I looked back. Now, the narrow gravel parking lot was empty, and a coyote-looking dog sniffed around the picnic table. As I drove by the new motel down the road, the No Vacancy sign was on.

I drove northeast, toward Madero, and by early afternoon, I was there. I went to the post office and took my key back. One last time.

PART SEVEN

Andrew Cottin

1

MOST DAYS, I THOUGHT OF THE STORY AS A BOOK I WAS WRITING FOR NEAL. Once I got the chronology straight, once I was able to make all the different versions of the same stories fit into a single time line, I'd be able to leave it sitting on a shelf somewhere. Hoping that he'd be able to find it, somehow, and read it and know what it meant.

Other days, I saw more as a piece of cut-and-paste artwork, a collage: a forty-year wide picture, with faces and buildings and rubber boots pasted in, sometimes barely paper thick, other times much thicker and deeper and denser. In places, it had color, like the brown skin of Navajos or the yellow stink of shame. Mostly it was grey, neither black nor white. It was wrinkled, with edges ragged and torn.

And as I pasted and overlaid, each day, I thanked the gods, the ides, the roll of the dice. Thanks for the center image, the keystone of it all. Thanks for that last photograph of the old man and his wooden chains.

———

Madero's afternoon rains became more predictable. Sharply clear blue and green mornings grew dim by noon, as fast-moving nimbus waves boiled over the high ridges. The rains came hard with the front edges of the clouds, and were gone in two hours. The skies cleared again by mid-afternoon, leaving the world deep green and warm and damp and fresh, fragrant like a handful of new, wet, dirty mushrooms.

Then the songbirds took over—chickadees, robins, jays, finches, blackbirds, juncos—damned happy in those special hours: the little frosting of sun that got slipped in between the darker cakes of rainfall and night.

Lower down on the hillsides, below the steep belts of spruce, the stands of aspen were taking over the world. Bone-white trunks by the thousands spiking up out of a green sea of leaves, ferns, grasses and berry bushes.

The peak of the summer: had Madero ever been more alive?

——————

I wanted to stay right there until it was all written, hammering away on those rainy afternoons, waiting for the colors of the fall. Taking my fly rod down to the river in the evenings and rolling a few rainbows over. Beers, sometimes, at Ike's. But I knew I couldn't. And not just because I had to get on with life. I was drawing close enough to the end to see, clearly, the sharp edges of unfinished business: the last chapters, or the last pieces pasted in. I couldn't write them, or use them as that unifying color that artists always strive for. Because I didn't have them. They were not in my hands. Not in my collection of paper and buttons.

Those last pieces were stuck in the mind and memory of my father, and I couldn't hang a frame around that patchwork of fading images until I pasted in the little newspaper clippings, and connected them to faces and deeds in a way that pleased the eye and satisfied the soul.

The time would come, soon enough, when I'd have to try to pin my father down. Go to him, and try to open him up. To strip him naked and tie him spread-eagled to the top of a piss ant pile of memories in the hot summer sun. If that's the kind of persuasion it would take.

2

I SIT OUTSIDE THE MINE PORTAL ON AN OLD CHAIR. HE'S INSIDE THERE, working, and I can hear the dull ring of metal striking metal. Smell powder smoke in the air. Feel a shaking in the ground. Every few minutes, his compressor kicks on, runs for a few minutes, and shuts off.

He doesn't know I'm here.

After an hour or so, I hear the sound of steel wheels rolling on steel tracks, coming closer. An old mine car appears first, and then my old man, pushing it. He passes me by without seeing me, pushes the car to the end of the track, unlatches the bed, dumps the waste rock down over the hill.

He starts back, pushing the car from the other end, and he sees me. Stops a few feet away. And I can tell from the set to his jaw that he's about to remind me: I told you not to come back. Ever.

I cut him short.

"I'm finished," I say.

He just stands there, bent over a little, his hands curled over the top edge of the bed. Like he's holding himself up, tired. And I suspect that he is.

"I found Alphabet's old lady," I say. "It was blurry, but she knew a lot."

I look for something in his eyes, but his hat brim makes a shadow, and I can't see in there.

"I know how things worked. How they happened."

He takes a deep breath, then starts pushing the ore car again. When he reaches the portal, he speeds up. Then shoves the car hard and lets it go. It rolls into the darkness and, in there somewhere, slows to a stop.

He turns toward me.

"So what do you want now?"

"I brought some bourbon," I say. "I want a drink of that."

Afternoon is just breaking into evening. The shadows are starting to sneak out from between the rocks again, and lay themselves out along the canyon floor. The world is starting to split: some in the sun, some out. Yin and yang.

We sit on the bench on the rim, drinking whiskey and water out of coffee cups. He lights one Camel after another one. I've never seen him do that before. He's not angry. Yet. But he hasn't said more than a dozen words.

The crows are talking, and each caw multiplies and divides, echoing over and again. It's warm, and there's barely a wind.

Like so many times before with him, I'm unsure where to start. Unsure what boxes or wounds my words will open up. But I have to get the rock rolling again.

"I figured something out," I say. "It took a while."

I sip a little before I go on.

"When you set off that powder in those mills. You weren't just trying to play hell with Cable Minerals. You were after Alphabet."

A pained sort of a smile tips up one corner of his mouth. Small. And he squints his eyes almost closed. He seems to be arguing with himself. To answer, or not to answer.

"Son of a bitch wasn't worth much," he says, finally.

"What were you trying to do?"

He doesn't answer. And as we sit there, I begin to wonder if the end has come. I feel like I'm dealing the last hand, card by card, in a winner-take-all poker game. The last ace and the last jack. The last bet. The last best chance to win or lose it all.

I give him more time. Try to wait him out. But it isn't doing any good. He looks away, studying the rocks, as though I've left. Or never been there at all.

My last card is an envelope. Medium-sized. Brown. New. And from it, I pull out a photograph and hold it in front of him until he takes it. It shows a storekeeper, his wife and a young boy.

He stares at it for a moment, then half-squints his eyes again, as though he's trying to see through it, or perhaps throw it so out of focus that so he can't see it at all. The look is one of pain.

"That's the way it was, once," I say. Slowly, forcing my voice into a low, flat sound: here's the truth. "Before they took it away. The company. And the company man."

And it is the truth. Then, they had a future. They had a chance at life. The man. The woman. The boy. And even those yet to be born. The future was laid out to be a lively walk toward the sunset, not a crippling run down through the dark.

"And when they'd taken about all they could get, this is what was left." I hand him a second photograph. The last one. The one of Old Tom and his wooden chain. "What we all have to live with. The week before he died."

And that's the truth, too. A truth that will always be there, as it should be. Despite the torture of every line. Despite the pain.

He slumps forward, resting his elbows on his knees. He holds the photographs, but he stares down. Down into the dirt. Down at the black rubber on the toes of his boots. The pictures shake and flutter a little, in his hands.

"Nothin' but a goddamned shame." His voice has cracks in it, like an old record that's worn out. But it's the only record you own. And the dancers are waiting. Waiting for a sound.

I give him all the time he needs to say more, but he doesn't. So I hand him a copy of the first newspaper clipping: the first mill explosion.

"So tell me," I say. "Tell me what was really going on."

He looks down, out and across. Toward the sandstone spires. Toward the gulf. And beyond.

"Them old fuses," he says. "They ain't worth a shit."

———·•·———

Andrew Cottin was loading trucks in the mill. Night shift. A solitary job that kept him down in the dim light of the concentrate bins. Pulling the handles on a little tram. Dropping copper into a chute, down into the trucks below. He'd been there about a year, and he'd only sworn bitterly at the bosses a couple of times. He was getting by.

One evening, though, he noticed a new signature at the bottom of the day shift loading report. Jozef Wyszyanski, assistant mill foreman. He'd been transferred in from some other of the dozens of hard rock operations that Cable Minerals ran in that part of the country. He was there, suddenly. On the day watch. In the mill.

Over twenty years had passed. Madero had long ago shut down and gone over to the dogs. Dreams and nightmares had blurred. But the first day that he saw that face, heard that voice, just as the shifts were changing over, Andrew Cottin knew that time had not healed. Not scabbed-over any of the wounds. He felt infected, bitten by something that brought on fever, and worked its way through him, cell by cell. Anger. Bitter anger. Like a gangrene that had taken hold in his fingertip, and, each day, would work a little further through his hand, up his arm, into his core.

Alphabet owed a lot of people. And somehow, in a way Andrew Cottin couldn't explain, but in a way that made his stomach churn, the job of collecting on all those debts seemed to have come down to him. The last man with the last shot. It felt like a command, coming clear and loud out of a cloudy sky.

———·•·———

"Left the son of a bitch alone, though," my father is saying. "Let weeks go by. Might have left him alone forever." He's talking into his cup, telling a story to the bourbon there.

But Alphabet made the mistake of sitting down next to Andrew Cottin in the San Juan Bar one night.

"The bastard was drunk," my father says. "Slobberin' drunk. All the places he'd been. What a helluva miner he was. No goddamned mill he couldn't run. Finally, he started jabberin' about Navajos."

And, eventually, he got around to the time that he'd had a whole town full of them under his thumb. Ran the whole damned tribe of them. All he'd had to do was find himself a "chicken shit little store-keeper and his dumb fuck of a wife."

Andrew Cottin did not sleep that night. It came boiling back through him. All of it. He could hear his father, and see his mother's face. He could see Navajos, and hear Arvo Belke's scream of agony. All of the pain of Madero seared through him, and he rolled around in his own sweat until the sky lightened in the east. Then he drove back to a little mining claim that he owned. And he spent the week-end there, working out his rage.

During the day, the mill crawled with men. But at night, only a handful worked. A ball mill operator. A flotation cell operator. A night assayer and a night watchman. A truck loader. And an assistant mill foreman.

Like the other assistant mill foreman, Alphabet had to take his turn as night crew shift boss. Four weeks of days, four weeks of nights. His turn rolled around.

At 9 p.m. each night, the shift boss left the mill and walked over to the crusher plant, where one solitary man, the crusher operator worked. And while that operator walked over into the mill to eat his dinner, the foreman stood at the controls. Watching giant steel jaws smash rocks, over and over again. Watching for spills on the network of conveyor belts that ran over and around each other, moving the rock from crusher to crusher and on into the mill.

One of those belts ran from down in the bowels of the plant, past and just behind the operator's station, and on to a bin higher up.

At 9:15 on a Friday night, Andrew Cottin left his loading station, slipped across the shadowy space between the buildings, and let himself into the bottom of the crusher plant. There, he laid a half-stick of dynamite on the conveyor belt, and lit a length of fuse that he'd carefully measured off earlier in the night. Stuck down among the pieces of rock, the powder rode the conveyor belt slowly higher, toward Alphabet, while Andrew Cottin went back to loading trucks.

———•———

"That old fuse, the kind you light, ain't worth a shit," my father says again. "Sometimes it burns regular speed. Sometimes it don't."

That night, it burned too slowly. The half stick of dynamite rode past Alphabet and, just as it fell off the conveyor belt into the bin, it went off.

"Tore hell out of things," he says. "Blew out the crusher and one side out of the building. But all it did to Alphabet was throw him through the air a little ways and knock him on his ass."

He takes another sip of bourbon and his eyes fall out of focus. He's looking back, and he's disappointed in himself. But his jaw is relaxed and he slumps down a little. He almost looks amused.

"Caught me," he says simply.

The night watchman had strayed off his regular rounds because the batteries went dead on his flashlight. On his way back to the mill, he could look down into the crusher plant from the tracks running out of the mine. He could see the light of a match, the flush of a face, the work of a pair of hands.

"Saw the whole damned thing," my father says. "Hauled me to the slammer before I could even get my goddamned sandwich ate."

3

Madeline was still awake, reading a magazine, when Jozef
Wyszyanski got home from work shortly after midnight.

"You're early," she said, barely looking in his direction. She stayed
up late, some nights, just because she couldn't sleep. Not because
she was waiting up for him.

He walked by, into the kitchen, and laid his lunch bucket on the
counter. It was only after he'd poured himself a drink and sat down
that she noticed the half-dozen small cuts on the side of his face. And
the little tremor in his hands.

"What happened to you?"

"Some crazy son of a bitch blew up the crusher plant tonight."

"How?"

"Threw a stick of powder in the number three bin."

"Anybody hurt?"

"Went off right next to me. Almost got me."

She thought about that for a minute.

"Navajo?"

"White."

He gulped his drink, almost draining it.

"Christ, my head hurts."

"What's his name?"

"Collins. Somethin' like that. You don't know him."

"Do you?"

"Seen him around."

"Collins."

"You don't know him, I said."

"Okay."

"My head hurts like hell. I'm goin' to bed."

She sat up a while longer by herself. Thinking. You never know, when they leave, whether they're coming back. And, after so many days, so many nights, you never know, quite, whether you even give a shit.

4

WHEN HE'S NOT TALKING, THERE'S ALMOST NO SOUND. A LITTLE RASP FROM the breeze. A bird, now and then, down in the canyon. Way down below, a piece of rock falls off and shatters. Then nothing. I don't want to talk at all, in case he wants to believe that I'm not here. I just want to let the silence build, and see if that doesn't draw out his words. He can talk to himself, or he can talk to his cup. Or to me. Either way.

He studies the wild turkey on the label of the bottle. Then he pours himself another shot, and slops in a little water out of his old coffee pot. After a few minutes, I pour a little more into my cup.

"When I got out, he was gone. Moved on to some other half-assed operation in Colorado." He still doesn't look at me when he talks. "In jail, I could see his face, though. I could hear the son of a bitch laugh, just like he was standin' five feet away."

———·+·———

Andrew Cottin was never going to be on a Cable Minerals payroll again. He knew that. But he found work easily enough with the company that was hauling ore out of that Colorado mill. A truck driver, down a steep dirt road. He'd done that before.

He'd grown a beard in jail, and he looked different enough. Still, he stuck with his truck, stayed out of the mill, when Alphabet was on shift. The other drivers wandered around inside when they were waiting for a load. But not him. He sat behind the wheel and waited for his load to make.

When the other mill foreman was on, though, Andrew Cottin walked through the mill as much as he could, without being noticed.

Watching. Remembering. Trying to figure something out.

———•·—

"Spent eight or nine weeks," he says, just looking at part of his own reflection coming from inside the cup. Not seeing the sun dropping down to the top of the buttes, or thin clouds coming in from the west. Not feeling a cooling change to the air. Not hearing anything but the long, dull echoes in his own mind.

"Kept lookin' for ways to catch him alone. Didn't want to hurt nobody else."

He lights another cigarette, sucks in the smoke, and coughs hard enough to slop a little of his whiskey onto the ground.

"Wanted to cost that company a dollar or two and send Alphabet all the way to hell and not hurt nobody else. A hard thing to do." He takes another sip.

"Then I was goin' to Mexico and never comin' back." He pauses. "I'd a done what the Big Man put me on this earth to do."

I'm surprised, a little, by those last words. He didn't like bosses of any kind telling him what to do.

———•·—

The flotation process used chemicals—liquids that would sear the skin and eat into anything they touched—to separate the metals from the waste rock. And they were stored in thick metal tanks along the south side of the mill. Above them, a floor made of steel mesh. On that floor, the mill foreman's office.

When the acids in the flotation cells ran low, sensors spoke to a switch at the tanks. A pump kicked on. More acid moved down the line.

In his wandering, Andrew Cottin picked up on that chain of events. And a couple of other things, as well: the mill foreman was always in his office filling out the day's tonnage reports from 4 to 5 p.m. And the pump on one of tanks seemed to kick on some time around 4:30.

———•·—

It was day shift. About 3 p.m. Andrew Cottin climbed the ladder from the loading pit, and slipped along a catwalk. When he got to the chemical tanks, he climbed the welded-on ladder rungs to the top of one. The one that dumped out at the right time. He taped a stick of powder to the top, stuck a blasting cap crimped onto the end of an electric fuse into the dynamite, and dropped the end of the fuse to the floor behind the tank.

He climbed back down. He pulled a simple voltmeter out of his pocket and tested the wire that run to the pump motor. Nothing. Good. It wasn't supposed to be hot. Not yet. He cut away an inch of insulation, cut the fuse to the right length, and taped the end of it onto the wire.

———•—

"A *helluva* good idea," my father says. He leans forward, with his elbows on the his knees. He spits, and wipes his mouth with his shirt sleeve.

"When the switch turned on the pump, it would all go off. By then, I'd be sittin' down in my truck. Didn't even give a damn whether I got beat up a little when shit started to blow."

He looks over at me.

"Just like before," he says. "My timin' was off."

———•—

Maybe Andrew Cottin had never been around the tanks at 3 p.m. before. Maybe he didn't notice that the tank pumps kicked on every hour and a half, or so. Maybe he wasn't thinking clearly enough.

Whatever. He'd barely walked around to the other side of the tank. Barely gotten part way down the catwalk. When the pump kicked on.

The blast threw him off the catwalk, down onto the floor by the flotation cells. Unconscious. With tape in one hand and voltmeter in the other. With a piece of electric fuse stuck in his back pocket.

———•—

"Still in the hospital with a punctured lung when they figgered it out," he says. "So they came and got me."

That small, wry smile again.

"Alphabet, he was over in the assay office when she blew. Dumb son of a bitch probably never did understand what was goin' on."

5

"WHAT WERE ALL THOSE SIRENS?"

Jozef Wyszyanski had just put his lunch pail down and was washing his hands in the sink.

"Helluva explosion in the mill," he said. "Blew one of the re-agent tanks out. Spilled acid all over the goddamned place. Blew our goddamned office into little pieces. Tell you one thing. I'm damned lucky I wasn't sittin' there."

"What caused it?"

"Maybe an electrical short. Insurance company men are comin' in the morning to try to figure it out."

"Anybody hurt?"

"One guy. A truck driver. Don't know what in the hell he was doin' back in there anyway. Serves the bastard right."

———·—·———

When Alphabet found out that the mill was going to be shut down for a couple of months, he asked to be sent back to New Mexico. He never did hear what caused the explosion, or what happened to the guy that was hurt.

6

THE SUN IS GONE. THE PEAKS OVER IN THE ABAJOS ARE STILL IN THE LIGHT, but everything else that spreads out before us is muted. In shadows. The horizon is growing dim.

He gets up and takes a piss alongside a dead juniper snag. He looks a little unsteady, but maybe it's just me. We've put almost a half a bottle away.

Then he takes a couple of steps back toward his trailer.

"We've got more time."

"That's enough," he says. "Long goddamned day."

I could let him go, and take my chances on tomorrow. Let him rest, and finish it in the morning sun. But I know how it's always gone before. He might remember who he is, and who I am. He might realize how naked he got, just for a little while. And fear that. And never let me see that flesh, that blood, again.

"Let's have one more," I say. "Then I'll rustle us up some food. We got time. A little time till dark."

He pauses.

"Or do you want me to hit the road?"

The game might be over, but I'm still throwing out cards. And this one is a deuce of clubs. My weakest. Gambling on his loneliness, his fascination with his own voice. Stay around, for another minute, another drink, another night. Words not to be said. The odds say that I can't win.

But he turns, and he sits back down. We pour out just a little more, and we swirl it around and we watch it reflect back the little orange that has crept into the sky. Last call.

"When I left here last time. I said I was going to go find Alphabet." It's me talking.

He looks at me, and waits.

"You knew I couldn't do that," I say. "Didn't you?"

He takes a small sip. Barely. And holds it for a moment, before he lets a swallow haul it away.

"Didn't know what in the hell you might find."

"Alive, I mean."

"Can't say."

He's felt the cool evening breeze, and he knows that he's been bare before my eyes. It's chilling him. I know it is.

"He disappeared."

He looks away, and his hands don't move, and his eyes barely blink. For a long time.

"Maybe he just rotted," he finally answers. "Maybe his guts just fell out and his skin come off."

——————

Andrew Cottin saw Jozef Wyszyanski gassing up his jeep in Mexican Hat. It was a hot day. Too hot. And he didn't know what he was going to do, or why it had to be then. In that sun. But he pulled off the side of the road and waited.

Alphabet passed him, after a few minutes, and Andrew Cottin trailed along behind. They crossed the river and drove deeper into the reservation. The pavement shimmered in the heat, and the air that blew in through the windows only cooked, not cooled.

Then Alphabet turned north, toward some old copper mines that had reopened in the lower part of Copper Canyon, down a rough dirt road. The other man followed. But at a distance. Out of the dust.

About five miles along, he rounded a sharp corner and found Alphabet's jeep parked in the middle of the road. The older man was standing behind his rig, looking at a rock sample that he'd picked up. Probably fallen off an ore truck. When he saw Andrew Cottin coming, he dropped the rock and walked back toward the driver's side, intending to pull over out of the way.

———•+•———

"I stopped him," my father says. "Showed him my old .38, and told him to sit on his bumper with his hands in his pockets. Then I asked him if he knew who I was."

———•+•———

The older man squinted, and then his eyes opened a little. A sign of some recognition. He tried to smile, but it fell into a frown.

"Collins, ain't it? Ain't you the guy that blew up the crusher plant?" Fear was starting to take the place of anger and vague recall in Alphabet's eyes.

"Cottin, not Collins," the other man said. "Cottin, like in Tom Cottin. Like in Anne Marie Cottin. Maybe you just can't remember anymore, Alphabet. Maybe you just remember them as part of your great Navajo stunts. As your chickenshit storekeeper and his dumb-fuck wife. But they were my parents, Alphabet. My parents. You and me go back to Madero. We go back a long ways."

It took awhile, but Alphabet was digging. It showed in his face. Sorting back through a lifetime of old files and faces and places. He would have been sorting hard, and he would have eventually come to the boy. The boy in the store.

He just nodded.

"What do you want with me?" he asked then. A simple question. Almost innocent, like there'd been some mistake.

"You owe, Alphabet. You owe. And now's the time to pay up."

———•+•———

"Made him park his old jeep back up in a dry gulch, out of sight," my old man says then. "Made him get behind the wheel of my truck, and we drove. All the way past the old tradin' post at Piute Farms, then west above the river. Till the road petered out. Kept goin'. Through the brush. Till we couldn't go no more."

He licks his lips and stops for a minute.

"While he drove, I made him help me remember a few things. What he did to the store and my old man. To me and my mother. To them Navajos. About beating up old man Belke. All the shit I saw him pull."

He picks up the last picture of his father and stares at it for a minute.

"All that," he says.

It's hard for me to see. My father talking. Making words. Drawing pictures in the hot, dusty air. His voice grating, no pity. His words beating down on the other man. The devil holding court.

———————

"Get out," Andrew Cottin said, when big slabs of red rock blocked their way. Leaving them no way to turn, no place else to go. End of the line.

"What are you gonna do?"

Andrew Cottin stood in front of the other man, still holding the pistol, aiming it at his stomach. The rasping, grating sound of cicadas and the buzz of flies were the only sounds. Nothing appeared to move in the blistering sun.

"Go stand over there against that rock."

Alphabet's face was pale, and sweat ran down alongside his nose. Down both cheeks. He stood there, stiff, saying nothing. Waiting. Just waiting.

"I said move, goddamn you," and Andrew Cottin kicked the legs out from under the other man. Dust boiled up from the spot where he fell.

"Now stand over there. Face that rock."

Alphabet moved slowly, sluggishly, until he was up against the rock. His head was thrown partly back, like he was trying to get a message through to the sky.

"Now, I'm gonna count to ten."

He paused.

"One . . . two . . . three . . ." He could see Alphabet's back stiffen.

"Four . . . five . . . six." He opened the door and got into his truck, counting out through the open window.

"Seven . . . eight . . . nine."

At ten, he slammed the door closed, and Alphabet jerked forward and rested his face against his arms against the rock. Then Andrew Cottin turned his starter over, and the engine kicked in.

"So long, Alphabet," Andrew Cottin said, putting his truck in gear and leaning out the window. "Quite a little walk from here. You'll have plenty of time to think 'er over. Maybe you'll do 'er different next time." He started to move away. "Who knows," he said as Alphabet turned part way around. "Maybe one of them 'stinkin' lousy Navajos' will come along and give you a drink."

Darkness has fallen on the rim. No sounds. No coyotes. No last words from the crows. No owls. Just a little wind that comes more as a feeling than a sound.

"What happened to him?"

"Can't say. Thirsted to death, maybe. Navajo came along and put him out of his misery, maybe. Ever' Indian on the north half of the reservation knew who he was. What he'd done. Doubt they would have helped him much."

He thirsted, or he didn't. A Navajo killed him, or he didn't. Madeline Wyszynski was right, or Ruby the clerk was right. Or both were right. And wrong. Many versions of the same story. All of them true.

We stand and walk back toward the trailer, barely visible in the falling dark.

JOZEF WYSZYANSKI HEARD A VEHICLE OF SOME KIND COMING ALONG THE road. It was just at the end of dusk, and the headlights were on. Alphabet ran out into the middle of the road, waving his arms in the glare.

His mouth and throat were stuck, too dry to speak. To yell. To make any sounds. So he just waved his arms.

Inside, Chee Nez and Tommy Manygoats turned the radio down, and looked at the man with wild eyes and white hair sticking up in tufts and spikes from the top of his head. They slowed down, nearly to a stop.

"*Chindi,*" Chee Nez said. The evil soul that stays behind to roam the world after a man is dead. The Navajo ghost. Tommy Manygoats nodded, and Chee Nez sped up. They drove around the man. On down the rough dirt road. And they turned the radio up.

Alphabet sat down on a big rock and watched the tail lights grow smaller in the dust. He thought for a second that they were coming back. But no, they were not. It was just an illusion caused by failing light and the dust.

Off to his left, he could hear a coyote bark. On his right, another coyote answered back. Then the tail lights were gone.

IT'S MORNING, AND THE SUN IS WARM. AFTER A COUPLE OF CUPS OF STRONG black coffee out on the rim, I load my bags into the back of my truck and get ready to go.

He's standing there behind me, just as he did before.

"I warned you," he says.

"I know."

"You shoulda just left it alone." The old weariness has returned to his voice. Maybe it was just the night. Both of us have red eyes. "It's been a long time now. Didn't need to dig it up. No good can come from draggin' out them old carcasses."

I turn around and face him. "No," I say. "You're wrong about that."

"Am I?"

"I see, now, what you've gone through."

"Wasn't the way I had 'er planned."

"No. It never is. Not for any of us. We just live it out, and wait for the wind to change. Sometimes it does."

I dig around in my tool box until I find a hammer and half dozen small nails. Then I haul out a box and walk over to his trailer. He's behind me. Curious, probably.

Inside, I open the box and take out a wooden chain. The finest of the chains. Carved from an oak pool cue, I guess. It starts with a round, disc-shaped piece at one end, and tapers down, with the links smaller and smaller and smaller. At the other end, a tiny hook.

I hang it above his door, hammering clumsily with my left hand.

"You'll see this every time you walk out," I say. "Just remember the old man, and what they did. How he ended up." I pause. "And you'll always know. You had no choice. You did what you had to do."

He says nothing. Just stands there with the tiny wooden hook in the palm of his big callused hand. Looking down.

———•———

We stand by my truck. I'm ready to go. Maybe there's much to be said, but the words are gone. Moved into the shadows. Out of the heat. Maybe we've just used up all of our words, and we'll never need them again.

I hold out my left hand, the one without the plaster cast.

He stares at it for a moment. Then grabs it with his left hand, and we shake.

"I'm going to send you some new clothes," I say. "Then you come and see me. Anytime you can."

He nods his head. And we both turn away just in time.

PART EIGHT

Old Pictures on Old Walls

NEAL AND I LEFT MADERO EARLY ONE CLEAR MORNING—BRIGHT BUT WITH
no real heat coming from the sun—and walked the old road up Demon Creek. Above and below us, and across the canyon as well, old
ore dumps cascaded down the steep hillside, softened at the edges
by attacking bushes and small trees. I wanted to try those mines, go
under ground once, get as far back in as my courage would allow.
But most had caved in right at the surface, their timbers barely showing through slides of dirt and thickets of brush. A couple that hadn't
caved were locked tight with heavy doors and heavy chains.

So we went higher, further up the jagged canyon, peering into old
loading chutes, wandering around nondescript tin buildings, wondering who had been there, and why. Finally, we reached the Demon Creek mill, the last one in the mining district to close its doors.

The mill's collection of random metal buildings, one huge, most
small, stood behind a locked gate, but no one could know or care
who passed there. We crawled through, and moved along between
rows of rusted 55-gallon drums, past a rusted-out old dump truck,
and around signs that told us over and over again that we were breaking the law. That didn't matter.

Although the wind was weak, hardly noticeable, it was enough to
break the silence: not with its whistle, but by banging a piece of tin
against a building, somewhere back there, over and over again. Bang.
Bang.

The metal door that dangled awkwardly on one hinge wasn't keeping anyone or anything in or out of the big building, and we slipped
through into a wide and high darkness, the feel of a rectangular hole

leading out into space. Small square windows three stories above, edges of jagged glass, cast some light into the gloom, but only enough to produce a somber layer of shadows. Where was the organ music, and the candles? Where were the biers, and their coffins?

The place had its own dead: giant pieces of equipment—ball mills, rod mills, water tanks, others I couldn't name. And they loomed like brownish whales washed up on a dirty, littered shore, long-dead but safe against birds and worms and even time. Waiting for a tide that was never coming in. Bedded in flotsam that would never float: rusted pipes and rails, machine parts, wheels, gears, chain.

The air was sharp, edged with the smell of concentrated ore and the acids used to process it—a stinging smell that would cling to every board, every piece of tin, long after the mill had been crushed by the winter snows and buried in the sliding rocks. And even in the heat of a sunny and calm morning, the empty structure felt clammy and cold.

We picked our way around the buildings, kicking through dirt and broken glass, through old rubber boots and piles of rusted drill bits, through cobwebs and dusty shadows. There was part of a ledger book, rows and rows of numbers filled in with a fine and precise hand. A broken pair of small round spectacles. A tin cup speckled with rust. A canvas glove with fingers worn through.

As we walked along, I dug back into memories of the Hollander book. All of the jargon that I'd read. And I tried to recite the process to Neal, to make him see how it had all worked. Sounded. Felt.

Part was easy to recognize and remember, and part took invention and guess.

It all begins at the grizzly, the grate made from steel rails, where the rock is dumped out of the ore cars. All but the biggest fall through, and those that hang up in the slots between the rails are broken apart with sledge hammers . . .

Who stood there, balanced on these rails, careful not to slip through, swinging a twelve-pound sledge with back-breaking force? Curtis Lee? Nelson? Which of the other Navajos? It was a tough job, and a dangerous one, and surely one that the whites would have forced onto the dark skins, the ones with no choice.

. . . and the jaws of this crusher hammer together and pop the hog-sized rocks as easily as a man can squeeze a crust of dried bread . . .

Don't fall in, Jack Elton, the fuzz-jawed operator just up off the ranch, would have been told. Or perhaps one of the younger, smarter, Navajos. If you do, your head will pop like a grape, your bones will be ground to powder, and we'll be lucky to even save your boots.

. . . then this conveyor belt takes it over to these rod and ball mills, which turn like giant drums, and steel rods and balls rolling around inside crush the rock to sand . . .

After time measured in months, rods the size of telephone poles would be reduced to pieces smaller than candy bars. Balls the size of grapefruits would be worn down to little marbles. And when the mills were cleaned out and the rods and balls replaced, men like Alphabet and Abrahams would be there, anxious and somber, for the sands in the bottom always held flakes and tiny nuggets of gold. It was a moment, an event, barely discussed in advance, and quietly.

. . . then it goes into these floatation cells, where chemicals separate and concentrate the metals—lead, zinc, copper—leaving all the rest, the tons of waste, to float off and be disposed of . . .

Separate and concentrate. Whites here, Indians there. Miners on this side, company on that side. Life versus falling rock. Madero against time. What was of value, and what was just tons of waste to be floated off? Who was of value, and who was just years of waste, to be dumped over the side of the hill? Some, like Sam Benally and the Lazlo brothers, were quickly gone. Others, like Arvo Belke and Jay Rogers, had been more slowly hauled away.

We cleared the far end of the buildings, past the last of the loading chutes that held the concentrated ores, and walked out into a sunshine that blinded me and made me stumble. It was warmer out here, and we sat on a big rusted pipe, watching the leaping, frothing waters of Demon Creek.

I looked back toward the empty shells, still quiet except for the tin that banged in the light wind. And I couldn't shake that feeling that it had all been built and welded together and dug simply to chew up and spit out until there was nothing left. No rock. No men. And, ultimately, it had all been built to be abandoned, left behind.

"So that's how it went," I said aloud, as though someone else was really there. "In one end and out the other."

Bartered. Traded. Spent. Month after month, year after year, until the bones cracked and broke. Until the muscles gave way. Until the eyes were too filled with pieces or rock and dirt. Turn in you light. This is your last shift.

And the mountain. It was spent there, too. Gutted and turned inside out, bartered away for a few decades of shaky prosperity. And then prices fell and the veins ran out. Somebody must have known that none of it, not the men nor the mountains, could ever last.

We talked about it for over an hour. Talked about the rock and the decay and the rust, and how all of that was in our blood. Talked about abandonment and waste. Talked about useless lives and unmarked graves. And we wondered if they weren't all connected in some unexplainable but important way.

Then the wind picked up a little and got cooler as the noontime storm built, and we headed back down the hill, toward town.

2

THE NEXT MORNING, I ASKED RICHERT IF HE'D LET ME BE ALONE IN THE store for a half-hour or so. He looked at me like I was using words that rang no bells, and I thought for a minute that he was going to turn me down. But I explained as best I could, and though he still didn't seem convinced, he agreed to go for a walk anyway. I could sense that he wished he had a chance to gracefully count the money in the drawer, first, just in case.

I took Neal with me in there, too. We climbed the eighteen steps that led up to the little office, and I sat in the chair behind the desk. It wasn't difficult to visualize the place busy, filled with miners and their wives and children. Claire Sadler behind the counter. It wasn't difficult, either, to imagine Navajos there, standing in line, waiting for their money. But it was much harder to pretend, I found, that I had a gun in my hand and that a Sam Benally was coming up the steps. And that I was pulling the trigger with the gun pointed toward a human face. I couldn't, in fact, lift my hand and act that moment out. Billy Yazzie's words hung there in the way, and I couldn't lift them, nor push them aside.

Then we went to the back of the building and found the stairs leading down. I flipped on a light switch, but it was still dark and dank and shadowy. There were no rooms filled with coal, but in rooms filled with boxes of canned goods, the everlasting sulphur smell of coal lingered, and seeped from the walls. No coal-burning furnace, either, but we could see where it had stood, just where a small modern heater, connected to the outside with gas pipes, stood now.

Our father has labored here, I said to Neal. Every morning before school. Our father as an innocent. His coat hung here. His books stacked over there. Not knowing what we all know now: his path led from these walls to a copper mine out on the edge of the desert. How could it be? How could it be?

The floor grate was gone, too, but we could see where the hole had been filled in with a piece of plywood. I stood under it, and tried to imagine blood dripping, and I was strangely reluctant to look up. What would it feel like, I asked Neal, that blood, to a young boy down there in that half-dark, alone? What questions and guesses, and maybe even hopes, would run through his mind? I decided that we didn't want to try to know, and climbed the stairs quickly and turned off the light.

We stood behind the meat counter and walked the aisles and rang up "no sale" on the old cash register. We opened the backs of antique display cases, and stood at the big front window. We looked at a tin wheel that held compartments full of needles, and at a bucket full of ax handles. At times, I closed my eyes and imagined smells and sounds.

Then Richert was back, and I thanked him and we left. But leaving was not that easy, and though we were out on the street, walking in the clean air, I was still back in there somewhere. Part of my mind was inside old photographs, inside old stories, and I was fighting to stay in there until I'd seen all the faces and heard all the voices. Old songs went through my mind, and I could see labels and old products that were no longer on shelves. Where was all this coming from? I seemed to walk for years before I began to give in to the cool air on my face, to smell the rain, and to see the clouds building on the edge of the earth. I felt good.

3

WE WALKED DOWN TO THE OLD MAN'S SHACK. BUT, LIKE SO MUCH OF WHO he'd been and what he'd done, it was gone. Only part of the floor remained. Who had torn it down? The town? The county? Firewood scavengers? It didn't matter, not who had torn it down or even that it had happened. The shack had stood for nothing, except perhaps cruelty, and mistakes.

We walked on past, along the path that was growing over now, down to the river. The short piece of log he'd used as his stool was still there, and the coffee can on a rope. We sat on the log and watched the river, slow and grey now, with ice building up along the edges, and I told Neal about the last time I'd walked this way. The old man had been sitting there in the afternoon sun, carving his wooden chain, and that moment, that image, had been the one I'd been able to grab and hold.

The temptation was strong to let that moment stand for everything, I explained. But no. That's just sentimental. Only a fool would try to read too much into it: he knew how to carve chains, that's all. It could have been kachinas, or ships in bottles, or wooden masks.

I cut the can free, filled it with rocks and dropped it into the bottom of the little lagoon. Then I carried the stool to the edge of the river and threw it in. I watched it bob and glide down through the current until it was out of sight.

"This is what you do," I said to Neal. "This is part of how you say good-bye."

4

THE ROAD OUT OF MADERO RAN PAST THE CEMETERY. WE PULLED OVER, I put on my jacket, and we walked up to Tom Cottin's grave. Light rain was falling, and the cemetery was cloaked in a strange wet silence. All we could hear were the raindrops as they bounced off the marble stones and iron grave fences.

I had nothing to say, really, and no thoughts that I hadn't run through my mind over and over again. Regret. Understanding. Even a sort of love. So, for a quarter of an hour, we just stood there in silence.

Then we walked around, looking at the grave markers, until we came to one marked:

SAM BENALLY

b. 1924

d. 1950

We stood there in silence for awhile, too, even though we knew we were only paying last respects to an old pistol, rusted by now, and to a pair of black rubber boots.

I left Neal there, and drove on alone.